The Bear of Pichesham

The Bear
of
Pichesham

Jonah Larchwood

Dedicated to Francis Edwin George Bradley,
my grandfather, who has made his presence felt
in the book in many subtle ways.

Brief Author's Notes

The pronunciation of Pichesham may not be obvious. It doesn't really matter, but I stress the Pi-, and just pronounce the -chesham the way it looks.

This book was written using UK English spelling. Readers accustomed to US spelling may notice some small differences. Thanks for your understanding and happy reading.

Contents

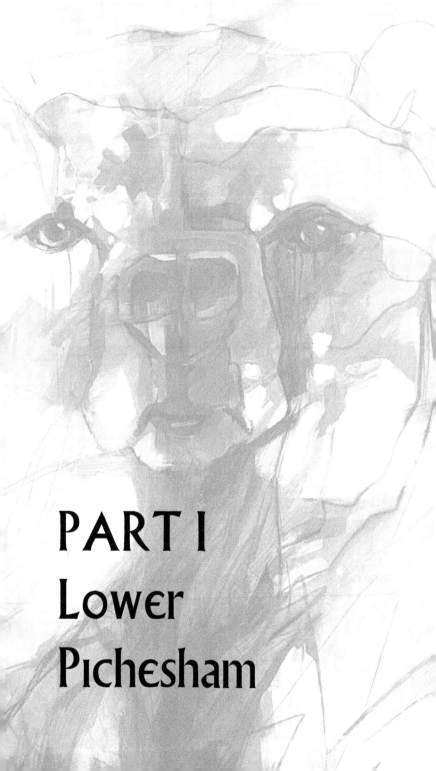

PART I
Lower
Pichesham

Meteor

P H I L O S O P H I C A L

T R A N S A C T I O N S.

XIX. A Further Account of the Meteor of the 4th of October 1783. In a letter from Rev. Jas. Alderman, to Alex. Aubert, Esq. F. R. S. and S.A.

Read Jul. 18, 1784.

DEAR SIR,

YOUR previous account of the meteor of 4th Oct. 1783 prompts me to write and supply additional observations made by my-self and also my curate, whilst atop the tower of St Joseph's, Pichesham inspecting rain damage. Although I could scarce believe my eyes in the moment, my own estimate of time was forty minutes past six and I am in no doubt that I was witness to the same event as your excellent account.

Vol. LXXIV.   Our

Our poſition was much cloſer, and as a reſult, more detail was available to be ſeen. The initial light was much as you deſcribed, a blue-tinted oblong, but occupying near half the evening ſky in our field of view. The light faded rapidly, leaving a red trail. It was followed by a ſtrangely-coloured light, deep violet in nature and ſmaller, but ſtill clearly viſible to us. This body appeared to deſcend into woodland to the eaſt of Picheſham village, and I was affeared that fire might enſue. Immediately after it diſappeared there was a wave of light radiating outwards from that area, in form ſomewhat like a rain-bow but compoſed of only blue and violet ſhades. No noiſe was apparent, although my curate ſayed that a preſſure was felt inſide his head. I my-ſelf did not apprehend this.

The following day, accompanied by Mr. Chas. Charting of Chartings Hall, I reſolved to locate if poſſible the landing place, and recover whatever may be found of the object. South-eaſt of Chartings Hall, we located an area within the woodland that was affected most ſtrangely. An area forty-five yards acroſs previouſly containing much valuable timber was reduced to nought but grey duſt. Trees at the edge of the region were variouſly damaged, ſome ſplit in the line of the main trunk top to bottom. In the centre of this area was a deep circular pit meaſuring three feet and ſix

inches

inches acrofs at the level. A man was lowered on a rope, but no bottom could be found. Later attempts to meafure the depth were ineffective, as no rope long enough was prefent in the locale. In the days fince, the pit flooded, and further exploration is confidered impractical. The pit was capped at the beheft of Mr. Charting for the fafety of his workers and liveftock. I did prevail upon him to preferve an entrance should any defire further exploration.

I beg the favour that, fhould you confider thefe obfervations of fufficient intereft, they be prefented to the Royal Society; with great regard, &c.

Rev. Jas. ALDERMAN, Vicar of the Parish

Arrival

I swear the village didn't want to be found.

Lower Pichesham is in the heart of England, less than two miles from a superstore as the crow flies. But since I can't fly, I had to find it by road. The junction was miles along the old London Road, itself long bypassed by the highway, and led rapidly to a narrow lane with grass growing in the middle. It then descended through dark conifers, so dense that the lights on the car came on. At the end of it I found myself facing a forbiddingly high barbed wire-topped gate and a grim-faced armed guard. He glared at me and talked quietly into his radio.

I opened the window and gave him my friendly smile, the one that makes me look harmless. It usually works well, but barely registered on this iceberg.

"Can I help you, miss?"

"I think I'm lost. I'm looking for the New Star Inn in Lower Pichesham?"

"Go back about half a mile and take the road between two brick pillars. It looks like a private driveway. Easy to miss the turn if you aren't from the area."

"Thanks, sorry to bother you. May I ask where I am, or would you have to shoot me?"

That went down like a lead bucket of cold sick. He stared back frostily. "This is the secure area of Chartings Military

Hospital, miss. The entrance for the general public is in town."

I'd seen it of course, but had no idea the grounds spread this far. I thanked him again and turned the car, uncomfortably aware of the disapproving glare in the rear-view mirror.

Even knowing what to look for, I struggled to find the pillars. When I did, they definitely gave off a private vibe, so much so that I still hesitated. I persevered, and, after an alarmingly steep and twisty drive down, emerged from the gloom of the pines to be greeted by the sight of the village ahead.

It was not what I had anticipated. My vision had been of a picture-postcard place, all beams and roses. Below me, the arc of a broad river bent around ranks of sturdy brick houses set in shallow curves that overlooked the water beyond. The overall impression was of tranquil simplicity, and the evening sun cast a pleasant glow over the scene.

The pub was visible directly ahead, backing onto the river, next to a small hump-backed footbridge. Seeing no obvious car park, I left the car on the street. Inside, the main bar was warm and cosy. Some of the customers glanced over at me and then returned to their conversation.

Seeing a bell on the bar, I gave it a slap and was rewarded with a satisfyingly loud ding. A burly man with a rather grand moustache and a wide smile appeared, as if from nowhere. "Good evening."

I was briefly startled, but he was friendly. "Sorry, I didn't see you there. Can I check in, please? Annie Maylor."

"Yes, we're expecting you, Miss Maylor. We don't get that many direct bookings."

I used my smile for the second time that day. "I prefer Ms, but Annie is better. Why not?"

"We're not on the tourist trail here, so casual visitors are unusual, especially from the US."

"Oh, I'm not here for the sights. I'm doing some work and personal research. In fact, I'm hoping you might help with that. I'm looking for historical records of the area."

"Of course, but before you settle in, I noticed you brought a car. Mrs T is very strict about parking."

There had been something about this in the booking email, but the thought of having to carry my case around by hand like a backpacker had not appealed. Money usually solves these problems. "OK, well, I'm here now. Surely there is somewhere I can put it? I don't mind paying."

He looked embarrassed. "Actually, it is a problem. Our garage is full, and there is no on-street parking allowed in the village at all, except by special arrangement. Can I suggest you go over to Ferry Cottage now? Mrs T is the law in Pichesham and she enforces the rules with a rod of iron."

I was surprised, but he seemed serious enough, and I wasn't here to offend the locals. "Sure, of course. What should I do?"

"The personal approach would be best. Margot Trimble is tough, but her bark is worse than her bite. Ask nicely and be prepared to ..."

"Kiss a little backside?"

He pulled a face. "I was going to say eat humble pie, but whatever works for you, Ms, er, Annie. Anyway, if records are what you are looking for, that's the place to start. It would be worth your while to lay on some charm."

As promised, Ferry Cottage was just a stroll away, next to a small jetty with an open boat tied up, its warm orange bricks glowing in the setting sun. It was obviously older than the rest of the village, but not ancient. Pretty, but not spectacular. Looking back at the more modern pub and the nearby houses, you could tell where the village's architect had found their inspiration. The crude iron door knocker looked even older than the cottage, rusted and warped. I rapped it harder than necessary, slightly nervous.

Margot Trimble looked much as I'd imagined. Greying hair, early sixties, dressed in a tweed jacket, jeans, and sensible shoes. She didn't exactly glare at me, but it wasn't far off.

"Hi, Mrs Trimble? I'm sorry to disturb you this late, but I'm staying at the New Star. The guy who checked me in said that I should come and apologise for the car."

"That would be Grant, I assume. Vehicles are not permitted overnight on the streets here. He should have explained in advance. This is most unlike him."

"It's my fault, Mrs Trimble. It was in the email, I should have read it more carefully. I'm afraid I was exhausted from the flight. Would it possibly be OK for me to move it tomorrow? The email did explain that I should have arrived using the river ferry, but I assume it has stopped for the day now."

She looked at me intently. For a moment, I thought I'd blown it. "Why are you here, Annie Maylor? Why Pichesham? We don't encourage uninvited guests here."

Wow. And here was me thinking that Brits were polite. "I'm following up on my family history, Mrs Trimble. I believe my great-grandfather came from here. In fact, Grant suggested I should talk to you, that you might have access to old records."

"Did he indeed?" She snorted. "Very well. Put your car in the boat shed tonight and make sure it is removed first thing in the morning. What was his name?"

The jump was jarring. "My great-grandfather? Clive Maylor. He came over to Washington State in 1929."

"Hmm. You'll have to drive round to the opposite bank tomorrow morning. Dr Hunt runs the ferry from there. I'll call him and let him know to expect you. You can leave your vehicle there. Last crossing tomorrow morning is at nine a.m. If you miss it, he restarts at three p.m." She started to close the door, hesitated. "You do have a look of him. Come for afternoon tea tomorrow if you like. Four p.m. would suit." She shut the door in my face before I had a chance to say thanks.

Grant seemed surprised and a little impressed when I returned from moving the car and told him about the encounter. "She must have liked you. She was so rude the last time that happened that they left early."

"You could have fooled me. But I got an invite for afternoon tea."

He pulled a face. "A mixed blessing. I've known Margot for ten years. She is, despite appearances, the kindest person you could meet, but her cooking is atrocious. Now, I've taken your bag upstairs—can I get you something to eat? I can get you a sandwich. Sergio made profiteroles and there are some left."

I let my genial host force a dessert bowl and a whisky on me and was shown to a small room overlooking the river. Outside, it was quite dark by now. Beyond that, all I could see were sparse lights from the town on the other side.

I checked my WhatsApp. Farzad had sent a 'Welcome to the UK' message. There was nothing else about the story proposal. *Secretz!* magazine was not too bothered about journalistic integrity, but they were always on the lookout for a juicy story with a hint of oddity to entice the shoppers at the checkouts. It would be even better if it involved a popular celebrity. I wasn't happy at having to revert to providing copy for a low-quality publication like this, but I needed a restart somewhere. I messaged him back with smiley face, airplane and cake emojis.

There was still nothing from Paul. I could tell he'd read the last three messages. I started a reply.

Dammit, Paul, I've said I'm sorry. What else can I do? I'm in England. Are you still in London? Call me. We can meet up, talk it through.

I looked at the message, deleted the first word and sent it. One grey tick. I threw the phone on the bed and went to the window seat, feeling irritable. I blamed myself, but he was being unreasonable now, throwing away three years together over one mistake. Asshat.

Outside, a large black bird winged its way across the river. I tried the bed. The room was plain, but the mattress was comfortable. The whisky did its work and I was asleep before I realised.

The Companions–I

Central Europe, 1281

My earliest memories are very clear. The smell of my mother and the taste of her milk. Dense fur to burrow into. Later, the excitement of my first meat, hot and bloody. Bears progress through early life faster than humans, and without your symbols and words to worry about, these early impressions last. At least, they did for me.

I was soon making my way alone. They say that the maternal instinct does not last long in bears, but occasionally I wonder how my mother felt after I left her side for the final time. Perhaps she had more cubs and never thought about me, but I doubt it is that easy. I hope she was happy.

My life then was simple enough—sometimes hungry, sometimes asleep, mostly just doing what bears do. There should have been more of that. There should have been time to carry my own cubs. I think I would have been good at it. My mother taught me well.

That was not to be my fate. One morning, the stench of humans and dogs filled the forest. They came in large numbers, making noise, driving everything before them. Another bear, a big male, turned to fight back only to fall to their weapons. Too small to fight, I ran into the river, hoping to escape on the other side, but was caught in a net held by more humans in boats. I bellowed and struggled until a hard blow to the head silenced me.

I awoke to pain and confusion, my legs restrained with ropes and blood streaming from my nose where a ring had been inserted. The pain eased eventually, but there was no hope or happiness to be had in this time. Most of the time I stood tethered to a wall in the foulness of my dung, waiting ravenously for the occasional scraps of food and my daily bucket of water. It took a while for me to understand what my captors required of me. At some point, I realised that food would follow when I had done something they wanted. In such a way, I learned to tolerate the muzzle, to follow when told, and even stand on my hind legs and 'dance'.

Once they were satisfied, they led me into the streets to perform. From then on, we travelled from place to place. The daytimes were easiest; they were predictable. The younger of my two captors would play a small wooden pipe while I stumbled around. Once in a while a child might throw bread to me; more often they would throw stones. I had no understanding of music then, but I hated the high-pitched squealing that pipe made. I don't think I was alone in that. On many days, his hat would remain empty when other street performers seemed to do well. On these days, he would use the stick more harshly.

It was the nights I came to dread. Not every night. Special nights.

The first time they came with the dogs, I did not understand what was happening. I was chained to a wooden pole in the centre of a village. Men gathered around, many of them with dogs held on ropes. They talked loudly, excitedly, making strange gestures with their arms. Pieces of metal changed hands; laughter filled the air.

Then the other captor, the older one, started speaking and the crowd formed a circle. Men with dogs lined up in front of me, the dogs baying and straining at their ropes, trying to reach me. As the dogs were released, instinct took over. I fought back with teeth and claws, fending them off as best I could. But no matter how hard I hit, how far I sent them flying, they kept coming back. In rage and frustration, I grabbed one dog around the torso and squeezed. It squealed in agony as ribs cracked, but I kept squeezing it, ignoring the other dogs worrying my legs. When it was dead, I dropped it and grabbed for another. But this was the prompt for the men around to step in. My captors came with the sticks and beat the dogs back. They were put back on ropes and led away. I at least had the satisfaction of seeing some limping and bleeding as they went.

The younger human stayed with me that night. Normally they left me alone, but he stayed to tend to my wounds. I was just grateful that they had made it stop. I didn't understand that they had started the attack in the first place. Not then.

The second time was similar. If anything, I was even more frightened, because I knew what was coming. I was no better at fending the dogs off, but it was over more quickly. It was just by chance that when I flung one of the hounds away, it landed headfirst on something sharp and wooden. I heard the bone snap, and it fell dead immediately. As before, once this happened, the dogs were gathered up. I was only bitten once that time.

After the third attack, I stopped counting; I had no concept of numbers beyond that. I could always tell when they were coming though, because the day before we would not perform in the streets and the food was better, more plentiful.

I grew larger and stronger. One time, I grabbed the stick during a beating and snapped it. After that, things changed.

The humans were more wary, even scared. I could smell it on them.

Sometime after this incident we reached a new town, but instead of performing, I was tied up and left for several hours. At last, the older one returned, accompanied by a different human. This new person examined me from a distance, then they talked and argued for a while. Metal was passed, and they led me to a large building at the edge of the town, through a gate to an area open to the sky, surrounded by walls. I was chained to a post and my captor made as if to leave. As he did so, the piper ran into the yard and started shouting and pushing at him. More men arrived, overpowering both of them. I roared in approval as they were dragged away.

I assumed at first that more dogs would come soon. But the days passed quietly. I was left alone. Food and water were brought regularly. Humans came and went about their business. I tried to ignore them, happy to have some rest for a while, but the strangeness of that place worried me.

A pit was dug in the centre, lines and curves cut into the surrounding earth. One human in particular seemed to direct the others. When he came near to my area to inspect me, I could smell flowers and something unidentifiable underneath. When he was in the yard, the fear among the other humans thickened the air. Eventually, the activity came to an end.

That evening, the flowery man did a final tour while his servants stood silent, some trembling. Everything seemed to be to his satisfaction, and he stalked away. Relieved, people scattered, leaving just the small female who usually brought my food. There was more than before, better tasting. I ate with enthusiasm, but partway through the meal, a drowsy feeling flowed through me. I remember falling heavily, and then nothing.

When I awoke, things had changed. I was surrounded by earth walls, but looking up, I could see the sky. The smells of the yard were still there, and I realised I was in the pit. Frightened, I started bellowing loudly.

A crowd of voices started chanting. The rhythm was slow at first, then accelerated, louder and louder, to a single shout. This was followed by a piercing shriek. The sound of sobbing from a human changed into another cry of pain, followed by still one more. Silence fell. Above me, the face of the flowery man appeared, peering down into the pit. He started speaking, and a small dark circle appeared in the sky above the pit.

The circle fell towards me, and kept on falling for an impossibly long time, coming closer and becoming larger and larger. Eventually, it was no longer falling, but I was. I no longer had any comprehension of what was happening. The surface of the circle was now below me. My legs seemed to extend towards it. I could see my paws in the distance, tiny blobs on the end of long, dark, curved lines of fur. They connected, and the rest of my body seemed to flow down, like honey from a bees' nest dripping down a tree trunk.

I seemed to regain something like my own form and found myself standing in a dark grey rocky landscape. Something had changed inside my head. It was as if fire filled my mind, racing up and down, burning new paths, but with nothing to fill them. Fury raged in me, but there was no enemy in sight. In frustration and anger, I attacked the bare rocks around me. A sound from above distracted me and, looking up, I could see three objects falling. They hit the ground nearby with a loud thump. Three human bodies, broken and bloody, limbs at all angles. They were clearly dead. I felt nothing but more anger and ran to the nearest, intending to rend it to pieces.

I grabbed at it, biting into the still-warm flesh. The taste of the blood was too much, and suddenly ravenous, I started eating. As I ate, new thoughts flowed into the holes burned into my head. Fragmentary memories of a woman. I knew her slightly. It was the one who had cleaned my pen and fed me. A brief life of misery and fear, interspersed with a few bright moments of hope—a joke shared with another girl, the time a visitor had looked at her with interest and taken her to his bed, a last moment of joy at being chosen by the master for a special task, shortly followed by betrayal and death.

Bright pain flashed through me, complex human emotions crashing through my animal instincts. I fought it back. What did I care about this dead human? I roared into the air and grabbed at the next body. I knew this one better. It was the piper, my tormentor of years. I laughed to see his pitiful dead face, and bit straight into it. Again, knowledge and ideas that were not mine flooded in. His name floated to the top. Timo. Greta—his name for me! The concept of names was new and the idea that I had a name at all stunned me. My rage dimmed a little, and, dazed, I fell into a sitting position, watching the memories storming my mind as if I were an onlooker. A little boy travelling with his father and his performing bear. Pride at learning how to handle old Bruin by himself, able to call himself a bearward in his own right. The argument, running away. The forced service in the army, the death and the blood, the injury to a leg that never healed. The comfort and squalor of drink. The final attempt to recover some of the joy of childhood—the chance to work with a new bear, a faithful companion to travel the world with.

Nausea gripped me. This human I'd hated with a vengeance, this Timo … loved me? Had believed I was his friend! The thought was unbearable. My poor wracked head could no longer cope, and I descended into unconsciousness.

🐾 🐾 🐾

When I came to, I was calmer. My mind was still alien to me, but I found myself able to think clearly and coherently. Somewhere in a well of memories, parts of Timo and the female swirled and merged. I left them to one side, trying to understand what had happened.

I could think! This was the strangest sensation. My animal instincts were there, as were my old memories. But sitting precariously above them was a delicate layer of symbols and words, drawn from the two unwilling donors still oozing their life fluids onto the grey rock.

The flowery man now had an identity, of sorts. The girl, Crina, had known him as Count Stevas (or more usually 'Master'). She was hardly more than a child, I could see now. Timo had just thought of him as 'thieving scum'. I could now make some sense of human hierarchy and symbols. Stevas wore clothing that gave him status and put fear into the minds of his servants. Crina had believed he was in league with 'the Devil', whatever that was. Still, there was nothing in their minds to explain how or why I was in this barren place.

I considered the third body. This one was dressed similarly to the count. I understood now that the biting had infected me with thoughts, and perhaps answers lay in taking a mouthful of this more important corpse. I had no moral issue. Morals were a novel concept and meat was meat. What stopped me was the suspicion that this was what Stevas wanted.

As if the thought had been heard, something *wrenched* me sideways. I found myself back in the courtyard. Count Stevas sat there in an ornate chair, protected by a barrier of wary men armed with blades. I growled, trying to see a way through to tear his throat out. Cursed with more knowledge now, I paced around them rather than risk myself against steel directly.

He spoke. "Welcome, spirit."

What was that supposed to mean? I consulted my new memories, prowling, trying to keep all the danger in view. A hazy understanding of invisible beings came through, but it made no sense.

"Welcome, spirit. Are you ready to serve your new master?"

"No." I was startled. The word had come from me, although it was not clear how. Unnerving as it was for me, the effect was gratifying. He had clearly expected a different answer.

"Spirit, obey me!"

"I will rip you and eat you first," I snarled. He shrank back in his chair.

"You will keep your distance! Back, beast!"

I lunged toward him, but something was interfering. My legs were folding against my will. I swore and cursed using the vilest words Timo could supply, but my head sank lower until I was lying face down in the dirt.

He rallied, braver now. "That's better. You will obey me. You will address me as Master, and you will do my bidding."

"I will call you maggot and piss on you." Pain like I had never felt seared through me. I cried out in agony.

"Stand up."

I stood on my hind legs.

"Dance for me, spirit."

I stumbled around, much as I had done for Timo.

"You can do better, spirit. Dance!"

Distant memories of a small girl watching her mother dance. I tried to imitate the memory, a grotesque parody. It seemed to satisfy him. "Enough. We will start again. Are you ready to serve me?"

I tested another refusal in my head. Even the thought brought pain. I could somehow sense what he wanted to hear. Reluctantly, I gave in. "What is your wish?" He waited pointedly. "What is your wish, Master?" *Maggot.* The minor rebellion in my mind seemed to pass unpunished. It was of little comfort.

"Return to the underworld, demon. I will summon you when I am ready." He gestured, and the world slid sideways again. I was back in the grey landscape.

For a while, I slumped, despairing. As well as the iron ring in my nose, I now had a new shackle through my whole body, and my mind was a stranger to me. Count Stevas seemed both cruel and mad, and I was trapped in a confusion that neither I nor the intruding memories had any understanding of.

But time passed, and practical concerns interjected. I was hungry and, more importantly, thirsty. There was meat, if I could still stomach it, but it was water I needed. I roused myself and decided to explore. The land rose steeply to one side, so I climbed to get a better view. All was grey, as far as I could see. Dark grey land, grey sky, diffuse light that came from nowhere in particular. I skirted around the contour line and on the other side of the hill came to the base of a cliff face, split by crevices. Caves. Instinct drove me to explore, seeking the comfort of shelter even though there appeared to be no weather to shelter from. In the first I found nothing but dry bones. The second was empty. In the third cave, I could hear a promising trickling sound. As I followed my nose in the darkness, my foot splashed into a puddle. It was shallow, but enough. Thirst quenched, I returned to the entrance. The light had dimmed a little and a soft damp mist filled the land below. Up here it was dry. It came to me that for now, I was free from danger. Drab though it was, the grey world was calm and restful. I drifted into a deep sleep.

🐾 🐾 🐾

Water drips from trees overhead into an open grave. It is not deep, but deep enough. Father is dry in his shroud, but rain is falling from the end of my nose.

"Are you crying?" A little girl is standing beside me. I don't know who she is. I shake my head. It is none of her business.

I reach up to hold his hand. He is very tall, but I think not very old. I am sad for him, but also for myself. No one will shed tears for me. "Shall we bury him now?" I ask. He nods gruffly and reaches for the shovel.

She reaches for the shovel as well, and now we both have one, the work is easier than last time. The rain stops. We finish planting the onions and sit for a while together. I look at her face. She is very pretty, but so sad, and I cannot see her eyes. I offer her water. It is hot in the midday sun.

The onions are ready to harvest. I cut one in half, and we share it. It is sweet and pungent, and my eyes sting. He takes me in his arms, and we hold fast while tears water the soil.

🐾 🐾 🐾

I started awake. The vision persisted. I'd dreamt of simple things before—chases, insects. This type of dream was new. Whatever was left of Crina and Timo seemed to be getting on well inside my head. I felt sorry for Crina. She had barely lived and had never done me any harm. I wasn't ready to forgive Timo, but it was hard to stay angry at a dead man, and now that I knew him a little, harder still.

I came out of the cave. I could no longer ignore the hunger, though I did not relish the thought of my meal. But then the world turned again and I was back in front of Stevas. Something was different. He and the guards looked bigger, like giants. He smirked unpleasantly.

"Good, it worked. The old fool was right. You'll be no threat to me that size, demon."

I surmised that by some means he had made me smaller, not himself larger. It was no more fantastic than everything else happening, so I dismissed it as just another mystery. What was more interesting to me was the 'demon' word. Its meaning had begun to penetrate. It seemed he truly believed me to be this unnatural creature. I decided to let him believe what he liked for now—it might be useful. But I was still hungry.

"I need food and clean water. Will you give me some, Master?"

He scoffed. "What does a demon need food for? I have tasks for you."

Thinking fast, I said, "This animal body needs sustenance, Master. Give it food, and I will do what you ask. Without food, it will die."

He hesitated. I could sense him weighing up my request. He ordered one of his servants to fetch bread and fruit. I bolted it down. "Thank you, Master. What is your wish?"

"I want you to bring ruin upon Grand Duke Daumantas. I want you to bring me the contents of his treasury and his head in a sack."

The name meant nothing to me, but clearly this person had annoyed him. "Master, I am your willing servant, but this duke you speak of is unknown to me."

I could see the anger and disappointment growing. He had expected some powerful, all-knowing demon, and I wasn't that. There was a tingle of pain starting. What could I do?

Play for time, Greta.

Bow and cringe. The count likes to see obeisance.

"Point the way Master, tell me his weakness and strength."

Demons are cunning.

Yes, they are known for this. Humour him.

"We demons have our ways, Master, wiles and strategies. Tell what you know, and we will make a plan."

Placated by my grovelling, Stevas sighed. "Belbek never really believed this would work. He was wrong and right, apparently." He dismissed his attendants and poured some water for himself. I sensed the chance to get more information.

"Who is this Belbek, Master?"

"The priest? You should know him well. He joined you in the pit with the other two."

The third corpse. "Master, there were two others in the pit. Their memories are in me. I know nothing of this Belbek," I lied.

He seized on the lie. "So, the old fool was not so green! Somehow, he has escaped. Though how he did that with a knife in his belly… But this means the spell is not complete! Beast, beggar, crone and scholar. To summon a demon to do my bidding. Perhaps it is not too late. But I have no other scholar to hand." He paced the room. "Belbek said that his translation of the scroll was not perfect. 'Bodies', it said, but death was implied, not stated. He begged me not to kill the girl, tried to persuade me that only a little blood was needed."

Fury swelled within the part of me that was Timo. I suppressed it. "Master, this is true. Their thoughts came with the blood." I didn't know whether it was true or not, but it seemed to do the trick.

"Very well. There is a scribe in Daumantas' retinue. I will somehow get blood. His knowledge will then be yours and Daumantas will fall. Go now."

I was pushed back into the grey world. The wrenching sensation was becoming familiar now, not so disorienting.

We need the scholar. We don't understand enough.

If I still had my own hands I would ...

You would do nothing. The bear cannot get near him. We need information.

Crina was right. I needed to know more, so I traced my steps back to the bodies. Timo's ruined face stared at me reproachfully.

You made a mess of me.

I growled. The nose ring still pained me at times. Still, I straightened the broken limbs as best I could. He was still warm and so was Crina's body when I tidied it.

I never saw myself before. Am I a crone?

No, you are beautiful.

I snorted. Humans. "Are you both ready for company in there?"

We need him.

And the priest tried to save you?

Yes, he did, it is true. I remember.

Then do it, Bear.

The third body was still oozing from the stomach wound. I licked at the blood gingerly. Why was it still warm?

It was different this time. Rather than a flood of knowledge, there was a hesitant trickle.

Is this hell?

You tell us, priest, you are supposed to know about such things.

Welcome, Belbek. Join us.

Slowly at first, then in a rush, my mind expanded again. An old mind, years spent in a monastery library among ancient books and scrolls. A solitary life, caring for fragments of the past when no one else did. A sudden mad rush to save precious remnants from the invading horde. The flight from Constantinople. Gratitude for the shelter and interest in the rare manuscripts from his friend, Count Stevas. A passion shared for years by correspondence and now in person at last. Excitement and growing dread about the blasphemous experiments. Guilt and horror at the end.

Sorrow sorrow sorrow. The girl, the blood.

I could see him now for what he had been. Cultured, educated, intelligent, but naive and sheltered too long from reality. More innocent in some ways than Crina. Head swimming, I shushed the voices and curled up to sleep it off.

There were no strange dreams this time, but when I awoke, I could tell that my new memories had found their niche. There was knowledge, education, and a powerful urge to explore. Belbek had known nothing of the grey world, and I felt his fascination with this unexpected twist of fate.

So, what can your knowledge do for me, priest? He had not truly believed in the spells contained in the manuscript that had led to this, even when the knife went in. But there was no denying that magic had been done. Was there something in the books? I knew where Belbek had stored them, but trapped here I could do nothing.

But you do remember how the turning felt. Look, it is here, inside you.

I closed my eyes and relived the sensation. It came to me that it was just another direction to turn in, invisible but there. I extended a paw to step around the remembered corner. It just felt like pressing down on the floor. I tentatively poked my head around and looked. Belbek was chortling with delight somewhere inside as Stevas came into view, lying on a cot snoring. I was still in the grey world, but looking into his bedchamber in the real world.

Do you see?

Recent events in Belbek's life unreeled. The talisman had been in Stevas' possession for years. He had known it had power before the arrival of the priest and his treasured books. I watched as they pored over the text, for all the world like two friends playing a game. The shared joy when the connection was made. Belbek's amazement the first time the opening appeared.

It is all connected. The talisman and this world are part of the same thing.

I cautiously crept forward into the room. But as I grew closer to him, the pain started again. I pushed on, but my limbs betrayed me, much as they had done before. Fearful of waking him, I stepped back. Maybe I could just leave through the door? Something told me it wouldn't work, and it proved so. As I moved that way, I felt my feet sliding, and fell back into the grey world with a thump. Disappointing.

No, this is useful. We know more than Stevas does now.

Now it is time to explore this world. There are other mysteries here for us to understand.

Their curiosity—*my* curiosity—needed sating. Grumbling to myself, I lumbered to my feet.

The Village

I awoke very early, my body clock still adjusting from New York time. Mist hung over the river, and hazy pink light filtered through clouds on the distant horizon. Rather than disturb the whole building, I put on running gear and crept out as silently as I could. The streets of the village didn't appeal, so I crossed the little bridge, pausing to admire the rocky stream tumbling under it, then jogged up the hill along a narrow grassy track. The air was still full of night fragrance, and I kept startling small rabbits that darted into the foliage. I apologised to them silently, puffing from the exertion of the climb. It was idyllic, a world away from the city parks I was used to.

On the way up, I passed a group of buildings in various states of disrepair and filed them in my mind for later. Spotting a promontory ahead, I sprinted up a final steep section and stopped breathless to take in the view across the river. It wasn't that high, but still seemed to tower over the jumbled blend of town and countryside below. From here, even the industrial units across the water seemed at ease with their surroundings.

Still buzzing from the exercise, I wandered down, stopping sometimes to take a picture. Arriving at the buildings again, I saw an old-fashioned water pump by one of the semi-derelict houses. Fragments of a wooden pub sign still swung from an ornate bracket attached to the side, the design long faded. I walked over and tried the handle of the pump and was surprised to find it working.

"Would you like a cup, or are you happy to drink from the spout?"

Looking around, I saw an elderly man with long hair and a beard sitting on a bench outside the building. From the other side it had looked like it might fall down at any moment, but it was clearly occupied, with solar panels on the roof and a well-tended garden.

"I'm so sorry. I thought the house was empty."

"It will be soon enough, I daresay." He shuffled inside and came out again holding a glass and a large jug. "Here, you can fill this for me. I was about to get some anyway and you'll save me a job. The glass is for you if you want a drink."

I thanked him and filled the jug. The water was cool, fresh and very welcome and I carefully avoided thinking about bacteria. I introduced myself and explained my mission to find out about Clive. "Do you mind talking to me? You seem like someone who might be able to help with local knowledge."

"Always happy to chat, but I'm not really a local boy. My wife was born here, she would have been able to tell you things, but she's been gone for some ten years now."

"I'm so sorry. Must be tough here on your own."

"It was difficult for a while after Junie passed, but my daughter over in town visits every couple of weeks, and the people in the village help out a lot with things like groceries. That Margot Trimble made me get a mobile phone and arranged for the panels to keep that and the fridge going. All mod cons here, you know." He chuckled. "Junie wouldn't have approved. She was a proper earth mother. We met at Woodstock in 1969. I'd been a roadie with Led Zeppelin on their '68 tour, but got fired when I dropped a case of instruments. So, I just bummed around America for a few months. Junie was a wild one. We had some adventures. But eventually she said she wanted to come home and live off the land."

We chatted for a while. The man interested me. There was a story here, maybe not my story, but something that might make a good article. Right now, I had places to be and a car to move, so I quickly took a picture of him. "You don't mind, do you? I like to keep a record for my interviews."

He muttered that it was fine, the usual response I get. I thanked him for the water and promised to look in again. He seemed pleased.

Back at the inn, I showered and went looking for some breakfast. A good-looking young man was serving plates to other guests. He greeted me cheerily and seated me by the window. "Good morning, Ms Maylor, my name is Sergio. What can I tempt you with today?"

"Call me Annie, please. Was that Eggs Florentine I saw you serving? It looked amazing, if that's not too much trouble. Oh, and compliments on the profiteroles."

He assured me it was no trouble at all and disappeared into the kitchen after directing me to the coffee bar.

A family in Middle Eastern clothing sat at a table nearby. A teenage girl was trying to encourage a small boy to eat cereal. She looked tired, as did the rest of her party. I recognised some Arabic words, so I risked my rusty language skills.

"Sabah el Kheir."

"Sabah el Noor." She was surprised, and continued the conversation in her language. "You speak Arabic?"

"A little, not well. I worked in Jordan for a few years."

"Could you help me with this menu, please? My father is worried we might order something forbidden."

"Of course."

We went over the menu together. I pointed out things to avoid and did my best to translate 'porridge'. I pleased myself with how much I remembered. Sergio soon returned with a steaming plate of eggs, so I passed on their order and excused myself. The dish was excellent, every bit as good as in some of the high-end hotels in New York. After I'd finished, Sergio approached me.

"Excuse me for asking, but would you mind translating for me?"

I went over to their table again. "Sergio here says to tell you that a translator is arriving later today, and that he'll be able to help properly. He hopes you are comfortable, and you are welcome to use the office computer if you want to use email."

Smiles and thanks were exchanged, and I left to retrieve my vehicle.

🐾 🐾 🐾

It took longer than I expected to find the ferry point on the other side. It was hidden at the back of an industrial estate and I thought I'd missed the last morning crossing. I arrived to find the boat waiting with the engine already running. A sandy-haired man I vaguely recognised as one of the customers in the pub last night was waving at me to hurry. A small round white dog was standing at the prow, for all the world as if it were in charge. It made an appealing image, so I snapped a picture before I clambered in, apologising to the other passenger. I sat at the back next to the helmsman. "Just made it!"

An attractive grin stretched his craggy face. "Tansy and I would have had to come back for you. Tansy would not have been amused, but Margot said to make sure we picked you up." The dog looked back at us disdainfully at the mention of its name.

"Ouch. Sorry, Tansy," I called. "You must be Dr Hunt? Sorry for holding you up, I'm not used to your roads. It was so much busier than I expected."

"We gave you a few minutes. I have some time today before my appointments, and Margot calling for a favour like that—well, let's just say it's unusual."

"Grant at the pub said something similar. I don't know what I've done to deserve it. I thought I'd offended her."

"I suppose you might have. Margot is hard to read."

"Appointments?" I ventured.

"I run a GP surgery twice a week in the village. I'm not really a practising doctor these days, but it's good to keep a hand in."

"Really? You seem young to be retired." The smile seemed to stiffen a little. *Oops. Awkward. Change the subject.* "So, you must know this place well. I've been here less than a day and it strikes me as very odd. Even for England."

He relaxed again. "Lower Pichesham is a rare place. Once you meet some of the residents, you'll see it more."

As we arrived, the old man I'd met that morning was waiting. The other passenger, a pleasant-looking middle-aged woman I assumed to be the daughter he'd mentioned, waved and called a greeting. Dr Hunt tied up the boat at the little pier by Ferry Cottage and helped us out. As the others walked off, the old man turned and looked at us with an odd, rather sly expression.

The doctor and I walked into the village, preceded by the dog, him towering by my side. I made light conversation, telling him about my encounter with the old man and the morning's language refresher. "I mean, elsewhere that wouldn't be so unusual, but Grant said you don't get tourists here."

"That's true. It's because this whole place is owned by a charitable trust, even the New Star Inn itself. Most of the people who come through are those who need a little help in life. My guess is that you met some refugees—from Yemen, maybe? There have been a few lately." He looked at me appraisingly. "Conversational Arabic? That's a useful skill. If Margot finds out, she'll have you on the staff."

I laughed. "Yeah, I don't think so. I already have a job. I'm a journalist, generally lifestyle articles now, but I've done more serious stuff in the past. That's where the languages come from. This trip is mostly personal, but I'm hoping to get a decent article as well. I kind of need it." I explained about the family history quest, as he seemed interested.

"This is me." He gestured at one of the blocky little houses. "What are you doing today? Before your appointment with the boss, I mean."

"I'm not sure. I was hoping there might be somewhere with records. A church maybe?"

"Oh, there is a church up in the old village. You were near it this morning, a bit beyond the house where Lance lives—that's who you met this morning. The church was abandoned a long time ago. But there is a graveyard, and it's well cared for, so maybe some of the names on the headstones will help?"

I thanked him. He was nice. A touch old for me, maybe, but my type. "Maybe I'll see you around?"

"I expect so. I'm invited to afternoon tea as well." He turned back as he went inside. "Dominic, by the way. If you were wondering. Dom to my friends."

"Annie. See you later, Dom." Yup, definitely a little spark there.

The Companions–II

Polatsk, Grand Duchy of Lithuania, 1285

It was a long time before Count Stevas summoned me back. I made good use of it, testing the limits of my invisible tether. Moving along the new directions turned out to be a little like swimming. It took practice, and sometimes I ended up falling with a thump when I misjudged the levels. Eventually I worked out the shape of it. An intangible surface, like a thin skin, surrounded the talisman in a sphere. It reminded me of the way that water beads up on some leaves. Once I understood, I found I could approach that surface from any angle, but could go no further. Usefully, there was a balance point where, if I was careful, I could see into an area without going into it.

The room underneath the count's chamber was a pantry, meaning I could try my new skills unseen by him, and steal food and other supplies when the room was unoccupied.

Once, a cook caught a glimpse. She had been Crina's friend.

"*Delia, remember me,*" I whispered in Crina's voice. The poor woman jumped and ran out, clutching an apron to her face. After that, the servants avoided the room.

I made an attempt to get Belbek's books, sure that they would be helpful. They were in reach, in a strongbox bolted to a wall in his chamber. I tried to open it while he was sleeping. To my frustration, my claws couldn't be made to manipulate the lock. I could have ripped the whole box away with little effort, but I could not do it without revealing myself.

Since it didn't seem to matter where I stood in the grey world while secretly visiting Stevas' house, I was free to explore there as well. Despite the barrenness of the land, it was littered with objects—banal things like sticks, rags and broken pots. There were many remnants of once-living creatures, mostly skeletal. More disturbing were the occasional animal carcasses that were recognisable. Small birds, squirrels. A rabbit that smelled fresh enough to eat, coated in dust. Another bear, much larger than me, long dead and dried out, flesh like leather, still covered in fur. A human leg, still oozing at the torn end, sent my hackles rising, but there was no visible danger. I moved on, working on a circular route around the caves. Interspersed with these were things that might be useful if I could work out a way to pick them up—a box of candles; a hammer; a length of fine cord.

Under a rocky ledge, I found a large pot full of crudely struck silver coins protruding from the dust. Nearby, a slightly wrinkled turnip sat incongruously on the ground. At least that was edible, and I reached for it.

"DO NOT."

I spun around in alarm. A mound was shifting behind me, dust pouring away from its limbs as it rose onto four legs, its movements clumsy and awkward. It towered above me, a great shaggy beast with widespread horns.

"Do not. That is mine!"

Terrifying as the beast was, it made no threatening moves. I looked more closely. It was big, but I saw signs that it was old and weak. And it was speaking. I braced myself against a rock. "Who or what are you? Are you the demon?"

There was a deep sense of laughter.

"Well, are you?"

"I am like you. I see your minds, bear. I have my own companions. There are no demons here." It bent down and ate the turnip.

Curiosity fought the fear. Perhaps this creature …

"Can answer your questions? Surely. I mean you no harm. It's always pleasant to meet someone new. It's been a long time."

"You can hear my thoughts?"

"You are shouting them at me, youngster. Hard to avoid it." It shook off the last of the dust. "I'm thirsty. I slept too long. Come, join me." It walked stiffly towards the caves. I followed at a safe distance.

We reached the wet cave, and as we entered, the walls lit up, revealing that the puddle I'd found earlier was actually a large pond. The creature drank deeply from it. When it was satisfied, it stood on its hind legs and stretched its arms. I was bewildered. The creature now had the shape and dimensions of a human male, though it still resembled the beast it had been. The transformation had happened without me noticing.

"How long, bear? What year is it?"

I consulted the companions and found a reply from Belbek. "It is the year of our Lord 1285."

"Seventy-four years since I last visited the world." He sighed. "Well, I'll tell you some basics now. You may need them if you are summoned. First, don't fight your master's orders. If you can obey, you must. You can resist, but it only leads to pain and misery. I have watched others like us try to resist and fail. Your abilities will grow with experience. I see you have already started to learn to navigate the boundary. You are a quick learner."

"Is there no escape?"

"You might trick your way out of slavery for a while, but your old life is over. Your master will have control over an object of some sort, and you are now tied to that object. Even if it is not held, it will seek out new masters. I do not know how or why this happens, but it does. I have outlived many masters. After the first died, I tried to return to a herd of my kind. They rejected me. I was too different. Still, at least I was free to choose my own path. But over time, my anchor stone was rediscovered repeatedly. The last master was generous. She unleashed me and ordered my stone cast into a deep lake. That was nearly eight hundred years ago. I hope to die of old age before it is found again."

"How old are you?"

"Perhaps three thousand years. It is hard to keep track. Time passes differently here. Ageing is slow."

"As is decay?" I said, thinking of the warm corpses.

"Sharp mind." He nodded approvingly. "But wounds and illness also take a long time to heal, so try to not get injured."

I had so many questions, and Auroch (as I came to know him later) was happy to oblige with answers. But he was not troubled much by the question of why things were the way they were. When I asked how he had changed his shape, he seemed surprised. "I didn't notice. It's just something I do, helps fit into the caves better. I forget where I learned that. Falcon, maybe." He tried to show me, but I couldn't understand. I asked where the others he'd mentioned were. "We come and go. When I arrived, there were five other bound folk, all gone now. There were seven like us the last time I was awake. They usually gather down in the forest cavern beneath the lake. It is warmer there."

The what?

He answered my unspoken thought. "See that path?" His hoofed arm gestured to one side of the cave. "Follow it down sometime. It is too hot for me, I prefer the cool desert air up here. Some are friendlier than others, but none of the bound folk will harm you. Though I would advise you to stay away from the wolf pack. They are not quite like us. Troublemakers, all of them, especially Erik."

"Thank you. You are being very kind."

He grunted. "I was not always. Age has mellowed me." Turning away, he bent down and slapped the surface of the pond. "Last, there is always the Thing-under-the-Water." After a moment, a glistening greenish bulge rose from the water, followed by a long, slender tentacle. I recoiled in alarm, but then felt something like a voice, saying something like a greeting. Despite its disturbing appearance, a feeling of welcome radiated towards me.

"Thing was here before I arrived, before even the bound folk I first met all those years ago, and for all I know before their predecessors. It can be hard to understand what it is saying, but it looks after us."

The tentacle reached towards me. I reached out a paw and touched it gingerly. There was a short sense of amusement.

"And that is everyone I know of. Some of us die. Some go to the real world and just never return. Lion-with-Long-Teeth helped me when I was sent in. She looked so fierce, and it was hard at first to stop myself from running away. But we became great friends."

"Where is she now?"

He sighed. "She returned from a summons one time with a missing eye and a deep slash across her belly. Even here, where wounds bleed slowly, it was too much. It was the end for her, but Thing eased the pain, and she went peacefully. It was long ago now."

This was sobering. "So, we aren't magically invulnerable then."

He rumbled in grim amusement. "Far from it, bear."

He seems lonely.

"Your young lady has a sweet nature. Be assured, I am never alone. Ahn-na and Muhn-na would like to meet her. Do you accept?"

"I suppose?"

The hazy figure of a woman emerged in a space somewhere that was both inside my head and not. It held out fuzzy arms. I watched as my Crina emerged into that same space. The figure embraced her, and then Crina was weeping. Thoughts of her mother, her lost friends, the hurt at the betrayal poured out. Ahn-na consoled her, somehow managing to rock her like a baby. The emotions bled over to all of us to some degree. A male figure reached through to Timo and stood alongside him, projecting reassurance and understanding. Belbek looked on interestedly, seeming to have no equivalent personality in the great beast. All the while, Auroch and I stood where we had been all along, looking on as outsiders for the moment.

Auroch seemed pleased. "Your companions are strong and well matched. You have a good chance, I think. I'm still hungry. Do you have any more worldly food, by chance?"

I had a small stash of stale bread, so we wandered outside to find it.

🐾 🐾 🐾

Later, Auroch was explaining the lighting in the cave when I felt a tug of summons. "I have to go."

I was back with the count. He loomed above, even larger than before. I began to feel the pattern of this, how I might make these apparent shifts in size myself. Another piece of knowledge to ask my new friend about. I stayed silent, staring up.

"This knife has the blood of the scribe. Take it, complete the spell. I must have my revenge. Hurry, we don't have long until they find the body."

He laid the knife before me. To my eyes, it seemed as long as a broadsword.

Don't worry, nothing will happen.

Despite Belbek's assurances, I remained nervous about what might happen. I licked at the stain cautiously. Just the familiar tang of blood. Relief flooded me. We were complete and whole, and there was no more disruption in my head.

"Well?"

Auroch and I had planned what to say. I decided a little show would add to the effect, so I twisted back and forth, reappearing full-sized. He jumped back in alarm. I bowed as best I could without entering the pain zone.

"Master."

He eyed me with suspicion. "Has it worked?"

"I am ready to serve."

"You remember my orders?"

"I do."

Belbek knew of Daumantas, though not why Stevas was so keen on doing him harm. He was the latest in a series of rulers of the increasingly unstable lands that made up the Grand Duchy of Lithuania.

"Then do so. Do it now!"

I stayed prone for a moment. "Master, I find I cannot part from your presence." This was true, at least while he held that anchor.

He swore under his breath. "Very well." He retrieved a scroll from his strongbox, and, reading from it, muttered some words in badly accented Latin. "That should allow you to travel. Daumantas' encampment is in the valley north of here. He is gathering yet more tribute. He will not rob me again." We walked outside, and Stevas gestured in the right direction. "I will summon you at sunset tomorrow if you are not already returned. Do not fail me. You will suffer if you fail me."

I moved stepwise, flickering in and out of the real world until his house was out of sight. Then I relaxed a little and ambled through a woodland very like the forest I was born in. I knew I wasn't free. He had extended my range but could summon me back at will. Still, it was wonderful to walk alone in the fresh air for the first time in years.

My brief time to myself ended too soon. The encampment appeared ahead, a busy place surrounded by guards. I had my plan, but would it work?

It was easy enough to get in. I changed size until I was small enough to slip past the sentries, and, by eavesdropping, found out the location of the Grand Duke's tent. I entered his quarters in my reduced form and then waited for night to fall. Finally, Daumantas sent his servants away. Alone and unarmed as he was, I made my move. I appeared behind him, grabbed him, and took him back to the grey world with scarcely a sound made.

There was predictable yelling as I dumped him in the dust, and a strong reek of fear. To give him credit, he recovered poise quickly once he realised he wasn't injured. I put on a suitably diabolical voice.

"Welcome to the edge of the underworld, Daumantas. I am the demon of Count Stevas." The words were ludicrous, but I needed his attention.

He was brave. Being confronted by a talking demon-bear should have made him quake. "What evil is this? Where have you brought me?"

I glared down at him. "My master sent me here to take you to Hell. I may yet choose to do so. Are you ready for death?"

He narrowed his eyes. "Am I not dead already?"

"Not quite. There is still a chance for you. I detest my master and wish only to be released from his control. If you will help me, I will return you alive."

"Your master claims to be a great sorcerer. It seems he was telling the truth. I know nothing about these matters. What can I do?"

"He only succeeded in trapping me with help. He is careless and stupid."

A ghost of a smile appeared. "So I always thought myself. A disloyal subject, and not even competent. Very well, take me back and I will have him tortured. He will reveal his secrets and you will be released."

Ha, small chance. This man was as untrustworthy as Stevas, and a lot smarter. "Not so simple, Duke. I am bound to obey my master's commands on pain of death. His orders were to 'bring ruin upon Grand Duke Daumantas, bring me the contents of his treasury and his head in a sack'. I must fulfil those orders."

"But ..."

"He did not say your head must be detached from your body, and I didn't ask for clarification. If you agree to my terms, I will bring you a weapon at the right time, to carry inside your sack. He is no warrior. Direct me to your treasury so that I can take it now. Once he is dead, I will be released. Your treasury will be returned. I have no use for it."

He was reluctant, especially about the money. "How can I trust you?"

I reared up to my full height and glared at him. "You have no choice!" I roared. "If I have to rip off your head, I will." I cuffed him with one claw, and he staggered and fell, blood flowing from his lip.

He stood and spat at the floor, fuming. "Very well. It is agreed. Look under my bed. There is a shallow pit, with a locked box concealed there."

I turned myself back into his tent. Pushing the cot aside, I quickly found the box. It was heavy and awkward to lift, but I managed, and dragged it back to the grey world. "Here. Open it."

Taking a key from around his neck, he unlocked the chest. Sure enough, there was coin in there.

"Wait here. I will return shortly." I turned myself back toward the campsite. Finding enough sacks to carry my loot turned out to be harder than convincing the duke. I sneaked around the camp, taking them one at a time back to the duke, and instructed him to put his treasure in one. He really did not want to, and I had to shout some more. A head-sized rock went into another. A third, the largest, was meant for him. "What weapon shall you have?"

"Bring me my sword. It is hanging on a stand."

Timo's voice interrupted my thoughts.

No! We cannot allow him a weapon like that. Something smaller.

He has only one chance. The duke will have been trained in the sword.

We must take the risk. Trust Bear, Timo.

Timo was right, it was a dangerous moment, but I would have to trust my captive. "You must maintain surprise. If he has time to order me to defend him, I will have to kill you. And then he will know what I have done. If you cannot take him immediately, separate him from the talisman he wears. That is the source of his power over me."

"I understand."

"Very well." I fetched the sword and threw it toward him. "I will be back soon. Be ready."

I ran back from the encampment through the forest to Count Stevas' house and beat upon the gate. Terrified servants led the way to the chamber he was waiting in.

"Well?"

Without speaking, I switched worlds. I scooped up the sack holding Daumantas and took him into the pantry beneath. "He is upstairs. I will distract him. Hurry." Daumantas nodded.

One more crossing to take the other sacks to Stevas. Spilling the money across the floor, I dumped the one with the rock noisily to one side. He grabbed at the coins first, as I'd hoped. "Master, your order has been fulfilled. Are you pleased?"

"I thought there would be more. Are you sure you got it all?"

"Master, he swore it was. He begged for mercy, promising everything." I could see a shadowy figure emerging behind Stevas. "I took it all, and just before…"

Daumantas grabbed him from behind, ripped the talisman from his neck, and punched him violently to the floor. Stevas looked aghast at me.

"Traitor! Liar! How is this possible? Belbek said you had to obey."

Daumantas drew his sword and held it to his throat. "Oh, Stevas. I hoped this monster was lying, but here you are, just as it said, picking over my purse."

I realised my mistake too late. "Kill him quickly. Release me."

Daumantas smiled. "No, I think my old friend Stevas is going to gift me this talisman, demon. You seem too useful to be let go. I have enemies you can help with."

"My lord," Stevas gabbled, "it tricked me. I summoned it for your use, I just asked it for treasure. I didn't know it would attack you. Please, I am your faithful servant. I will gladly give it to you."

Daumantas stared down at him. "I will choose to believe you, Stevas. If you tell me how to control it."

"You already do, my lord. Squeeze the talisman in your hand and speak your wish. But choose your words carefully, my lord. See how it twisted mine?"

"Lying worm," I growled. "Release me, Duke. You will never know peace if you don't."

He laughed. "I can be careful, monster."

I lunged at him. It was no use. I fell to my knees again.

"So, it is true. Thank you, Stevas. I accept your gift. But the demon is right, you are a lying worm. Demon, kill Count Stevas."

The miracle happened. I felt nothing more than a slight urge. The talisman was unreachable, but the duke's order had no real compulsion. I stared at them both. Then I leapt at Stevas and snapped his neck. He dropped to the floor in a heap. I was almost sure I could have ignored the command, but that vile creature wasn't getting a second chance.

The duke watched with interested. "Very good, demon. Now, gather my money back into this sack."

It felt the same. I resisted the urge. I wanted to see what would happen if I disobeyed.

"No." There was just a slight tingle in my head, like a fly buzzing in my ear.

He squeezed the talisman hard. "Obey me, you unholy creature," he shouted. The tingle flared briefly, then faded away.

"Pick up your own mess, Duke. I'm leaving." I turned back into the grey world.

There was a ghostly sensation of summoning. I ignored it for a while, but Belbek reminded me about the books. I switched back. Daumantas' face lit up for a few moments. I tried one more time to get near enough to take a swipe. Pain flared, so I drew back and stalked over to Stevas' strongbox instead, keeping Daumantas in sight. It wrenched from the wall easily enough. "Goodbye, Duke. Thank you, it seems you kept the agreement after all. You'd better keep that talisman with you now. It protects you from me. Useful, eh? But I can check if you still have it. If I ever find you without it … well, let us part as friends. You have all of Stevas' wealth and property, so you are still up on the day."

He roared and ran at me, brandishing the sword. I flipped out before he got close enough for the pain to start. I swivelled mid-change and reappeared behind him. This was fun.

Bear, tell him…

Crina was worried about her friends. "Look after his servants, Duke. They are innocents, and they are under my protection. I cannot hurt you directly, but I can do other damage."

He tried one more time. Honestly, I was beginning to like this man. He was no quitter. I laughed aloud, withdrawing as slowly as I could, letting the real world fade away.

Afternoon Tea

Following the doctor's advice that morning, I wandered back across the little footbridge and up the hill. I soon found the church, which was in ruins. The roof was long gone, as was the east wall. A hand-lettered sign gave a cheerful warning about the dangers of falling masonry, but the surrounding graveyard was indeed well tended.

In the most recent section, I found a small memorial stone bearing the single word 'June', with a small arrangement of wildflowers. Further back there was a rather grand area with a number of headstones bearing the name 'Charting', presumably somehow linked to the hospital. There were no Maylors that I could find. I took notes and photos, but I felt disappointed. I'd been pinning my hopes on church records. If any still existed, they were probably in a dusty archive miles away. The weather decided that I'd done enough, so I scurried back to find a towel and an early lunch.

It was beginning to seem like my spur-of-the-moment trip was going to be a washout. The investigation into Great-Grandpa and his diary had been on my list for years, but never a priority. Since the bust-up with Paul, my name was mud back home anyway. Having lost the goodwill of both the NYPD and most of my journalistic contacts, I needed to lie low for a while and find something fresh to restore my reputation. A good human-interest story could be my ticket back in, but so far, I'd discovered the square root of zip. Still, it was a good place to de-stress. And the accommodation was exemplary. My request for a 'light salad' for lunch had arrived as an exotic confection of leaves, mango, and edible flowers that even cynical old me had felt the need to photograph.

I spent a leisurely couple of hours on the covered veranda, writing on my laptop and watching the Great British drizzle float across the view. Someone in the village was practising the violin, and snatches of Vivaldi drifted over.

"Good afternoon, Annie, enjoying the ambience?" It was Dominic, holding a tray. "Mind if I join you?" I gestured, pleased to see him, and he sat down next to me. "Can I pour you some tea? Sergio put an extra cup on, and I think the second cake is for you as well. Apparently it's his version of Tarta de Santiago, whatever that is."

"Good job I made the effort to run this morning." I took a small bite of what looked like an almond tart and was rewarded with an unexpected burst of orange zest. "The food here is superb. I'd have thought Sergio would be in London at some fancy restaurant."

"He was a sous chef at the Ivy for two years. Met Grant and followed him here. I think he misses it a bit, but they seem very happy together." We sat and listened to the music. "That's young Osman Tankye playing. I'm no expert, but he sounds pretty good. His father told me he's auditioning for the Royal College next month. I hope he makes it. They're due a bit of luck."

"Aren't you here to escort me to afternoon tea? Should we be eating cake?"

"You'd be glad of it, but I'll have it if you don't want any. And you might get lucky. Sometimes she makes scones, and they are usually edible at least."

I compromised on half, and we sat chatting. An enormous black bird clattered down from somewhere and stalked around the table, exuding menace. "Dear Lord! What is that?" I exclaimed.

Dom chuckled. "Annie, meet Arthur the raven. He's a bit of a fixture here. Even has his own pad." Dominic gestured up to the roof of the inn, where I could see a platform jutting out below the eaves. "Here boy." As he scattered some crumbs, the bird picked one up with a delicate motion and jumped away to eat it.

Arthur had the other half of my cake, and we strolled down to Ferry Cottage. I was unaccountably nervous as we knocked on the door. I'd met this woman once for a few minutes, but it felt like we were dropping in on Queen Elizabeth herself. We were ushered brusquely into a bright room lined with shelves adorned with books. A small collection of vintage children's toys occupied a glass-fronted cabinet. On the table was a large open album filled with black and white photos. Tea was served in large white cups, and a dainty cake stand holding some flat grey disks was proffered. Margot sat across from us, her eyes sharp and assessing, taking in every detail of my appearance as I diffidently reached for the tea. I tucked my hair self-consciously behind my ears, wishing I'd remembered to get my roots done before I arrived.

"Please try a lavender shortbread, Ms Maylor. It's a new recipe for me, but I think it's a winner."

I took one with trepidation and nibbled at the edge. It tasted of soap and sadness. Oh, well, maybe scones another time.

"Now, tell me about your great-grandfather."

"Well, as I said last night, his name was Clive Maylor. His diary mentions Pichesham a few times. I tried all the usual databases but came up blank."

"And do you have any pictures of him?"

"Yes, here." I'd brought some documents. "This is my grandfather's christening photo. Clive and his wife Lillian are holding him."

She peered at it. "Oh yes. I have an album here that my aunt left. She was chair of the Trust before me. Here, look at this photo."

On the open page was a group picture of several men in military uniform, standing in front of a grand doorway. Some of them looked very young—boys, really. One of these was unmistakably Clive, standing beside a baby-faced youth who could not have been more than sixteen. I pointed . "That's Clive there."

"Yes, I thought so. This is a picture taken at Chartings House in 1914. The older man beside him is his father, Major John Charting. The other uniformed men are staff and estate workers. It's all written on the back. Take it out and have a look. You might see a name you know, Dr Hunt."

"Really? How curious."

I carefully slid the picture from its mounts and turned it over. Sure enough, a handwritten legend put names to the faces. James Wick, Gareth Beckett, Major John Charting, Clive Charting, Henry Duchamp, Norman Bendigo. And at the bottom: 'Taken by Peter Brownlow.'

Dominic said, "Brownlow is my mother's maiden name. Is there a connection?"

"Peter was the major's cousin. He was the estate manager and wasn't able to enlist because he suffered from clubfoot. I have reason to think he was your grandfather."

He looked doubtful. "It's quite a common name."

I spoke up. "But my great-grandfather was Clive Maylor, not Charting."

"I assume he changed it when he left here. Clive moved to the US after the government took control of the hospital. It was not a happy parting. From what my aunt told me. Perhaps he wanted to put it all behind him and start anew."

This was very interesting. My enigmatic ancestor had acquired whole new dimensions—a military past and a family of landed gentry. I was in my very own episode of *Who Do You Think You Are?* "This is amazing. Are there other pictures?"

"A few. These were gathered from various places by a resident in the 1970s who wrote a brief history of the Trust. It was useful in getting grants."

We leafed through the pages. Most were shots of a grand country house from various angles. There was a blurred image of a hunt gathering; horses, hounds and men standing around in traditional garb. Another photo was of a row of young women in nurses' uniforms, bookended by a stern-looking matron and an elegantly dressed woman carrying a parasol. "That one was also taken by Peter Brownlow, in July 1915. There are no other names, but the woman on the right is probably Agatha, Clive's mother."

I got busy with the cellphone camera, making the best copies I could. My family back in the States was going to want to see these. "There must be family photographs then?"

"I'm sure there were, but they have been lost. Chartings House was severely damaged by fire between the wars."

"And what is it that makes you think Peter is my grandfather?" Dom asked.

"I need to check something first. If I can, I'll explain later. But Ms Maylor, I would like to know more about your interest. I have made some calls, and I'm aware of your occupation. Please don't be offended. I am responsible for the welfare of the people of this village, and we do not court publicity for the Trust."

I was more surprised than offended. I turned up the charm a notch. "Well, to be honest, Mrs Trimble, I'm between jobs at the moment. I have some time on my hands, and family history is interesting to look into anyway. It's certainly turning out more promising than I could have hoped for. But if you are asking whether I'm looking for a story, yes, I did have hopes. I have Clive's diary, and it says very little about his early life, except near the end, when he writes about some rather ... unlikely events. Maybe it will make a story, maybe not, but it all happened more than a hundred years ago. I don't think there is anything to concern you."

I smiled reassuringly. But I felt a small tickle run through my story sense and decided to look into this Trust. Wouldn't hurt to follow up a bit.

"I'm intrigued. What do you mean by 'unlikely', Ms Maylor?"

I debated internally what to tell her. "Most of what Great-Grandpa Clive wrote in his diaries was work-related. Quite interesting, if horses are your thing. He was a bloodstock agent, very successful. My father wrote a small memoir using the diary and it sold quite well locally. But towards the end, the entries start to get strange. Stories about his childhood that make no sense. Pop says the dementia came on rapidly, and you can see that in what Clive wrote. Even so, some of the stories are very detailed and they have a ring of truth about them."

"What are the stories about?"

"Well, to put it bluntly, impossible things happen, and they usually revolve around a bear. Which is ridiculous, of course. I was hoping to find out if there was any basis for the stories, maybe some local folklore that might have influenced his mind. I've been thinking about an article, or maybe even a book, for years, but you know how it is. Real life usually gets in the way."

I had a strong sense that I had said something wrong. There was a long silence before Margot spoke. "I wish you well with your story, Ms Maylor, but it causes me some unease. Lower Pichesham is a quiet place for good reasons, and the non-residents who come here are quiet people. A few hikers, new staff at the hospital, people visiting their relatives there. Publicity that attracts visitors looking for the sensational … this would concern me. Would you be willing to let me see the article before you publish it? Assuming there is something to write, of course."

I had been asked for similar concessions many times. "No, that's not something I would be prepared to do. I am a reputable journalist, Mrs Trimble. I think you'll just have to trust my judgement. But I appreciate your concerns, and I will think about what you've said and whether I can take account of such sensitivities."

There was another long silence. "Ms Maylor, while I accept you may believe in your own judgement, is it not true that one of your stories directly led to someone being attacked?"

How in God's name did she know about that? I responded coolly. "The story you are referring to was a clear case of corruption in office. It led to the city councillor in question being prosecuted. Without the story, he would have continued to take those bribes."

"Yes, but from what I understand, this led to him making an attempt on the life of your informant. I imagine this must have weighed upon your conscience?"

She had pricked a nerve. The person she was referring to was Paul's ex-wife, who had been the inside person as the councillor's lover. She'd gone to Paul hoping that he could do something about it in an official capacity—he was a detective in the NYPD. When his superiors said it was not worth the resources, he'd let it slip to me and I'd jumped on the story. I'd worked it up into a top-notch piece of investigative journalism. Perhaps I should have told him before it went to press, but it was *really* good. I'd been careful to keep Sandra's part anonymous, but the councillor had jumped to an unwarranted conclusion. The violence of his reaction had come as a complete shock to everyone who knew him. Sandra hadn't been badly hurt, but Paul blamed me for what had happened. He'd made damn sure I was persona non grata in New York, telling everyone that I'd revealed a source. Most of my previous contacts had blanked me directly to my face.

"The story was entirely factual, Mrs Trimble, and I believe in the truth. What others do with that is their concern."

☗ ☗ ☗

That was more or less it. Margot was stiffly polite but had nothing to add and firmly refused to be photographed. We left, crumbling grey cookies discreetly concealed in Dom's jacket pocket. When we were out of sight of the cottage, he tossed them toward the riverbank. Arthur fluttered over from his perch on the pub, inspected them, and stalked off in apparent disgust.

We strolled back to the inn, lost in thought. I was feeling bruised and dissatisfied. Dominic was the first to break the silence.

"That was… I don't know what that was. She was pretty rough with you."

I didn't want to talk about that, so I changed the subject. "Is it likely to be true about that guy being your grandfather?"

"It is certainly possible. From what I remember, my mum never met her own dad, he died before she was born. And I was born with the same condition, had therapy as a little kid for it."

"Clubfoot? Is it hereditary then?"

"Not always, but it does run in some families. Talipes is the medical name. Back when that man was growing up, treatment was primitive and he would have been quite badly affected. So, it is possible, but that is quite a coincidence. I've been living and working here for four years. I'm paid by the Trust, but this is the first time I've ever heard about it."

"It's odd, I agree."

"Baffling. On one hand, it doesn't matter, it isn't as if I was trying to trace him. On the other hand, I don't like my employer knowing such things when I don't. If it's true at all!" He gave a sigh. "Well, at least you have some answers. You must be pleased with that, even if Margot was sniffy with you."

"Yes. In a way. Pop will be hyped, and the stately home thing will bring some pretty big bragging rights."

He laughed at that. "You can probably trace back to royalty now. That kind of family will be documented far more than most. Even bigger bragging rights."

I shrugged. "It is pretty cool. But it's not really what I came for."

The Pichesham Trust– Pioneers of Care

A brochure, apparently written in 1972 or 1973

The remarkable history of the Pichesham Trust is intimately intertwined with Chartings Military Hospital. The Trust's origins can be traced to the Great War. While her husband John was away serving in the Army Remount Service, Mrs Agatha Charting was determined to find her own way to contribute to the war effort. With John's agreement, Chartings House, built in 1725, was first used as a war hospital supply depot in 1915. As the number of casualties in France increased rapidly, it was made over as a convalescent hospital in August 1916.

Many hundreds of men recovered there; sadly, others succumbed to their wounds. Six men from this time are buried in the churchyard of the now-ruined St Joseph's Church in Pichesham. A commemorative window in the church was commissioned from noted glass artist Mary Lowndes, a close friend to Agatha through her connections with the suffrage movement. One panel, similar in design to the Lowndes window in St Mary, Sennicotts, West Sussex, featured an image of a solemn nurse tending to an injured man and it is believed that Agatha posed for this herself. Sadly, the church was destroyed by a stray bomb in 1944. Fragments of the window were later reused during the restoration of the east wing of Chartings House.

By July 1918, with the war coming to a close, one particular casualty arrived. Captain Clive Charting, only son of John and Agatha, suffered horrific wounds at what was to become known as the final German offensive, the Second Battle of the Marne. Though the battle was a success for the Allies, Captain Charting was caught in the path of an exploding shell. Miraculously surviving, he was brought home with severe and lasting injuries.

Sparing no expense, the Chartings brought in expertise, including doctors trained under Harold Gilles, the celebrated pioneer of facial reconstructive surgery. Surgeons at Chartings developed novel techniques aimed at alleviation of restricted movement due to scarring of the limbs. So successful were they that Captain Charting recovered almost all movement. After the war, with many severely disabled men needing help, the hospital continued its work. Considerable resources of the estate had been put into supporting the hospital, so in 1920, the family established the Chartings Hospital Trust. They devoted themselves tirelessly to raising financial support among their peers and were highly successful. Their work was recognised in 1926 when Agatha Charting was made a Companion of Honour to King George V.

Tragedy was to strike soon after. A fire broke out in the family wing of the house on the evening of January 22nd, 1927. Among the dead were Agatha, John, the estate manager Peter Brownlow (a cousin) and a maid, Jennifer Grady. The patients and hospital staff were all saved, but the building itself was largely destroyed. Only the east wing and gatehouse now remain.

Despite his grief, Clive Charting tried to continue the work. The hospital was rebuilt, but in the interim the specialist surgical team had relocated to London, never to return. Without its particular niche, and having found no alternative purpose, the Trust could no longer attract enough donations to continue.

It was at this point that the Ministry of Defence stepped in and offered to purchase the hospital and estate. Mindful perhaps of the strong reputation acquired by the Trust in its humane treatment of servicemen, but also with an eye on the land, a substantial sum was offered. There was a catch. The Ministry wanted *all* the land, including the village of Pichesham itself. The residents would have to leave and make way for a new barracks and training centre.

Clive Charting sought alternative ways forward, but, on the verge of bankruptcy and still suffering the lingering effects of his injuries, was forced to accede to the sale. He managed to obtain assurances that the hospital would continue in some form, and to this day Chartings Military Hospital continues its work, these days being focused on mental health. He also retained a stretch of land along the river front with a view to creating new homes for the displaced villagers. Exhausted and depressed by the turn of events, and facing anger from many of his former tenants, he endowed the Trust with the majority of the sale proceeds, and persuaded Miss Margaret Stanground, former chief nurse, to take over chairmanship of the Trust, before departing for a new life abroad.

The Trust was renamed the Pichesham Trust. Margaret Stanground immediately set about finding a new mission. She saw the development of the new village of Lower Pichesham as an opportunity to create a new kind of community. As well as former tenants, people who needed help with their troubles would be welcomed and given space and time to heal. She saw it as critical that the community contained diverse people from all social backgrounds. Although the approach imposed very low limits on the numbers that could be helped directly, her reasoning was that, strengthened and nourished, people would move back into the world, taking the spirit of Pichesham with them to reach others who also needed help.

The ethos of those days persists. The Trust reaches out into the world supporting projects in forty-five countries, both with guidance and financial support. Individual projects cover a wide range of specialisms, including education, addiction services, mental health and women's health. Working within these disparate groups, project leaders have access to a closely knit mesh of knowledge where they can learn best practice and pass on their own experiences.

Lower Pichesham still welcomes people and families in need and brings its quiet magic into their lives until they can stand alone again.

Pr Trevor Jameston, grateful former resident of Lower Pichesham

Violante-I

A ropewalk near the Arsenale di Venezia,
1449

"... discendat in hoc speculum virtus spiritus sancti ..."

The little group of hooded figures was still working through the incantation and it was going to be a while yet. I ducked back home to Greyside, wondering if there was time for a snack.

These summonings were never convenient. I had been practising my flageolet work with Thing, and it was finally beginning to sound reasonable. Ever since I discovered that Thing-under-the-Water liked music, the part of me that was Timo had wanted to re-learn how to play. Auroch had taught me the basics of shape-changing, but it wasn't his best trick. Hooves are not easy to modify. My human shape was rough at best, but unlike him, I could do proper hands now, although the thumbs were less than ideal. Getting the airflow right to play an instrument was another challenge, but Thing and I were almost ready to put on a performance for the Greysiders. We'd decided on a madrigal by Jacopo da Bologna. Thing was reproducing the vocal line (without words, of course) while I had adapted the most interesting instrumental lines.

I sighed and wished Thing farewell for now. There was always a chance that this would be our last meeting. It was a feeling that I had become accustomed to over the decades. I wrote Auroch a note and drifted moodily back to my cave to await the latest master.

I sneaked another look. They were gathered in a cleared area of some sort of factory building. I didn't know Venice well, but I knew it must be somewhere near the Arsenale, because it stank of tar and was stacked with reels of rope. The leader was a female, dark-haired, her body concealed in heavy robes. She was so tall that she loomed over the others there. I could tell she was going to be trouble. Even over the background smell, the aroma of magic was strong on her. Still, she was running through the usual rigmarole, so maybe I could play on her superstition.

The summons finally came, and I emerged into a neatly constructed and unusually roomy pentagram made of rope.

She gasped and smiled triumphantly at her shocked minions. "I told you it would work, Radulphus!"

I picked my teeth with a claw, affecting boredom with the whole proceeding. "Tell me your desire, Master."

She did not care for my attitude. "Surely you know already, all-knowing, all-powerful demon."

"Well, about that …"

"Silence. I know your true name, Ursa. I know all about you. You are the least of your kind, despised weakling among demons. But you will serve me well yet."

I don't know why I was surprised. It made sense that the humans would have been keeping records over the years. Still, I took umbrage at the word 'despised', so I farted loudly. "Fear you not the sulphurous pits of hell, mortal?"

The woman hadn't expected that, and gave a small giggle that turned into a proper belly laugh. It was infectious, and I found myself laughing as well. The hooded group around the room looked at each other, unsure whether they should join in. One essayed a nervous chuckle, and she snapped round at him, glaring. "Enough. Ursa, I ask only this now. Do you know the location of the Cave of Wonders?"

This was not a casual question. The force of compulsion lay behind it. I had no idea what it meant, but I had to answer. "Master, I know of many caves, but none with names. I live in a cave myself, but there are no wonders in it."

"Then you are incorrect, for there is at least one wonder there in the shape of your own self, is there not?"

Again, I could not disagree. This human was sharp, more so than any I had encountered before. And oddly attractive. I felt a strange sensation stirring inside.

"Legend has it that the Cave of Wonders has walls of glittering gold. In the centre, an enchanted lake conceals the entrance to a garden containing trees bearing magical fruit. Beyond the garden lie great treasures. Do you know of such a cave?"

I was uneasy. Thing's cave had a golden tinge to it when it was lit, and there was a glittering effect from the reflections of the water in the lake. Not to mention the route into the cavern where the forest trees grew. I tried to hold back, but she knew. I could feel fingerlike sensations crawling inside my head. This woman not only had abilities, she knew how to use them to get to the truth.

"Speak, demon. You know, I can see it."

I gave in. "I know of a cave that resembles what you say in part. But I know nothing of magical fruit or treasures."

"Take me there."

"As you desire, my lady. Lay down the talisman you hold, for I cannot approach it. Then step nearer." The thought of holding her was doing odd things to my stomach.

She laughed again. I stared back. She tilted her head slightly and worms slid through my mind again.

"Interesting. You speak truly." There was a quizzical look on her face, which made her eyebrows arch in a way that caused my breath to catch. If she noticed, she said nothing about it, but stuck to business. "You could carry me there in this way, but would you complete the command if I did not have the talisman?"

I thought I probably would if it pleased her, but I kept my counsel. "Try, Master, and find out," I said sarcastically.

She shook her head. "We cannot risk it. I need another plan. Advise me, Ursa."

The reply was plucked out before I had a chance to resist. "Another could go in your stead."

She tutted. "Obviously. But who?"

One of the hooded attendants spoke up. "Aldino should be the one to go, sister. It must be family."

She looked at me. "Is it dangerous?"

I shrugged. "Humans survive in my world, but they suffer and sicken if they are there for long. A few days and they will die. There are also the inhabitants. Many have reason to hate your kind and will kill them on sight."

"I don't believe he would need to be there for long," she replied. "Will you defend him? And bring him back? I order it."

I tested the command. It had been a long time since I could resist direct orders. "Until the order dissolves. It will not hold there for long, maybe a few hours. I have no great love for your kind myself." I tried to inject a note of menace, but it wasn't working. I wanted this woman to like me!

"Very well. Wait, Ursa." She and the one called Radulphus conferred. I gathered from the conversation that Aldino was the man's son. Eventually, she turned to me again. "Aldino will be brought here tomorrow morning.

You will take him then. Until then, return to whence you came!"

☙ ☙ ☙

I did as ordered, but I came back to a viewing point where I could spy on them from Greyside. They returned to a house that must have been quite grand at some point, but had an air of neglect. I watched as the woman went into a bedchamber. She knelt in front of a cross as if to pray, and I appeared in the room. She jumped in alarm. "How?! I did not summon you! How are you here, and why?"

I laughed. "I am always nearby while someone holds the talisman. You chant your silly chants, cast your pointless spells. All you ever had to do was hold it and call."

She bristled, and anger flashed in her eyes. The effect was startling. Her already lovely face was alive with emotion, and I wanted more than anything to feel her emotions directed at me. And she knew it. Her expression changed to amazement as she read my feelings. "What devilry is this?" she whispered.

My mind was whirling with confusion. How could I be attracted to a *human*? They were nothing to me. I'd mated with many of my own species over the decades whenever the urge took me. A brief courtship, a moment or two of lust, and I'd been happy with that. This one wasn't even male.

She saw all of that. Every feeling I had was written plainly for her to see. I couldn't conceal it. Until that day, I never understood nakedness. Suddenly, I wanted to be hidden from her and had a desperate desire to retreat to Greyside.

"Wait! Don't go."

I stood there trembling, trying not to think of anything.

She stepped closer. "No one has ever desired me. No one. Even the few who looked could not stand to be near me for long. They cannot abide their inner selves being seen."

I looked at her again. It made no sense.

Don't ask me. Not my type. Crina is all the woman I need.

I ignored both Timo's impertinence and the silly giggle inside from Crina, but it was clear the attraction wasn't coming from him or even Belbek. "What is your name?"

"Violante," she stuttered.

"That's a beautiful name. I want to touch you, Violante. Will you let me touch you?"

"Demon," she whispered, "you are trying to trick me."

"Lay the talisman aside, Violante. Trust your senses. You know how I feel."

She swallowed nervously, breathing heavily. "How can I … ?"

"I can be different." I stood upright and shifted my shape to be like Crina. Not exactly like. I couldn't get rid of the fur. "I can be like this. Or do you want a male?" I changed again, this time to Timo. Her gaze fell at the top of my legs. "Do you want that as well? I can try." Concentrating, I pushed my sex outwards and looked down as well. Close enough. "I can be both. Or neither. Tell me what you want, Violante. I will be whatever you desire."

She lifted a chain from around her neck and dropped the talisman onto a table. I stepped forward and brushed her cheek. She shivered, but moved closer. I unbuttoned her clothing, letting it fall to the floor. My newly made thumb eased down her body as I breathed in the aroma of her musk. The exotic mix of woman and magic was heady and exciting, and she shuddered as the thumb reached its destination. I lifted her around my waist and carried her to the bed.

I will not say everything we did that night. Those memories are kept for myself, for when I am lonely or tired or sad. I have loved other humans since, but none have been like my one night with Violante.

Eventually she slept, just as dawn was breaking. Reluctantly, I returned to Greyside and curled up in my cave, contented and exhausted, ready for whatever the new day brought.

🐾 🐾 🐾

The morning came and I was summoned again. A bearded youth arrived in the factory accompanied by Violante and Radulphus. He was partially armoured, carrying a short sword and a leather satchel. His father clapped him on the shoulder. "You know what to look for. Godspeed, son."

Aldino stepped into the pentagram. The fear was pungent on him, but underneath was the familiar scent of magic. Nothing like as strong as Violante, but still there.

I grabbed him with an unnecessarily hard squeeze and took him back to my Greyside home. "Welcome to Hell, boy."

It was always worth a try, but it rarely worked. They were expecting fire and brimstone, and all I had to offer was grey dust. He drew his sword and prodded me with it, drawing blood. "Foul creature, take me to the Cave of Wonders, and fast."

The little shit. That was going to take months to heal. I growled and stalked towards Thing's cave. We entered, I made the gesture, and soft golden light flooded the walls and the surface of the pond.

"Gold!"

"It's just reflections, idiot. At least I think so. I've never looked closely. Come."

I skirted the pond, and we descended the path towards the forest. The heat down there was oppressive and I rarely came down myself. Most of the other Greysiders preferred it, hailing from warmer climates. I wondered if any of them were nearby. I'm tough, but all of them were more experienced than me, and I could lose badly in a fight.

We reached the tree line. "Which way are the magical fruit trees, demon?" Aldino asked.

"There are some cherry trees over there. And that one near them still has apples on it. Perhaps that is what you want."

We approached the trees, and as I looked, I realised that this was, in fact, an orchard of sorts. Interspersed between the trees I knew were others that were odd. I'd ignored these in the past, happy to eat what was familiar, but there was a pattern to the planting. Aldino pestered me with questions about these as we moved through and became increasingly irritated by my ignorance. To placate him, and to test if he had his aunt's ability, I started to make up stories.

"This one when prepared with certain seaweeds, gives the strength of ten men."

"The red ones are a deadly poison that only works in moonlight. The green ones are the cure for the poison."

"This one allows the eater to know the truth in men's hearts."

He gathered up samples of all, including a lot of the last one, which I knew for certain was just hawthorn. Clearly, he envied Violante's gift.

At the far end of the orchard, the rocky ceiling high above sloped down to a rough wall, split by a large crevice.

"This could be it!" He looked inside, but the light stopped at the entrance. Striking a spark with a tinderbox, he lit a small handheld lantern and crept inside, beckoning me to follow. "Come, you are sworn to protect me."

Inside was a large natural chamber, lined with crystalline facets that reflected the tiny light from the lamp strangely. Stacked within were heaps of objects and along one wall was a group of wooden chests of many sizes. Aldino walked over and opened one at random. It was filled with painted clay pottery. The next held coarse fabric and string.

I didn't hide my amusement. "Is this the treasure you seek? So glad it was worth coming for." I pulled out some of the fabric and settled down on the floor, bored with his antics.

He snarled back at me and continued to open chests. At the sixth one, he finally looked happier. It contained a large amount of rough silver coins. They looked familiar, and I recognised them as the ones I'd seen shortly before I met Auroch all those years before.

"Silver! I have never seen as much. This is a fortune." He scooped as much as he could into his satchel, ditching most of the fruits gathered earlier. He carried on opening chests, occasionally finding something that took his fancy, and scattering things untidily around. "I have enough. Where is the lamp, though?" He continued to search the cave, ignoring lamps and lanterns galore.

Belbek was interested, even if I was not, so I asked a question for him. "What are you looking for, exactly?"

"I will know it when I see it. It is old, far older than this discarded trash." Finally, at the back, tucked into a small niche, he stumbled across a bowl-shaped rock. He dragged it out into the room. "Can this crude thing really be it? Answer me, demon."

Belbek looked curiously at it through my eyes. It clearly was a lamp of sorts. A heavy rounded stone, only just liftable for a human. The slightly hollowed surface held a layer of what smelled like rancid animal fat. I could see strips of charred leather sticking through the surface. I felt slightly ill looking at it. "It's a lamp. What do you want me to say?"

"Is it the Great Lamp?"

"I don't know what you are talking about."

"Aunt says the Great Lamp controls the spirit of the true Djinn. That you are naught but an insect compared to it. We are to bring it back to her, and with its help, she will lead the family to new heights. I wonder …"

He opened the small lantern he held and lit a twist of kindling, holding the flame to the charred wicks of the bowl. One flared into life. "Aunt has ideas above her station. She is not the only one with power."

<u>Bear, it might be wise to stop this. I am not sure, but …</u>

Belbek's warning came too late. A soft scraping sound started and gradually increased in volume. Suddenly the cave filled with light and damp green tendrils as Thing-under-the-Water oozed from holes in the walls. Aldino shrank back in fear. I had braced myself to defend the human against another like myself. I stood no chance in a fight against Thing. I had never considered the possibility. But there was no attack. It waited patiently.

Aldino was the first to understand. "Are you the true Djinn?" he whispered. Something vaguely like a voice expressed something like agreement. "What is it saying?"

My voice seemed to have its own life as I heard myself say, "It says Yes." I was horrified. No one had ever suggested to me that Thing could be controlled. This felt like sacrilege.

Aldino's fear gave way to triumph. "Ask it, am I its master?"

Again, the word came out without my permission. "Yes."

With an expression of infuriating triumph, Aldino dropped everything he was holding and hoisted the stone aloft. "Great Djinn, take all of us and all the treasures here in this room back to the ropewalk."

A sharp yellow light stabbed straight through my eye, and everything in the cave drained through the hole it left, scraping agonisingly along the edges. Finally, I was drawn bodily through the same hole, turned inside out and put back to rights again.

We were back in the factory. Violante and Radulphus were waiting there, and stood up as we appeared, rearing back in panic as the vast bulk of Thing slithered across the floor toward them.

"Aldino, what in hell's name have you wrought on us!" Radulphus looked terrified.

"Father, be calm. I have it. Meet the true Djinn." Aldino gestured at Thing.

Violante recovered her composure. "You've done well, Aldino. That is the lamp you hold? Bring it to me, and we can advance our plans."

"I'm sorry, Aunt, but I am its master."

She rocked back, stunned. "But you have no magic. How is this possible?"

A wave of iron will pulsed towards Aldino, but he seemed to brush it off. "It has been hard to conceal it from you, Aunt, but I no longer need to. Did you truly believe I would willingly let a woman take such a treasure?" He turned to Radulphus. "Father, I cannot hold my tongue any longer. My friends tell me that the Inquisition are already circling Violante's blasphemous activities. Let me solve this problem for the family."

Radulphus looked scared, but from her expression Violante could already see agreement written in his mind. She thrust the talisman before her like a shield. "Demon, protect me!" I jerked into action and placed myself in front of her.

Aldino smirked. "Djinn, take that thing from her and bring it to me." Like a darting tongue, a thin tendril whipped out and grabbed the talisman from her neck, snapping the thin chain that held it there. I noticed the tendril blacken and shrivel as a wave of pain came from Thing. The talisman was dropped in front of Aldino and he bent to pick it up. "I will keep you at hand, demon. Djinn, chain this creature. I don't trust it."

Poor Thing. Poor me. It radiated regret and sadness as dozens of fine tendrils flew at me, pierced and penetrated my hide, forcing me back against the wall. I was lifted like a marionette. It hurt, but not as much as I'd thought it would. I hung there helplessly.

"Djinn, take this woman back to your hell. She would have ended there anyway once the Inquisition were finished. Goodbye, Aunt." The ground inside the pentagram twisted and bent, and Violante was dragged through, screaming.

Soup in the Garden

Lower Pichesham, August 2018

An evening spent on the internet had turned up a grainy PDF of the brochure that Margot had mentioned, and I'd emailed for an appointment at the main library in town to see what else I could find. I slept restlessly, trying to figure out what was bugging me.

Next morning, I did the hillside run again, and on the way back took a closer look in the graveyard. Sure enough, just as mentioned in the brochure, there were John and Agatha in the Chartings area. There was no mention of the fire, just a date and a short dedication. In a slightly older area I found Peter Brownlow, buried in a family plot with his parents. That headstone was slightly more interesting.

IN LOVING MEMORY OF
PETER AND SARAH BROWNLOW
D. AUGUST 14 AND 17 1871
AGED 36 AND 37.
TOGETHER IN DEATH AS IN LIFE, LET THEM REST IN ETERNAL PEACE.
ALSO ELEANOR BROWNLOW,
PRESUMED D. AUGUST 1871
AGED 9 YEARS.
LOST TO US IN BODY BUT NOT IN MEMORY.
ALSO IN MEMORY OF PETER BROWNLOW JR.,
PASSED FROM THIS WORLD 22ND JANUARY 1927
AGED 61 YEARS.

The Brownlows seemed to have had unlucky lives, and the inscription for the girl was odd. I made a mental note to follow it up sometime.

As I walked away, I was pensive and restless. The history of the Trust was bothering me. It was all very lovely, but it seemed oddly unfocused. I saw Lance sitting on his bench, smoking, so I stopped to say hi. There was a familiar pungent odour.

"Good morning. Is that what I think? I thought that was still illegal here."

"Shh. I grow a little just for me. Helps me backache." He opened a small tin and offered it to me.

"No thanks. Not before breakfast anyway."

"Saw you up at the church. Find what you're looking for?"

I told him about the outcome of my meeting with Margot and showed him the picture of my great-grandpa in his uniform.

"So, you were right all along?"

"Yes, but …"

"Something is bothering you?"

I didn't know how to explain. "Do you know about the Trust?"

"Of course. Everything below is about that. The old village isn't part of it. June and I weren't exactly allowed here, we just moved in after the army closed the training centre and no one chucked us out." He hesitated. "Truth is though, Junie brought us here because of the Trust. I was in a pretty bad state. Heroin. Her mum and dad knew old Miss Stanground well, and Junie got me into therapy. They've kept an eye on me ever since."

"So, it's OK? Nothing fishy?"

"Not sure what you mean. It's a bit much sometimes, the kindness gets a bit claustrophobic. But I'd be long gone without it. And they helped Junie so much at the end." There was a catch in his voice.

"Sorry. I didn't mean to upset you." I gave his hand a squeeze. "Forgive a nosy American?"

He smiled. "You're fine, love. No, you needn't worry about the Trust. Their only problem is that they can't help everyone who needs help."

I helped make tea by way of an apology. God knows what was in it. Not *Camellia sinensis,* that was for sure. Lance's special blend was apparently a great secret and I certainly felt more awake afterwards. We parted as friends. It was obvious that Lance believed in the Trust, but I was still itchy.

🐾 🐾 🐾

Dom had invited me to lunch at his house. I had intended to take the diary along to show him, but it wasn't in my suitcase after all, so I emailed Pop to ask him if he could forward the backup scans. In the end, we didn't talk much about the investigation. It was sunny, and we sat on a bench in Dom's tiny garden with mugs of chunky vegetable soup and a plain cheese sandwich that Tansy seemed to get most of. Ridiculous. We'd known each other for two days, and it had felt like two years. But suddenly, it became awkward. The casual meal had somehow turned into a date, and it seemed as if we both noticed simultaneously. I sought a safe topic.

"How old is Tansy?"

"I guess about nine. She isn't really my dog, as you can probably tell by the attitude. Arrived in the village this time last year and chose my garden as a base. Pets aren't encouraged here, but Margot gave her a name and said I'd better take care of her. I'm not entirely sure whether it was for the dog's sake or mine. Either way, Tansy has been good for me."

We fell silent again. He scratched idly at a scar above his ear before clearing his throat. "Do you mind me asking, are you in the UK for a while?"

I considered the question. "Maybe? I don't have to be anywhere, I'm between jobs. Why?"

He looked thoughtful, searching for the right words. "I'll just say it. I really like you, Annie, and it would be good to get to know you properly. Romantically, I mean. If you aren't interested, I'd get it. Or perhaps there is someone at home already?" I tried not to laugh at his embarrassment, but he could tell I was amused. "Dammit. Forty-four years old, and still terrified of talking to girls."

He was not as old as I'd thought. I smiled and patted his hand reassuringly. "It's fine to ask. And thanks for the 'girl'. No, there's no-one in my life. Or rather, there was. We broke up a few weeks ago and it's still raw. He's over here in London, but he's not returning my calls."

"Ah. And you are hoping for a reconciliation?"

I sighed. "I was. Otherwise, I'm not sure I'd be in England at all. But I don't know. Being away from home seems to be putting things into perspective. I can't keep saying sorry."

I was irritable again, and it wasn't Dom's fault. I checked my phone once more. Nothing from Paul. He hadn't even read the last message. Had he blocked me? I threw caution to the winds. "You know what? There isn't anyone anymore. And I would like to get to know you too. Yes, I'm on the rebound. Are you OK with that?"

"Life's short, Annie. And I haven't felt like this in quite a while."

There was a tentative kiss. Before I knew it, it turned into a more confident one. It was passionate and comforting at the same time. My pulse pounded and my body tingled with unexpected intensity. We broke off, breathing rather heavily. He looked stunned.

"That was…"

"Yes. It was, wasn't it."

We sat holding hands. I wanted more, but the intensity of emotion was alarming, unlike anything I'd felt before. I didn't trust it.

"Annie." His voice was a little shaky. "Before we … before this goes further, there are things you should know about me. Baggage."

"How about we save that for another time?" I didn't want to know anything right then. Animal instincts were overriding any higher thoughts. I pulled his head towards mine, and soft, purple light seemed to fill my mind as we connected.

Eventually he pulled back, flushed. "No. We have to … Annie, it's been a long time. I don't even have any … protection. Not within its expiry date, anyway." He was beet red.

I couldn't help myself. I burst out laughing at the pained look on his face. The spell was broken, and perhaps it was just as well. He smiled wryly. I stood up.

"I'm going now," I announced. "Call me later. And maybe visit a pharmacy or something. Just in case. Not that I'm promising anything." I walked off, blushing furiously myself.

Clive's Diary

Edited extracts from the diary of Clive Maylor towards the end of his life, from December 1972 to March 1973

27th December 1972

I should not be feeling so sad. It has been a good Christmas. But the house is empty now the family are all gone home. January stretches ahead, and I have nothing to look forward to. I think it was that game of chess that has done it. Young Dougie was so pleased to beat me. Mark told him I'd let him win, but I didn't. He is good for eleven years old, but I just could not think of the moves ahead the way I used to even a couple of years ago.

Here Clive is referring to his son Mark (my grandfather) and grandson Douglas (my father).

1st March 1973

It has been a while since I wrote here, but Dr Stein says that keeping a diary going might help slow the deterioration down. Not sure if I should believe that. Maybe he is just trying to be positive. Retirement doesn't give you much to talk about in a diary, but he says to just put ordinary things down as an anchor when I get especially forgetful.

It was difficult to hear it. I knew it was coming really, but it was still a shock. Senile dementia. Both my grandfathers went that way, so it's no surprise. At least my father was spared that indignity.

14th March 1973

Today I forgot the word for tomato. I'm writing it now. Tomato, red, round, salad. Bloody stupid brain. Broken like the rest of me. <u>It</u> probably did this as well. Not fair. I know it was only doing what it was told.

Should I write it down? I said I wouldn't. Lillian knows some of it, of course. But if I don't, it might be lost. Hal is long gone and maybe it would be best forgotten. But I owe him so much.

Lillian Maylor, née Bradley, my great-grandmother. Lillian died in June 1972, nine months before this entry. It is unclear who Hal is, although it is evident he was an important person in Clive's life.

15th March 1973

I've decided that I must write down what I remember while I can. About the bear and Hal and me.

I'm fairly sure I was twelve the first time I really saw it. I was home from school for the summer and we'd gone down to the swimming spot in the slow stretch of the river. Hal had made me promise I would help him learn to swim at last. Some village boys were there as well, and started the usual teasing about the way he looked. But Hal didn't see himself as different. He hardly ever took offence and was quick to make friends. Before long, they were helping and encouraging him along. He managed a short distance, and laughed so much at his own achievement that he briefly went under, and had to be pulled ashore, still laughing. Then he sat on the bank happily watching us leap from Big Rock into the jumping pool. When Mickey Davidson pushed me off the edge, I wasn't expecting it and I dropped awkwardly into the branches of a small tree that was partly submerged.

I panicked a bit when I realised I was stuck with my head underwater. It was probably only seconds, but it felt like a long time struggling. I was lifted clear of the water onto the bank and found myself face to face with a huge bear. Before I had a chance to feel afraid, it vanished.

No one else seemed to notice that anything odd had happened, and I said nothing. We got dressed and walked back home through Pichesham. Hal was even quieter than usual. I knew he must have seen what happened and, as soon as we were out of earshot of the others, I asked him. He looked guiltily at the ground. It took a while to get it out of him, and I had to promise I would keep it a secret. "Bear looks after me. I asked her to help you. But she might be cross now," is what he said.

Looking back, I wonder why I didn't question it more. But as we walked home on that day, I remembered things from the past that I had accepted as normal that were not normal at all. There wasn't much point in pushing Hal. He always had to explain things in his own time.

Tired now, that's a lot of writing. I think Lillian is calling.

22nd March 1973

I think I have been sick, or maybe I just forgot to write. Anyway, I've just read the last entry again and I remembered about the magic cave. This would have been when we were quite young, still in the nursery. We were playing in a castle made of blankets draped over tables and chairs. And then I was in a cave with glittering walls. It was cold, the others were there as well, and there was a stranger. He was playing a game of hide and seek with us, but it was very confusing because I don't think he had a face. He gave me a red ball and I kept it a secret from the others. And then there was someone else, shouting something like, "How did they get in here?" and we were back in the nursery. But I still had the red ball. And I must have forgotten about this, or thought it was a dream, but now I think it was real. It explains things that happened later.

Is this a good sign? Probably not. My poor brain is digging up old memories to fill the gaps in my more recent ones. But it was nice to remember. I wonder where the ball went?

23rd March 1973

I try not to think about this one, but I feel I must. I was going out riding on Clover, and Hal wanted to come with me. He wasn't allowed to ride because he had these fits sometimes. But he hadn't had one for ages, and I was in a bad mood with Father for some forgotten reason and feeling rebellious. So, I told Hal to meet me in the woods, just out of sight.

Clover was a big old lad, and he was quite strong enough for both of us, and we rode off upriver from Pichesham. I wanted to see Miranda before I had to go back to school, and I knew Hal wouldn't mind looking after the horse for a while. We stopped in the lane, and I left Hal with Clover under a big oak. I sneaked up to the house, tapped on the window, and Miranda and I found a cosy spot in the garden shed. It all seems so innocent now, but no doubt at the time it would have been a scandal if her parents had caught us. We weren't there for long before I heard Clover neighing loudly. It wasn't the normal sort, it sounded distressed. I ignored it for a while, too busy with Miranda. I wish I hadn't. It went on, and eventually I made some mumbled apologies, and went back to see what was bothering the horse.

What was happening was Hal fitting. He'd somehow managed to wrap the reins around his own neck, and was dangling from poor old Clover's head, pulling him down to the ground. Clover was stamping around, trying to get loose, and dragging Hal around. I tried to cut the reins with my pocket knife, but Clover was too frightened to let me get near. I was beginning to panic when the bear appeared out of nowhere. It didn't even hesitate. It slashed a huge claw straight into Clover's neck. The horse collapsed to the ground and lay there, quivering, blood gushing out. Then the bear unwrapped the reins from Hal. It lowered him to the ground and bent over him, then turned to me and spoke. "He will be fine, his colour is good. Stay with him. I will alert your father." I didn't even register that it was speaking, I was so terrified.

And with that, it ran back in the direction of home. When Father found us, Hal was conscious again, and I was trying to keep him warm. We were both still sitting in the gore. Father said nothing at the time. He draped Hal onto his own saddle, and we walked home in silence. Father never raised a hand to me before that day, but later on I almost welcomed the beating. The only thing he said was to not tell Mother what had happened. I never had the nerve to ask how the bear told him, and we never spoke of it again.

Poor Father. We patched things up later. He didn't deserve what happened. I'd like to see him again. I must ask Lillian to call him. Perhaps we could visit?

27th March 1973

That's wrong. It wasn't Clover. And it was Lillian I was with in the shed, not Miranda. Or was it Clover? But the blood was real. A blood-red ball. I wonder if Lillian knows where it went?

The story about the swimming spot is repeated on April 4th but with less detail. Clive describes "Big Rock" as "Red Rock", but it is otherwise consistent with the telling on March 15th.

There is an entry that seems to mention "the bear" on April 22nd. The entry is largely illegible, but there are indications that it may have been about a battlefield incident. The only other interesting phrase that can be deciphered in the entry is a reference to something being 'dropped into Alderman's Well'.

Other entries are sporadic and either focus on daily activities or relate to his children and Lillian. These have been omitted.

The last entry was June 15th 1974. Clive was admitted to a nursing home in July of 1973 and passed away in early January 1975.

Violante-II

*A ropewalk near the Arsenale di Venezia,
1449*

I was strapped to the wall of the factory building for days, guarded by rough-looking thugs, hidden behind raised tarpaulins while the rope-makers busily plied their trade. No one approached me, and only Thing kept me fed and watered, even clearing my droppings when necessary. Aldino eventually reappeared late one night.

"The Djinn obeys me, but I don't understand what it says. I need you near, but I cannot have you looking like that. I take it you would prefer not to be chained here?"

"I can make myself look a little like another creature. Dog or monkey is easiest."

He considered and nodded to himself. "A monkey would do nicely."

I changed my appearance to resemble the Monkey of the East that I knew in Greyside. It was not a look I'd practised often.

"Dear God, you look like no beast I ever saw. But I suppose it will do." He called to Thing. "Make it a cage that it cannot escape." I felt the tendrils embedded in my body shift and reform, creating a latticework that was still attached to my body that a human could carry.

We were both transferred onto a large residential boat docked outside the warehouse. Thing's formless body flowed into the hold, while my cage was placed in their personal cabin. I could at least move around a little, but there was no way for me to go back to Greyside. In this way, I became a witness to Aldino's activities.

His ambitions were tediously unsurprising. A steady flow of nobles and ne'er-do-wells were entertained on the boat. A few of these visitors looked at me curiously, but I had no interest in them and kept silent. Radulphus and Aldino had more than a passing acquaintance with the city's underworld, and were heavily involved in smuggling luxury goods and bullion. But aided by the wealth stolen from Thing's cave, they were fostering new connections. One day a grandly dressed messenger arrived with an invitation for Radulphus to visit the doge's palace. Radulphus came back from the visit glowing with triumph.

"Francesco Foscari himself greeted me with friendship, Aldino. And he is open to persuasion. In times past, he would never have given me the time of day. But with his son disgraced and exiled, he needs to restore his standing in the eyes of the Council of Ten. It will take money and something more, but his youngest daughter, Benedetta, is recently of marriageable age. There is a path here. You could be doge yourself one day."

"Money we have now, but what do you mean by something more?"

"A grand gesture. Something to rouse the people's affection."

Aldino paced the room, musing. He strolled to the window overlooking the lagoon, crowded with vessels, and snapped his fingers. "I have it. Remember, Father, last year's Marriage of the Sea? When the canopy on the bucentaur collapsed on the nobility? The great ceremonial barge is falling apart. But with the bullion famine, the city cannot afford a new one."

"Even with the wealth you found, we cannot possibly afford that, Aldino. And it would take too long."

"The Djinn can create one for us. Can it not, demon?" He turned to address me.

I listlessly responded. "It can do almost anything. It would need some idea of what you want."

Radulphus found an excuse to dock their boat in the Arsenale overnight, and Aldino carried my cage up to the deck to inspect the old bucentaur. It was impressive in its way, gilded in many places, with a covered deck and two rows of oars. But you could see the worn sections of gilding and the deep cracks in the carved figurehead. Thing looked out through my borrowed eyes and made querying sensations while I interpreted as best I could. "Do you have plans? If not of this barge, then something similar?"

"Yes. But we do not want a simple replacement. It must be even greater, more magnificent. Like nothing ever seen before."

Thing understood clearly enough what they wanted. It was interpreting what *Thing* wanted that was difficult. "I am not sure, but I think we need to move. It seems to indicate a need to travel."

The following day, we sailed to a sparsely populated area toward the south of the lagoon. Occasionally, I would suggest a slight course correction. We approached a small rocky outcrop. "This seems to be right. Drop an anchor."

The pilot of the vessel came into the cabin complaining about the water depth. "It's not safe here, Master Aldino. This place is a known hazard. There was an island here with a monastery many years back. They tried all sorts to stop it sinking. Who knows what is down there to snag us?"

Aldino shushed him, but after the pilot left, questioned me again.

"All I can tell you is that this is where it wants to be. It is ready to start work."

"Very well, wait until nightfall," he grumbled.

As darkness fell across the lagoon, and the only boats that could be seen were faint lights in the distance, Aldino brought me to the deck. We watched as glistening green ropes slipped into the depths silently. "What is it doing?" Aldino asked.

I asked the question. The answer was complicated and involved many colours. "There is a vessel below the water already. I think it has been there for years. And there are other materials it needs—left behind, I suppose. That is why we came here."

The night passed, and the pre-dawn light slowly built. Just as the sun crept above the horizon, Thing broadcast a sense of satisfaction, with various green shades that seemed to suggest that the job was complete. I poked Aldino awake through the bars of the cage. "I think something will happen soon …"

Mid-sentence, the sea nearby started to bubble. Our boat rolled violently to one side, but righted itself within a few seconds. Everyone on board watched spellbound as, lit by the rising sun to the east, a great golden galley emerged from under the surface. Streams of water cascaded from the deck and through the oar ports back into the sea. Every inch of the ship was coated in gold, even the oars. Along the deck was a grand structure topped with what looked like statues of horses. At the front was a figurehead of … a bear. It was big and fierce, fangs bared and claws held out to rend an enemy to pieces.

Is that supposed to be me? I thought to myself. I felt a ripple of something like laughter in response.

Aldino and Radulphus were awestruck. "Look, Father! It's a replica of the Basilica. And those horses are like the Quadriga! How did it know?"

Radulphus' face was shining. "I don't know, son, but if this doesn't buy us a place on the council at least, I don't know what will."

🐾 🐾 🐾

The pair were riding high over the next few weeks. Radulphus took Doge Foscari secretly to see the new bucentaur. The doge was delighted and after some negotiation, a price for his daughter was agreed. Thing was dispatched to fetch more treasure. When it arrived, it came with a strong smell of the sea and many small muddy creatures attached. Shortly after this, Aldino returned one evening to his cabin with a bride by his side.

Sweet, spoiled little Benedetta. As distasteful as these humans usually were to me, how could I take against her? Sitting there in my cage in silence, I watched as she begged Aldino to be patient with her. It seemed she was only fourteen years old. I could tell he was tempted to bed her there and then, regardless. But Aldino was a vain man who wanted to be wanted. Most of all, he craved the respect of his superiors in society. Forcing himself on Benedetta would not have been a crime, but nor did he want to sully his newly purchased position with a poor reputation. He gave her a tight little smile and wished her a good night. As he lay silently beside her in the bed, she tried to stifle the tears and in the end he stalked off to sleep on the deck. I felt relief for her. It brought back some of Crina's less pleasant memories. She had not been so fortunate.

Benedetta was confined to the cabin while Aldino busied himself elsewhere. Her miseries were not confined to her new husband. The cabin was stuffy and overheated, and it seemed the girl had discovered for the first time that she suffered from sea sickness. After three days of non-stop crying and puking, I could no longer stand it. I asked Thing silently if there was anything it could do to help her. A few minutes later, a small corked vial of liquid appeared beside the cage, wrapped in a thin tendril. I uncorked it and sniffed. There was an intense burst of ginger with a touch of fennel, and something bitter underneath. "It's not going to hurt her, is it?" I asked. There was a reassuring blue and green response.

I spoke up. "Hey. Over here."

Benedetta looked up from the bowl she was hanging over. "Who's there?" she said, panicked.

"Here, in the cage. The monkey. I'm not really a monkey. They can't speak."

She recoiled in horror at the sight of me gesturing through the bars. "Am I going mad?"

"No, you are not mad. I'm Aldino's slave. I know I look odd, but I mean no harm." It wasn't the first time I'd had to get over this stage, but it was probably the least threatening I'd ever looked. "I have a remedy for you. For the sickness, I mean. I can't solve Aldino." I held up the vial.

She overcame her fear enough to respond. "What is it? Poison? I would welcome it."

"Don't talk like that. I think it's mostly ginger. The one who supplied it is a good person."

She came nearer and took the vial, sniffing it. "I hope it is poison. I have nothing to live for." She swigged it back whole. The heat of the spice made her clutch her throat, gasping. She sat down on the bunk rather red in the face, shuddered a bit, and then relaxed. "Oh. Oh. I do feel better." She burped.

"Better out than in," I said in my most cheerful voice.

She glared back, embarrassed. "How long have you been there, watching?"

"All the time you've been here, I'm afraid. You needn't worry, I've seen worse. I am sorry for your plight."

She poured water and washed her face, trying to recover some poise. "Thank you for that remedy."

"You should thank my friend, Thing. It is good at making potions and the like."

"It? I don't understand your meaning."

"It's complicated. We are complicated."

Realisation dawned. "You are Aldino's demon! This was the rumour from the servants. How else could a nobody like Radulphus have come up with so much money so quickly? And that barge!"

"Oh, I didn't make the barge. That was also my friend. But we come from the same place. You call us demon and djinn, but that is not how we think of ourselves. We are just what you see."

"It's your fault I am here! I have lost everything I cared about. My mother. My friends." She started weeping again. "My sweet Andrea."

"Don't be angry with us, Benedetta. We do not want to be here. Aldino holds us tight against our will. My friend is the most gentle of beings and is suffering as well."

I felt a wave of sad affection ripple through the cabin. It was so strong that Benedetta reacted to it with a start. I had an idea.

"Shall we play for Benedetta, my friend? It is not the audience we planned, but it may be our only chance."

Tendrils churned into the cage. One unfolded, and there was a miniature flageolet. Thing passed it to me. I closed my eyes and played the tune to the madrigal we'd been practising. Thing joined in with its gentle, high-pitched almost-voice. We did a good job.

Dominic's Story

Lower Pichesham, August 2018

I went back to the inn to freshen up. I fell asleep and came down later to the bar for a drink. Grant was there.

"There's a letter for you, Annie. Dominic brought it round a while ago. He specifically said not to disturb you." Grant looked quizzically at me, but I wasn't in a sharing mood. He brought me a Scotch and ice, and I took my letter outside. It was a thick envelope, with just the word 'Annie' written on it.

Dear Annie,

I wanted to do this in writing so that I didn't make a mess of explaining. It's been a long time since I felt this way about anyone, and I can't stand the thought of having to do this and then losing you later. Better now or never.

I joined the Royal Army Medical Corps after qualifying, and it was not long before I was deployed in Iraq. This was at a time when there was an uneasy peace in the region, and although I did occasionally have to treat wounded personnel, I spent most of my time doing general medicine for the troops. Part of our job was to visit the surrounding villages, running clinics. It was not easy. Some people were welcoming, but often they came because there was no alternative. The resentment could be oppressive, but I believed I was doing worthwhile work that would help win 'hearts and minds' eventually.

The last tour I was on started badly. Nearby villages that had been friendly were now quiet, with few patients visiting. The further out we went, the more open the hostility was. Everyone was on edge, expecting something to happen. On a road that should have been safe, an IED went off about ten metres ahead. The explosion was powerful enough to throw the vehicle we were in on its side. No one was hurt, but shots sounded, and we were now under sniper fire. The other vehicles in the convoy were undamaged and gave us cover, but we needed helicopter support.

I had never come under direct attack before, and I was, I am ashamed to say, paralysed with fear. I tried to hide it, but hanging there sideways, supported in straps, all I could do was beg repeatedly that the shooters stop.

I didn't witness the beginning of what followed, but I heard it. I've read the reports. The helicopter had arrived and was targeting the snipers. Then there was a noise so loud that our car was shunted about half a metre. The main rotors on the helicopter had cracked and sheared off, and it plummeted to the ground in seconds, smashing into pieces.

Silence followed. The shooting had stopped. For some seconds, no one moved. Then at last the training kicked in. The whole medical team scrambled out and dashed to the crash site.

It was carnage. The main fuselage of the helicopter had landed on a house, turning it into rubble. We stabilised two seriously injured crew, one of whom died later. The other crew were dead. The occupants of the house were crushed. Seven dead in total. There was a little boy with signs of life.

I performed an emergency thoracotomy, and he made it to the hospital. I don't know what happened to him afterwards.

I later found out that resistance fighters had taken over the house. They had set up three sniper positions at different vantage points along the road. Bizarrely, each of the widely spaced snipers had been killed by debris from the crash. We found one young man pierced straight through the torso by a fragment of rotor blade, pinned to the floor like an insect in a display case. This is the image I see in my nightmares most often.

It was a wretched business. We'd done what we could and eventually, having no one left who needed medical help, I made for the relief vehicle that was just arriving. A loose rock slipped under my feet, and I fell headfirst into its path. It stopped in time, but I banged my head against the winch in front and was knocked out.

The collision fractured my skull in two places. I was patched up, and physically I healed. But that was the end of my military career. I'd humiliated myself in front of my comrades with an abject display of fear, and then become yet another casualty through my own stupid clumsiness when good people had died trying to save me.

They gave me counselling, but what with the guilt and the physical pain of recovery, I spiralled into depression. It got worse when the enquiry found that the helicopter had not been attacked. The crash was due to mechanical failure, and it was sheer chance it had happened at that moment. I started to get delusions that somehow it was I who had caused the crash. I knew it made no sense, but no matter how I tried, I could not stop thinking about it.

During all this, I managed to take an overdose of painkillers. I still believe it was an accident, but to this day I don't know how it happened. Understandably, the medics did not believe me. Whether I really tried to end things unconsciously or not, the inevitable followed. I was sectioned and I found myself admitted to Chartings.

It was the lowest point of my life, but from there things slowly improved. The care I received at Chartings was first-rate. Their approach to PTSD has moved on a bit since, but the programme they designed worked for me. I'm better now—there's medication that helps when things head the wrong way. I still think about those people, about the waste and how, in the end, none of it helped anyone. But not all the time.

That's everything. If it's not too much, drop me a message.

x Dom

Later that day we walked along the river watching the sun go down, Tansy trotting ahead. Just before the path turned up the hill into the woods was a handy bench and we sat.

I broached it first. "Your letter. It was a lot to take in. When you said 'baggage', I was expecting a messy divorce or something."

"Oh, there's that as well. Although we weren't actually married. Cleo and I broke up when I was recovering. She was great, patient and supportive, but I could feel that her heart wasn't in it. It turned out that she'd met someone else while I was overseas and had been on the verge of telling me just before the incident in Iraq. She ended things with him to look after me. There were some tears when it all came out, but we parted on good enough terms in the end. She's married now and has two kids. It was more a relief than anything, that at least it was one life I hadn't ruined."

"And you've been here ever since?"

"The Trust and Chartings aren't formally connected anymore, but there's still crossover. I was about to be medically discharged from the service and didn't have anywhere to go. Mum is in sheltered housing. Elaine, my sister, didn't have room. The hospital put me in touch with Margot, and she offered me the house here if I was willing to be on staff. I'm paid a pittance, but it covers the rent, and I have a bit saved. When Lance stopped running the ferry rota, I took over. I love it—no stress, regulars to chat to, and I'm useful. I'll miss it."

He'd mentioned already that he was moving on. "How long is it before you go?"

"Three more months. I have a small house lined up in town, and I'm registered with a locum agency. The truth is, I've been here too long. The whole thing about the Trust is to make people strong enough to move on."

Tansy came and sat on my foot, staring haughtily at Arthur, who was standing on a nearby fence post straightening his feathers. It felt like a hint, but I'd already made up my mind.

"It's not too much, Dom. I really, really like you. I don't know why. I barely know you. You're OK-looking, I suppose."

"Well, thanks." He laughed.

I gave him a look. "It just seems like we were meant. I can't explain it better."

"I feel the same, Annie."

"Just promise me something. No hiding things. If you're in a bad way … you know …"

"Mentally?"

"Or otherwise. If you need help, I need to know."

He picked up my hand and pressed it to his lips. "I promise."

We went back to the village. As we reached the doorstep of Dom's house, he turned to me, hesitant. "Come inside."

There was no mistaking what he meant. I was feeling light-headed again and scolded myself for my ridiculous behaviour. I was thirty-seven, not some teenager. But right then that was how it felt, as if this was my first time with a boy, not with this rather lovely, damaged man. "Kiss me again. Don't stop this time."

He obliged. I felt his hand on the back of my head, pulling my face towards his, lips locked so tightly that it hurt. Before I knew it, one hand was pushing up inside his sweatshirt, while the other fumbled with his belt. He put me down long enough to unlock the door and we fell through before any clothes were removed.

The bedroom was too far, and we threw the couch cushions on the floor. Sex was anything but romantic. We were rushed, humping with the simple lust of animals. My head was pushed painfully against the baseboard and Dom's elbow banged into the edge of a table, sending a shower of flatware and a pepper mill falling to the floor.

Dom came quickly and loudly. I did not give him any recovery time, and pushed his head between my legs. His mouth and tongue seemed to know what I wanted, and when it arrived, my orgasm was raw and long. When it was over, he unbent and came up to kiss me, sharing his grinning, sticky face generously. Then his expression changed to pain.

"Ow. Ow. Sorry, cramp. Ow."

He got to his feet and walked stiffly around, trying to shake out the pain and nursing his grazed elbow. I lay there, getting cold on the floor amid the debris, and tried not to laugh too much. Eventually he stopped pacing and held out a hand to help me up. "Come on, let's get somewhere more comfortable. And warmer."

We rather primly gathered up the discarded clothes and retreated upstairs. It was only a single bed, but it was all we needed.

Violante–III

Two weeks passed, during which Aldino left the cabin to Benedetta. He had taken up residence on the new bucentaur. I was largely ignored, although once or twice he came back to ask me private questions. During these visits, he was cordial enough to Benedetta as he escorted her out of the room. Benedetta kept her distance from him, and her knowledge of me a secret.

We passed time amicably enough. I let Crina's memories come to the surface and take free rein. Despite their difference in social standing, daily life in a doge's palace was much the same as it had been in Count Stevas's castle, and there was much common ground to talk about. When she tired of that, I also told her some stories I knew from Greyside—Auroch's account of what really happened in the labyrinth, and the tale of Turold and his shameful fish pie. She laughed so much at that one that I thought she was going to choke.

Aldino started to bring gifts of fine clothing and delicacies. He seemed to be making an effort to woo her. "Perhaps it will not be so bad. He is trying," she said after one of these occasions.

I could smell that he was not going short of female company. But it seemed cruel to make things harder for her, so I said nothing about that. "While he's being pleasant, why not ask him if you can visit your mother?" I suggested. She clapped her hands at the idea.

When she returned from the visit on Aldino's arm, she was bright and cheerful, and even smiled at him. He bowed and took his parting from her, looking almost benign.

"You look happier," I said when he was gone.

She waved the comment away. "Mother was pleased to see me. She was furious with Father before the wedding, but he would not be swayed. Aldino insisted on staying with us most of the time, but when we were alone, Mother told me about a visit she has had from her childhood companion, *Lady Violante.*" She whispered the name. "You know she is Aldino's aunt? But she is no friend of his, I think. She says that Aldino tried to kill her. Mother was so frightened for me. It was all I could do to pretend to be friendly on the way back."

"How is that possible? Aldino sent her ... never mind where, but she could not have escaped." It was a shock, but I felt a flicker of hope. I kept my voice low. "Violante was the one who summoned me here. We were close. For a short while."

Benedetta looked excited. "Mother told me she is back in Venice under an assumed name. She is hiding from her family."

I thought furiously. "Benedetta, can we get a message to her? Violante has abilities. Indeed, she must have more than I realised. She can release me and Thing. Maybe she can release you from Aldino."

"Release me? I don't understand you. I am married now and he is my husband, for better or worse."

"If your father can be persuaded, there is annulment." I hesitated. I did not want to frighten the child. "Benedetta, you must understand. Aldino has his eyes set on your father's throne. With Thing under his control, he can achieve that. He would have no hesitation in using violent means against your father. And he only needs you as his wife while your father is alive."

She looked pale. I had made her bad situation worse, but I could see she believed me. "I could tell Father about Aldino's sorcery. The Inquisition …?"

"They would be useless against Thing. Aldino and his father may yearn for respectability, but in the end, they want power more."

"What do we need to do?"

"There is a stone lamp somewhere. It is large, far too heavy to carry around. He will have hidden it. That lamp is the source of his power over Thing. If Violante can get to it, she will take control."

"Where is it then?"

"Thing will not tell me. But Aldino will have kept it close at hand, and I think that means it must be aboard the new bucentaur."

Over the next few days, Benedetta showed how adept she could be at lying with a smile. She eventually persuaded Aldino to allow her a closer look at the bucentaur. She came back to the cabin, barely able to contain herself. "I saw it, just as you described. Just there, openly in the owner's cabin. He stroked it as we went in."

The arrogance of the man seemed astounding at first, but Aldino seemed to know how rare his gift was. Perhaps with Violante gone in his mind, there was no reason to hide a dirty old stone.

Communicating with Violante was slow and painful, but letters were written and surreptitiously passed from hand to hand. A plan was formed. Supplies were purchased. Easter came and went, and we waited as our opportunity drew near.

🐾 🐾 🐾

"You know, I can do other things than translate for you."

Aldino grunted. "What can you do that the Great Djinn cannot?"

I injected a sly note into my voice. "I could make Benedetta like you. Properly, as a wife should."

He looked interested, but sceptical. "You never mentioned this before."

"You never asked. But I am bored, having to listen to her endless weeping when you are not here. If you don't want me to do that, then take me out of this room. I beg you."

He ignored my plea. "You lie. She is in good enough spirits. She will come to love me."

"Oh, she pretends well, but she longs for her old home. I could make her long for something else," I said suggestively. It felt dirty, but Benedetta had agreed to this approach.

He smirked and dug into a pouch, pulling out my talisman. "Go on then, do that. I can rearrange my other entertainment for this evening."

"It will take time, Master. The spell builds slowly. And it has its best effect on certain special days. Annunciation, Epiphany and Ascension."

He frowned. "Ascension is near. But that is when I will present the bucentaur to the city at the Marriage of the Sea ceremony." He paused, then smiled darkly and chuckled. "Actually, that would be perfect. Take his daughter and then …" He walked off laughing. "Start your spell, Ursa!"

I was worried. The ruse had worked, but Aldino had something in mind that I was not party to.

After this, Benedetta's visits home were stopped, and we could not risk trying to send messages any other way. All we could do was to trust that Violante would play her part in the plan. In the meantime, I tried my best to persuade Benedetta to like Aldino, just as I had been ordered. Since I had no power over her mind, it turned into a sort of game. And she played her part well during his visits, delicately showing more apparent interest.

Ascension Day arrived. The boat sailed out to the ceremony site, and Benedetta described the scene she could see from the window. There was a small flotilla of vessels of all kinds. It was one of the most important events of the year to the city, a grand spectacle reaffirming Venice's relationship with the sea.

Aldino had arranged to visit that morning, before the ceremony was due to commence. Benedetta was agitated and nervous, and I had little comfort to give. There was no backing off from the plan. Whatever happened, Aldino would not be denied that day, and so many things could go wrong.

A servant brought in platters of food and a large flagon of hippocras. After he had left, she laced the spiced wine with the bhang and opium she had obtained from her mother. She took a tiny sip. "It tastes fine. The sugar and cinnamon conceal any bitterness."

"Be careful. It is very strong, and will affect you more than him."

She nodded and shuddered.

The morning wore on. At one point, there was a loud commotion that we could not see. Not long afterward, Aldino swept in without knocking. Benedetta pasted a smile onto her face and turned to greet him warmly. "Come, husband, sit beside me on the bed. I have made a breakfast for you here, see?"

He picked up a sweetmeat and joined her, clearly in high spirits. "So, Benedetta, you are welcoming today. What has brought this change of mood, I wonder?"

"I scarcely know, Aldino. Perhaps it is the ceremony today. The Marriage of the Sea seems an appropriate time to celebrate our own marriage in the way it should be."

He grinned and poured two glasses of wine, downing his quickly. Benedetta took hers daintily and sipped at it. "Perhaps you would like to know what I've been doing today, Benedetta?"

"Gladly, husband. Your business is my business now." She took his hand almost absently and started to stroke it, staring into his eyes. It looked very convincing from where I was.

Aldino was enjoying the sound of his own voice. "I have been entertaining guests aboard my new barge. Your father was there, and many of the Council."

"Did Father send greetings?" Her voice was dreamy and uninterested.

"No, he was more concerned with saving his own life. I have decided it is time for him to step aside. He and the Council are prisoners aboard the bucentaur. Do you know, the Great Djinn had to sink three ships before they would listen to terms? But don't worry, I don't intend to kill him. I thought maybe he would like to join your brother in exile. What do you think about that? Do you look forward to being wife to the doge, not a mere merchant?"

Benedetta turned her face to me, the mask broken, suddenly pale. I shook my head slightly. She took a deep breath and recomposed herself. "Oh, Aldino, you are so masterful. You must do as you see fit. Let me touch you."

Aldino looked at me directly with a thin smile and raised his glass in my direction.

"Here, let me fill your glass. Let us drink a toast. To you and I, wife and husband. Make me your wife, Aldino." She downed her own glass, and Aldino followed suit. They embraced, but I could see the drugged wine was having its effect on him. He was trying to undress her clumsily, and fell from the bed. He staggered to his feet, laughing inanely, and then fell again. Soon, the sound of snoring was heard.

"Hurry, Benedetta, make the signal!"

Benedetta was woozy, but dragged herself to the porthole. Flinging it open, she held out a bright yellow scarf and waved it frantically. She kept going for at least five minutes before slumping to the floor. And then there was nothing I could do but watch over them helplessly and hope Violante had received the signal.

Noises came through the open porthole. I could hear shouting, the clashing of swords and the occasional yell of pain. And then, unexpectedly, the ship shuddered. There was a tremendous groaning and popping as the great beams holding the ship together strained. The deck of the cabin splintered and broke apart, and the entire ship lurched to one side, making everything in it fall towards the wall. My cage fell as well, but as it did, I could feel the tendrils embedded in my body come loose, sliding out with a weird scraping sensation. There was a brief flash of yellow-pink farewell and I knew that Thing was gone.

I was numb for a moment, but then woke myself up. Benedetta was sliding toward the open porthole. I snapped back into my natural shape and scooped her up over my shoulder. Climbing up the near-vertical floor, I made it to the cabin door and came out onto the deck, water rising in the cabin behind me. Wedged into the woodwork, I waited as calmly as I could for the sea to take the ship. "Benedetta, wake up!"

She roused herself groggily, and I urged her on to my back. As the sea rose to reach us, I swam out and away from the doomed vessel, along with the other crew members fortunate enough to have escaped.

I could see small rowboats coming towards us from all directions. The first one to reach us held a young man in rich clothing, looking around frantically. He reached down and plucked Benedetta from my back, cradling her in his arms. "Benedetta! Are you all right?"

"Andrea? Is that you?" She looked up at him with an expression that said I did not need to worry about her anymore. I swam away before he could think about using his sword.

Not long after, I saw another boat. Standing at the helm was Violante, smiling triumphantly. "Hello, Ursa. Come aboard."

🐾 🐾 🐾

It felt good to be near her again, but Violante was cool, and it was clear that what we had shared was in the past. She told me the plan had worked perfectly. Safe in the knowledge that Aldino was incapacitated, she and her crew had invaded the bucentaur. The thugs on board had given resistance, but as anticipated, Thing had not interfered, having no orders. There had been little loss of life.

"I was tempted by the lamp. So much power."

"What stopped you?"

"Oh, I think I've had enough of that. You opened my eyes to the world, Ursa. My crew and I have other paths to follow. I just told the Great Djinn to go home and take his stone with him. You should have seen it. The sea boiled in front of us, and the noise when Aldino's ship exploded …"

Her crew—and in particular, I thought, the robust dark-skinned crewman sitting at the oars. He glowered at me with suspicion. I tried to suppress my jealousy. Violante looked at us both and laughed.

"Ursa, this is Lomelo. He has been my rock these past months. Perhaps the only rock I need." She spoke to him in a language I didn't know and smiled at him. He relaxed slightly.

Rather than confront how I was feeling, I changed the subject. "Tell me, how did you escape Greyside? I thought you were dead for sure."

"Your friend Auroch rescued me from that dark cave. I thought he was there to finish me. But he looked into my words and saw some of what we shared. I wanted to come back and stop Aldino. Release you if I could. Auroch took me to a village near a lake, somewhere in Africa. He stayed there, taught me the language, and asked the people to help me. Gave me resources. Everything I needed. It took many, many weeks to make my way back here to Venice. But here I am, with a ship of my own and a willing crew of adventurers."

"You look happy. Well." It was true. She had been lovely to me before, but she was blooming now, her hair wild and long, a touch of windburn on her cheeks.

"Flatterer." She smiled slightly and didn't look at me directly.

A sudden crashing made us turn around. We watched as, one by one, the golden horses on the new bucentaur splintered and fell from the roof to the deck. People on board were rapidly abandoning the vessel, getting into the myriad of small boats surrounding it. Ragged sheets of gilding peeled away and revealed the rotten timbers hiding underneath. The barge simply crumbled into the sea before our eyes. The prow was the last part to sink, and as the figurehead disappeared under the water, I waved it goodbye.

I hesitated. "I could not carry both Aldino and Benedetta."

"I understand. Radulphus will be a broken man. But if Aldino had survived, he would have faced the strappado. This way, Benedetta is released without shame, and the doge will find a way for the marriage to be conveniently forgotten. Perhaps I can persuade Radulphus to join me in exile. We will have to take our leave of this place soon. Francesco Foscari may be grateful for now, but he will not want reminders of his mistakes around for long. I think he would not be kind."

I made a decision. "I should go now. Promise me something."

She looked at me quizzically.

"If by chance you find Aldino's body and recover the talisman, will you throw it into the deep ocean somewhere?"

She nodded. She reached over and stroked my cheek. I will feel that caress until the end of my days.

Family History

My vacation in England turned into something else. Dom and I were more than good together, and I checked out of the hotel to join him in the little house. Maybe it was just a holiday romance, but he took the time to make some space in his closet. We spent a whole evening going over the mineral collection he had acquired in Iraq before he tucked it into a loft space, and it was both dull as ditchwater and enchanting to watch him light up with enthusiasm. It seemed to be the only thing from his time in the forces that he still took pleasure in.

Margot, apparently unabashed by that first difficult meeting, took the opportunity to dragoon me into voluntary work around the village. She told me outright that if I was going to be hanging around, I should make myself useful. Feeling a need to appease her, I succumbed as gracefully as I could, and found myself loaded up with random jobs of all sorts. Anything from dropping groceries off for elderly residents to manning the ferry seemed fair game.

The Al-Mansoob family I'd met on my first morning at the inn were now settled into the village, and one of my many activities was to help the children with their English at the tiny village school. Noura was quick on the uptake, and she was already keen to learn colloquialisms. Little Hani was cheerfully indifferent and couldn't wait to get into the playground. One afternoon, after I finally let him stop fidgeting, I followed him outside to find him with Osman and a few other boys. They were playing some sort of game involving fallen horse chestnuts threaded onto strings. Another group of children was skipping with ropes, and I wandered over to where Nadia Tankye was standing, watching with the other mothers.

> *Brown Bear, Brown Bear, turning round,*
> *Brown Bear, Brown Bear, touching ground,*
> *Brown Bear, Brown Bear, jumping high,*
> *Brown Bear, Brown Bear, reaching sky,*
> *Brown Bear, Brown Bear, eating bread,*
> *Brown Bear, Brown Bear, bites your HEAD,*
> *How many bites does it take?*
> *One, two, three, four, five …*

It was just a variation on an old skipping song, but the changes caught my ear. I asked Nadia about it, and she told me that there had been a local legend about a wild bear in the woods for as long as she could remember. The very young still used the story to scare each other. It turned out she was a true local, one the Fredericks, a family that had lived in the old village before it was rebuilt in the 1930s. It was an intriguing counterpoint to the entries in Clive's diaries and suggested a possible reason for his obsession with bears in his final months.

So, in between all the extra work and a new relationship, you might be forgiven for thinking that I didn't have the capacity to follow up on my various investigations. But there's love, and then there's work. The story about Clive's bear did not have any substance yet, but there was still the Trust. I arranged to meet up with Farzad.

Farzad Khan was an old friend from my days in the Middle East. He'd traded the excitement and occasional prestige of current affairs for a safer existence these days, as editor and part-owner of *Secretz!* magazine. I'd pushed the odd story his way over the years when work was thin, though I'd been careful to keep my real name off them. We met for lunch at a sandwich bar close to his offices in Birmingham.

"Hi, Annie, long time. How are you?" he said, reaching to shake my hand.

I stood up to greet him. "Hi, Farzad, I'm doing OK."

A slight frown. "I was sorry to hear about you and Paul. I met him at a party last week. He said … some things. Sounds like you've had a tricky time recently."

Farzad was constitutionally nosy, so I didn't take offence. "It's all water under the bridge, Farzad. I've moved on. And I need your help with another story."

He smiled. "To the point, as always. OK, what can I help with?"

I explained about the Pichesham Trust, showing him a printout of the brochure. "There's just something nagging at me. I haven't found anything to suggest it's not what it seems, but its mission is so vague. And it is publicity-shy, particularly the woman who runs it. Genuine charities are usually desperate for anything to bring in the dollars."

He looked at the brochure doubtfully. "Shady charities are ten a penny, Annie. They usually turn out to be a tax dodge. Even if there is something there, the magazine doesn't run that kind of story, you know that."

"Yes, and I am still working on the other story. It's coming along well," I exaggerated. "But you couldn't look into this, could you? Your contacts in finance are better than mine. I know I'm asking quite a big favour here."

"Well, I can dig up some background in my own time, I suppose. Email me the details. Now, let's order."

We chatted about mutual friends and acquaintances and the family history quest. It was a pleasant afternoon, and he let me pick up the tab without fuss. I made a point of telling him about Dominic. He made a point of showing me pictures of his recently born daughter. The old affair back in Jordan didn't need to be mentioned.

🐾 🐾 🐾

Back in Lower Pichesham, I had Clive's real name, and it was back to the databases. It turned out that while Clive might have been the son and heir, he'd had a sister. Angela Charting had married David Aberlome in 1919, and they'd moved to Canada in 1926. I finally tracked down a distant cousin, Marius Aberlome, living in Edmonton. Marius was a big family history buff, and was delighted when I got in contact.

"Annie, so good to see you at last! Is the picture OK? Still not quite got the hang of video calls." The camera shifted, and an elderly man in a suit and bow tie swung into view.

"It's fine, Marius, and good that we finally found a time to talk."

"Thank you so much for the copy of the memoir your father produced. I'm looking forward to finding out more about his life. It is so wonderful to find new family after all this time. And a little sad."

"Why so?"

"Well, that it took so long. I started this whole thing for Grandma thirty years ago. She so wanted to reconnect with her brother. Bless her, she held on as long as she could, made it to ninety-six."

"Wow. We didn't even know Clive had a sister. So, do you know how they lost touch?"

"Ah, it's a sorry tale of a family squabble. Clive came to visit them here in Edmonton sometime around 1929 or 1930. This was not long after he sold up the family estate."

"You know about that?" I asked.

"Oh, yes. Why, Doreen and I visited the old house about fifteen years ago. We took a pinch of Grandma's ashes, got permission to scatter them in the hospital gardens. They were very kind, made quite a fuss of us."

"How sweet." I made a mental note to see if I could find something in the local papers.

"Yes. Well, Grandpa had been expecting that Grandma would receive some of the proceeds from the sale. He was counting on it really, because the business was struggling. And then Clive told them about how he'd given it all to the Trust, and there was a tremendous row. Clive left, and they never heard from him again. Grandma never forgave herself. She said that she regretted it all immediately, but it was too late. And of course, now you've explained why we couldn't track him down."

"Nothing like families for holding a grudge."

"Sadly true. Of course, they were both still grieving their parents, and I believe there was also tension about their brother's disappearance. Grandma was sure that Clive must know more than he was saying. But if he did, he never let on. He certainly was not well. You can see it in the photographs taken during the visit."

"Wait a minute, another brother? I didn't see him in the birth records."

"Henry was adopted. Or something. I think it might not have been entirely legal, but reading between the lines, that wouldn't have stopped Agatha Charting." Marius chuckled, seemingly fine with the idea of his ancestor being some sort of child abductor. "His birth name was Duchamp. I have his birth certificate here."

The name rang a bell. "What happened to him?"

"Well, that's the thing. No one knows. He simply vanished during the Great War. Not in the fighting, they kept him at home because he was not fit for service. He just … disappeared."

The sense of a story was stirring within me now. There was something here.

Marius continued. "Now, you asked me in your email about a bear? I have a surprise!"

For a moment, my hopes were raised. But then Marius held up something to the camera, too close to see properly at first. He pulled it back towards him, and a teddy bear wearing a faded dress appeared in his hand. "Grandma brought this with her from England. She always called it Madam Bear. She is a genuine Steiff, very early and quite valuable. Grandma didn't allow us to play with Madam Bear. She would only take her out occasionally when she was in the mood to reminisce about her time in the nursery at Chartings. She's magnificent, isn't she?"

"She certainly is." I tried to project enough enthusiasm to cover my disappointment. "Marius, I'd love to see those photographs you mentioned."

"I knew you would," he said, "so I'm paying my grandson Scott to digitise everything. I've been meaning to do it for ages anyway, and he was looking for a holiday job. He started with the older papers that Clive brought here when he visited. Some of them are very fragile."

Papers. I'd given up hope. "What sort of papers?"

"Oh, all sorts. Certificates, letters, estate correspondence. Everything that was rescued from the fire. You know how it is. Somehow it is the daughters who usually end up taking care of all that."

Gold! We continued to exchange pleasantries, but it was all I could do to restrain the desire to ask him to hurry things along.

I needn't have worried. A few days later, I received an email from Scott Aberlome with a link to an online photo vault. Pure gold.

The Orphan

The following pages show a selection of letters from the family papers of Marius Aberlome, and from the papers of Mary Lowndes, with thanks to the Birmingham City Archives

Miss Mary Lowndes
Lowndes and Drury,
35 Park Walk,
Chelsea

18th October 1897

Dearest Aggie,

I hope this letter finds you well. Barbara sends her love, and wishes to thank you for your advice in the matter of J., as indeed do I. Alfred has been most accommodating, and the studio in Chelsea has gotten off to an auspicious start with a commission for a window in St Albans.

I write to you chiefly to recommend Mrs Eloise Duchamp, a protégée of Aunt Alice, for the position of governess for young Clive. Mrs Duchamp is the widow of Capitaine George Duchamp and arrived lately from Saint-Louis in Senegal via France. She is a most pleasant and educated person, with experience as a governess to a good family in the colony before her marriage.

It is perhaps a little early to be considering such matters while Clive is so young, but Mrs Duchamp has fallen upon difficult times through no fault of her own. I am told privately by Aunt that Capitaine Duchamp's family refused to receive her when she arrived in Paris for reasons you will perhaps understand, not unlike the situation of Miss Adewunmi, which ended so tragically. Aunt is most concerned to find Eloise a situation of safety and comfort.

Yours affectionately,
Mary

Mrs Agatha Charting
Chartings House,
Pichesham,
--------shire,

28th November 1897

Dear Mary,

I am so looking forward to Christmas. John has promised he will get the Yellow Suite redecorated in time for your and Barbara's visit. The Armitages are also coming. We shall have a merry party.

I have some exciting news to share with you, my dear friend. John refused to let me tell before, but by the time you arrive I will be six months gone, and I wanted you to know before anyone else from my Chelsea days. I have been unwell with it but I think the worst is over.

Eloise could not have arrived at a more opportune moment after Nanny Pargeter's unexpected departure. Clive is very happy in her care, and she has even charmed John's mother. No small achievement, I am sure you will agree! I can only hope that this happy state will continue once her own condition becomes more apparent. Do assure your aunt that she will be safe here. John is inclined to be a little pompous and disapproving, but he has the kindest heart I ever knew in a man.

Yours, as ever,

Aggie

P.S You may tell Barbara my news, of course. I know she is the soul of discretion. Do you think she might like to be a godmother? I am tempting fate, I know, but with you already being Clive's, it would be lovely.

Miss Mary Lowndes
Lowndes and Drury,
35 Park Walk,
Chelsea

24th March 1898

Dear Aunt Alice,

I hope you are keeping well, and that the rheumatism has eased now that spring is imminent. Thank you for the lovely card I received on my birthday. You always remember. Did you see the announcement from Chartings in the *Telegraph*? Agatha has dropped a line to say that the birth went well, and she is recovering. The child was baptised Angela Margaret, and Barbara is to be a godmother.

Eloise's time is not far behind now. Lieutenant Charting was not best pleased about our little deceptions, but Agatha knows her husband well enough to know he would not turn out a lady in need. Please give Jester a stroke for me, and send my love to Cook.

Your loving niece,
Mary

Mrs Agatha Charting
Chartings House,
Pichesham,
--------shire,

24th April 1898

Dear Mary,

   I write with such sadness. I must tell you that
Eloise gave birth to a son ten days ago. The birth
was very hard on both mother and child. We
thought the babe unlikely to survive, but despite
everything he has clung on, and Eloise was able to
nurture him for a short while. She came down with
the fever soon after the baptism, and succumbed
yesterday. We have arranged burial at St Joseph's on
April 30th and if you should be able to attend, you
will be most welcome. Eloise was not with us long,
but the household had taken her to its heart, and we
are bereft.

   Cruelty upon cruelty, Dr Peasemore suspects that
little Henri was damaged during the prolonged birth.
He does not breathe quite properly, and seems
listless, so unlike my darling Angela. Fortunately, I
am still in milk, and he feeds well enough.
Peasemore says that he knows an asylum suitable
should his diagnosis prove to be correct. But you
and I have seen such places and I will not
countenance this. Though I fear for Henri's future, I
promised dear Eloise that I will care for him, and we
will find a way.

   Much love to you, my dears,

   Aggie

Dr Reginald Peasemore,
The Larches,
Pichesham,
--------shire,

3rd June, 1902

Dear Lieutenant Charting,

Having examined young Henry again, I remain firmly of the opinion that he would be better placed in Hanwell Asylum, and would urge you to reconsider your decision to keep him in your own home. The management of imbeciles, especially those of the inferior races, is not a matter to be taken lightly. The institute is well respected for their humane treatment of such unfortunates. I urge this both for the child's welfare, and also that of your wife. I believe her excessive attachment to be detrimental to your own family, and speaks to a wilful character that must be reined in.

Should my advice be rejected again, I must respectfully withdraw from the case. I enclose my account and hope to hear an answer in this matter shortly.

Your servant,

R. Peasemore

Note to Peter Brownlow, found in the ledger of accounts from 1902

Peter, please do me the favour of paying Peasemore's bill, and informing him that his services are no longer required at Chartings. I think I might say something regrettable were I to write myself. Use the home farm account as usual. I suppose we must use him for the near term if the staff need medical assistance, but try to keep it from Agatha if that happens. She will, no doubt, be looking for alternative provision.

Cordially, John

Mrs Agatha Charting
Chartings House,
Pichesham,
--------shire,

6th June 1902

Dear Mary,

Such a drama. That pompous doctor was here again, demanding that Henry be sent to Hanwell. I am sure he stood to gain somehow. He sent John such a letter that my blood boiled, and John was no less exercised. I still suspect that it was Peasemore's incompetence that led to Eloise's untimely death, and he shall get no more work in this village. I have written to Dr Jex-Blake of our acquaintance, in the hope of a recommendation of someone more suitable to our needs here.

Henry was somewhat disturbed by the visit, but it was wonderful to see Clive and even little Angela gather him up and comfort him. He is such a brave little soul. The doctor sees only what he cannot do and takes no account of how hard he tries. I know he will never live a normal life and I confess I am worried about the seizures. But it is not as though Peasemore was ever able to help with those, anyway.

I will write properly tomorrow evening, but I know you will forgive my outburst!

Much love,

Aggie

Miss Mary Lowndes
Lowndes and Drury,
35 Park Walk,
Chelsea

16th January 1904

Dear Aggie,

Such a lovely surprise to receive the photograph today. Clive seems so grown up, and the spit of John. Angela is pretty as a picture, and of course Henry has his cheeky smile as always. I am so pleased that my Christmas gift to the children was a success. Madam Bear looks most handsome in her outfit. Where Clive had the idea, I have no notion. I never knew such things existed. They certainly didn't when I was a girl, and I was sorely tempted to buy one for myself during our visit to Hamleys!

I was sorry not to come and visit at Christmas, but work is busier than ever. I have had an enquiry for the windows of a new synagogue in New York, would you believe? And I have promised Christabel some illustrations for WSBU posters.

Affectionately yours,

Mary

Marthe

Chanac, Gévaudan region of France, 1764

The summons came, and I turned back into the world, resigned to another session as the plaything of humans. It was not the usual welcome. I found myself in a tiny house, confronted on one side by a snarling wolf, and on the other by an old woman being defended by a small dog. The dog was barking furiously and had blood on its muzzle. The wolf recoiled at my arrival, but something was not quite right about it. I looked more closely. There was a telltale scar around the eye.

"Svend? Is that you?"

The wolf stopped snarling but remained on guard, hackles raised. "Bear. Stand aside. I have my orders."

"Svend, please consider. You know how this works. I am resisting, but this human has me. I will have no choice but to fight and kill you. Back off."

He looked tempted to try his luck. I pushed my size up to maximum and bared my teeth. "Svend, I would not have you as an enemy. Talk to Erik, explain."

"This is not the end of the matter, Bear. I will indeed talk to Erik."

The wolf ran out through the open door. With the passing of the immediate threat, I turned my attention to the old woman. She was understandably terrified. To her eyes, I must have been a bigger danger than the wolf.

The dog ran at me and tried to take a bite. Timo had not forgotten how to handle over-excited dogs and I calmly moved to one side, tucked one foot under its stomach and hoisted it through the doorway of the house. I shut the door in its face and by the time I turned around again, the woman had fainted in fear.

I placed her on the small bed and looked around. The room smelled bad. Everything was dirty, and the woman looked ill. I found a jug of water, but it was stale and dead flies were floating in it. I took the jug and flickered past the door to a vantage point outside to find myself in an overgrown vegetable garden. The dog was frantically scratching at the door, trying to get in. I adjusted my shape to make myself a bit more human-like and spoke to it in peasant French picked up from the local taverns.

"Hey, dog. Hey. Come here."

The dog paused, agitated but curious. I retrieved a piece of bread from my carry sack and threw it over. It watched from a safe distance for a while, and, when I made no moves, trotted over to sniff the bread. The dog was thin and dirty, like the old woman, and clearly needed to eat.

"Don't worry, girl, it is safe. Go ahead."

While it was munching at the bread, I found a well and refreshed the water in the jug. It was a start.

🐾 🐾 🐾

This was the winter of 1764. I knew where I was. I kept careful track of the talisman these days. The house was in an isolated spot not far from Chanac, in the Gévaudan region of rural France. Forty years ago, when the talisman had arrived there, the farm had been thriving. Now it was neglected, the lime wash grubby and discoloured, with patches of the daub walls flaking off.

The talisman had been in the house for all that time, and I had felt no summons from there before. I guessed that the extreme danger had brought something latent to the surface in the old woman. If anything was going to do that, being confronted in your own home by a wolf would be it.

While the woman was unconscious, I shifted my form to as close to human as possible and covered up most of my fur with a torn dress I found in a chest. Then I kept guard while I waited for her to awake. I did not trust that Svend wouldn't return to finish the job with Erik and the rest in tow. I could handle one or two of them, but if they brought the pack, I would be in trouble.

Erik. I did not like Erik. The other wolves were reasonable enough when they weren't on the hunt. Svend and I had even shared a deer in Northern Spain many decades ago. There was, and still is, common ground between us and them. They must have been formed in a similar way, but unlike the bound folk, they carry only one human mind each. And they are not tied in the way we are, able to move wherever they please in the real world. I always thought that if left to their own devices, they would have reverted to normal wolf behaviour. But Erik was too much of everything—too human in his cruelty, too wolfish in his ruthlessness when tracking down prey. He led the pack into dark places.

The woman awoke. It was dark now, and I lit a candle.

"Who is there? Is that you, Jeanette?" She sounded confused and frightened.

I decided Crina's voice would be the most reassuring. "No, it is your rescuer. I was summoned here. I saw off the wolf."

The woman's eyes widened when she saw me, and she crossed herself. I'm sure I made a most unconvincing human.

"Barbotine? Barbotine, come to me." The dog ran over and jumped onto her lap, licking at her face. "What are you? What do you want with me? I am an old woman. There is nothing here."

"I mean you no harm. You summoned me here. Did you know you could?"

"I don't know what you are saying. I am old. Leave me alone."

I poured some water into a cup and offered it. "I am sorry to have frightened you. But I don't think it is safe for me to leave. The wolf may return. Since I am here, can I do anything to help?"

Her name was Marthe, and she had been ill with a fever for days, unable to get out for food or water. It took a while to gain her trust. I told her my name was Greta and explained my odd hairy appearance by saying that I had been born like this; had spent my life so far working in a travelling show, but had tired of it. I doubted she believed this tale, but she reluctantly accepted the help offered.

I could sense the talisman in the drawer of a dresser. Unusual that it wasn't in physical contact, but not unknown. She was harmless, and it seemed like a reasonable compromise to do her bidding without telling her of the power she could exert if she knew. It was easy enough, uncomplicated, and something new to occupy myself with.

At first, I just stole bread and vegetables from the surrounding area for her. As she regained strength, we settled into a comfortable pattern. I cleaned, did laundry and foraged for food and firewood. Marthe recovered enough to walk a little and would totter around the house tidying and cooking. Mostly talking. Barbotine became used to my presence and would even sit by me sometimes. Marthe was fond of a rabbit stew and I discovered to my surprise that I enjoyed the taste of cooked meat. Marthe had a way with the herbs she grew in the garden, and I could taste the different flavours, something I never had before. All in all, it was a pleasant interlude, and liking my master made everything very easy. One day, she told me she felt well enough to work again.

"Greta, I want to get back to my sewing. Before I was ill, I would take my wares to the market. Can you get me supplies? I need black thread and some linen. I used to get them from Jeanette in the village."

"I fear your neighbours are not ready to meet someone like me, Marthe. I could steal them for you?"

"No, I would not like that. Jeanette is a good person. Please, could you deliver a note?"

It was a risk to leave her, but after all, I was there to do her bidding. Jeanette's cottage was in the main village, so I took the note after dark, draped in the heaviest hooded cloak I could find and wearing Marthe's best gloves. I passed myself off as a distant relative of Marthe, come to care for her in her illness. Jeanette was suspicious, but I provided money, and waited outside the door while she found the requested supplies.

She returned. "Marthe does good work. I have an order for embroidered tableware for the marquis. She would be ideal to help me with it. Tell Marthe I will call on her in the morning to talk to her about it."

Jeanette called as promised, full of apologies for not having realised her old friend was ill. I retreated to a dark corner and left them to their discussions. A word caught my attention.

"… they think it was wolves. The poor woman was torn to shreds, they say."

I butted into the conversation. "I'm sorry, could you repeat that?" Marthe was looking at me wide-eyed in fear. I shook my head slightly, to indicate that she should say nothing.

"I was telling Marthe about what happened over toward Sainte-Énimie. The wife of Jacques Bonard was found dead near where she had been tending cattle. It's just the latest of many such atrocities. Marthe, you must move into the village. It's not safe for you out here."

I murmured something about how we were keeping the door bolted. It confirmed what I had suspected. Erik was on the trail of another cluster of humans.

I knew about their escapades in the north of Africa, and Auroch had told me of another such incident in the far reaches of the east. Erik was proud of it, boastful even. He was determined to rid the world of humans like those who had (in his belief) condemned him and his men to be 'cast in the form of wolves'. Auroch had tried to explain to him that the real Erik was long dead, and it was only the shadow of his memories causing him pain. But Erik was not to be reasoned with. He left the bound folk alone, but, blessed with a wolfish sense of smell altered by its exposure to Greyside, he spent his time scenting out those humans who could wield magic. Their innocence or otherwise was of no matter to him, and as he was leader of the pack, the other wolves followed his orders.

After Jeanette's visit, the people of the village called by regularly to check on Marthe. Now she was working, making delicately embroidered napkins, and earning enough to pay for food. Still, I found I was unable to leave. Not as a compulsion, that seemed to have passed, but I knew the situation with Erik would not go away.

To pass the time, I asked Marthe to teach me how to sew. My hands were human-shaped, but not sensitive enough to feel needle and thread the way she could. I found I could compensate by making the fingers thinner and longer than normal. Marthe watched this happening without comment. I would have told her the truth about me if she had asked, but she chose not to.

I became good enough with a needle to help with the hemming and other simpler tasks, while Marthe concentrated on the elaborate decorative work. One day she presented me with a surprise. It was a hood made of pale brown linen, embroidered with the features of a human face. It was beautifully made, with delicate pink lips and a shaped section for a nose. I was puzzled. "It is lovely, Marthe, but I don't understand. What is it?"

"It is a mask. I left holes in the eyes. I thought it might help you fit in more easily?"

My human emotions responded strongly to this unexpected kindness, and I felt a stinging in the corners of my eyes where a human might have shed tears. I still have that mask safely stored in my Greyside home. It was the first object I considered something of my own. And, rather to my amazement, the mask worked. Despite it looking nothing like a real human face, the villagers who visited accepted it, even at close quarters. Disfigurement was common enough in those days and perhaps they were relieved that whatever was underneath was hidden away.

Summer came, and with it came an unwelcome delegation. Late one night in April, Barbotine started barking in the garden. Her instincts were good. I could smell wolf markings in the vicinity. I gathered her up, and we retreated into the house, where I could keep her and Marthe close.

I watched through the window as Erik walked up to the door, stood on his hind legs, and waited. I opened the door cautiously. He looked even stranger than usual. I'd become accustomed to the bare skin on his head where he'd shaved off the fur. Now the tips of his ears had been rounded off. They looked sore and crusted over, as if it had been done recently. What had not changed was the cold fury he radiated that never seemed to relent.

"You know why I have come, Bear. We have cleared most of the scourge from this area. Just this one remains. I have left you this long, but we will be finished."

"I cannot let it happen, Erik. You know this, I am bound to her and have no choice. Leave this one alone. She is old and harmless and will end naturally soon."

"If you do not step aside, we will end you."

"No doubt. But I will take many of you down with me, Erik. Leave her. Move on to new prey elsewhere."

He stalked closer. Erik had learned some of the shape trick himself and he swelled to an unnatural size. "Last chance, Bear. My pack will follow me to death. I will not be cheated."

I believed him. "Erik, accept a compromise. I will end her myself in my own way. I do not care for your methods. Let us avoid bloodshed between our kind."

He paused. "You are not my kind, animal. Do you pledge it?"

"I do. You and I are here for the long term. These humans pass like mayflies. Let it be."

He considered and finally agreed. "The pack will rest in Greyside for a while, but I will be back here in winter. If you break your pledge, you will regret it." He left.

I reassured Marthe that the wolf was gone for good this time and kept the hollow feeling inside of me to myself. Summer passed into autumn, and life was calm and happy in the little house. And in the end, my agonising over how and when to do it was made easy for me. After the first snows, Marthe became ill again, and this time there was no relief.

The sickness left her gasping for breath and coughing up blood. I wrapped her up as warmly as I could and kept Barbotine close by for her comfort.

The final evening was heartbreaking. I was supporting Marthe upright to ease the cough, and when she finally recovered enough to lie down, she reached up and stroked my face. "I know who you are. I thought you were the Devil. But I know you are from another place. My angel. *Mon ange.*"

I shushed her and tucked her in again. But the brief respite was followed by a fit of coughing that left her wracked in agony. It was time. I slipped a hefty dose of Thing's pain reliever into her water and helped her to sip at the cup. The effect was rapid in the real world. She relaxed into a blissful dreamlike state and before I knew it was dead. It was over in seconds, and the smile on her face was beautiful.

🐾 🐾 🐾

Barbotine inspected her still form and looked at me mournfully. A wave of grief swept over me, but I knew it was not entirely my own.

It was only then that I realised my mistake. Marthe had never been my master. The compulsion had been coming from the little dog. I had been following her desires unknowingly all this time. Was Barbotine herself conscious of this? I didn't think so. She was, after all, only a dog. I had met my pledge, but my victim was not even the true target of Erik's wrath. He would be back, and he would know by smell that Barbotine was my true master.

Eventually, there was a sense of hunger, and I gave Barbotine some leftover stew. She fell asleep nestled up with Marthe's body. Unlike previous masters, Barbotine didn't hold the talisman, so I could have just given her some of the pain reliever and freed myself. But she was an innocent animal and had become a friend.

I took a risk. Wrapping my arms around Marthe and Barbotine, I carried them both back to Greyside, away from the influence of the talisman. She didn't even wake until we were there. It was immediately clear that Barbotine was something unusual. There were visible ripples radiating from her little body, something I had never seen anything like before, waves that seemed rooted in the earth beneath her.

I found a sheltered spot a little way from the caves and dug a grave for the body. Once Barbotine saw me digging, she joined in to help as best she could. Back in my bear form, I carefully placed Marthe inside and covered her over, all the while observed by the little dog.

"Will you stay here, Barbotine? It might be dangerous for you. My friend Auroch says humans go mad here. You are not a human, but you are a master. I don't know what might happen."

"Stay with you?"

"Yes, I'll bring you food and water. You can meet my friends. I think Thing will like you."

"Want stay here. With Marthe. I guard her."

"Very well."

Barbotine's ability to speak her thoughts in Greyside didn't surprise me. Dogs are shaped by humans; they are hardly natural animals at all. They have a level of understanding of human speech that doesn't exist in any normal wild animal. And everyone else I knew in Greyside could speak to me.

She settled into life there well enough, though I could sense her sadness. At night, she would sleep curled up against the rock I placed to mark Marthe's burial spot. Sometimes she would seek me or one of the others out for company, the rest of the time she would explore alone. What was unexpected was her effect on the land. The dust around the grave reacted to her presence. Over the course of months, walls of dust rose from the ground, surrounding the grave. Gaps appeared in the walls where windows might be, and objects shaped vaguely like furniture emerged. The shape of Marthe's old cottage became evident. It didn't look much like the house, but in Barbotine's mind I supposed it was more obvious. It was intriguing. Auroch came to inspect the structure, curious about our new resident. In his thousands of years, he had seen similar things, though none quite like Barbotine.

"Animals and humans turn up occasionally. Ordinary humans lose their minds after a few days. No one knows why. Animals aren't affected, they just adjust. But it's not a good place for them to live. They either starve, or they are hunted for food. Especially by the wolves, they enjoy a bit of sport on home ground. So, you had better find a way to keep her safe if you want her to stay."

Auroch promised to watch over her while I sought out Erik. I found the pack in their customary clearing in the underground forest. Erik was gnawing on a bloody limb at a distance from the others. He growled as I approached.

"You needn't get pissed about it, Erik. I don't want your dinner."

He stopped eating and bared his teeth at me. "Where is the old woman? You've hidden her."

"I did as we agreed. Her body is buried above, near the caves."

He looked at me piercingly. "Very well. I will check, but if you have done as you were told, then our argument is done. Just don't disobey me again."

I was enraged. I snatched the limb from between his paws and whacked him on the jaw with it. He went flying onto his back, landing at a painful angle against a tree. I leapt on top of him and put a claw right up to his neck, pressing hard.

"Stand back! I'll do it. Fall back, all of you." The pack slunk away, glaring at me. I looked down at Erik, teeth bared. "You listen and learn, wolf." He flinched. "You don't tell me what to do. No one put you in charge here. You and your little friends might be able to take me down, but I will take every single one of you on, starting with you. I'll break your legs and leave you bleeding dry first, so you can watch. Is that what you want?"

He grunted, but I wasn't finished.

"I don't interfere with you, but be clear, you don't interfere with me either. You leave me and my friends alone." I pushed the claw harder. "Do you understand?"

He tried to nod. I got up and stared down the pack. Erik tried to speak, but nothing came out. No one moved. "Good. Now, be good little pups and get on with your dinner. We'll say no more about it."

It felt good at the time. In retrospect? I should have handled it better.

Lance's Confession

Birmingham, October 2018

From the letters that Scott Aberlome had scanned in, I had picked out Agatha's correspondence to Mary Lowndes as especially interesting. An internet search had led me to an archive of her personal papers at Birmingham University. The university library wasn't far from where Farzad was working, so after I'd been to take copies, I took a chance and called into the office.

"Hi, Annie, that was quick. I haven't made much headway with the Trust yet."

"No, that's OK, Farzad, just thought I'd drop by as I was in the area."

"Actually, I'm glad you did, as I was planning to call you. I was talking to Leonard in the New York office yesterday. He was letting me know he's resigning to become CEO for a new current affairs magazine. It's all a bit of a mystery. A big investor has come out of nowhere, with a list of names. He asked about you, because you are on that list."

I was floored for a moment. "Seriously? What position?"

"Senior US editor was suggested, apparently. He was dubious because he doesn't know you, but I talked you up to him."

"I mean, I'm flattered, but that would be a massive step up."

138

"Annie, if I'm honest, I agree. But the way he describes it, it could have been tailor-made for you. I'm a bit jealous. I might apply myself if you aren't interested."

"Wow. No, of course I'm interested, but I'll need to think about it."

"Well, don't leave it too long. List of names or not, there will be stiff competition for this."

Bucked up by this turn of fortunes, I promptly put some work into my CV and sent details and an application. The correspondence I'd picked up at the university from Agatha Charting to her friend Mary really helped to fill out events in the family story and made Henry's disappearance seem more personal. I was on a roll, and things were headed my way.

Online searches threw up many news articles concerning John and Agatha Charting. Agatha had been quite a celebrity in her day, often featuring in picture magazines like *Tatler* and even in an article about the Chartings Hospital Trust in the *Times*. There was also extensive coverage of Henry Duchamp's disappearance in the regional press, with appeals for sightings that eventually petered out towards the end of 1917. And since I was searching for all the names I'd encountered, there was a rather odd parallel story about the Brownlow family that explained the inscription about Eleanor on the family grave.

🐾 🐾 🐾

19th NOVEMBER 1871
TRAGIC DEATHS OF FAMILY IN PICHESHAM
THE INQUEST

The quiet village of Pichesham was united in sadness and outrage following the conclusion of the coroner's inquest into the deaths of the Brownlow family, held today at the Falling Star Inn before the county coroner (A. P. Carter, Esq). The facts of the case are these. Mr Peter Brownlow, a noted violinist, commonly performing at Hanover Square Rooms in London, together with his wife Sarah, contracted a virulent strain of consumption and were confined together at their home, Ferry Cottage. Witness Mrs Fredericks declared that on calling with a laundry delivery, the daughter Eleanor, aged 9 years, did tell her that her parents were ill, not to enter the house for fear of her own life, and that she was caring for the little son of the house, also named Peter. There were murmurings around the room as the coroner asked why she had not entered the house, to which Mrs Fredericks stated it was not her business and that the family were known to avoid mixing with the common folk of the village.

Witness Freda Benson, village schoolmistress, then took the stand to declare that Eleanor was an unusually clever and accomplished child in all manner of things, and was perfectly capable of caring for the younger child, although she deplored Mrs Fredericks having not pursued entry. There was then an uproar in the room as Mrs Fredericks declared that Miss Benson should keep her counsel and was she not responsible for allowing the child such freedom as to wander the forest wheresoever she pleased. Mr Carter was forced to bring the matters to order with some force.

The next witness was John Charting, Esq, of Chartings House, elder brother to Sarah Brownlow. He related how on the morning of August 12th he had gone to the stables intending to ride out to visit his sister, only to find his nephew Peter wrapped in a blanket in the stable and waiting patiently with a note from the little girl asking him to take care of the younger child. Of Eleanor herself, there was no sign. Help was sent to Ferry Cottage immediately, but Mr Peter Brownlow Sr. later perished on August 14th, followed by his wife Sarah on August 17th. Dr Cedric Peasemore of The Larches, Pichesham, gave witness that he had certified death on both unfortunates. Mr Charting then told how he had mounted rigorous searches for his niece throughout the surrounding areas over the next weeks, involving dozens of estate workers and volunteers from the village. No trace of the little girl was found, nor any evidence of her belongings or clothing.

The coroner stated that on balance he believed the likelihood was that Eleanor had tried to return home after taking her brother to safety. Given the proximity of the river to the route, it was also highly likely that she had fallen in, possibly in a weakened state from having herself succumbed to consumption, and been swept downriver. He finally declared that in the absence of other evidence, he would have to find an open verdict on Eleanor Brownlow, but felt safe in declaring her also deceased. He commended Mr Charting for his efforts. Peter Brownlow Jr is now living at Chartings House with family members, and is well and healthy.

🐾 🐾 🐾

It seemed that the Brownlows were even more unfortunate than I'd assumed, and Pichesham had more than its fair share of mysterious disappearances.

And finally, fatefully, I added Lance's name to the search, almost on a whim. This was what came up from the Siracona Journal dated 18th September 1969.

SHOCKING REVELATIONS: Canvas "Palace" a Den of Sin and Vice

Following a tip-off that a woman was being held captive, police raided the hippie commune in the hills outside the town. Thirteen people were arrested. Charges were made for possession of marijuana and LSD against three men and one woman, and one further charge of distributing narcotics made against one Lancelot Brannigan, an Englishman present on an expired work visa. Brannigan is held in custody pending county court proceedings. Initial charges of kidnap against Brannigan were dropped following the refusal of a woman to testify.

According to an eyewitness, the hippies have constructed an extraordinary tent around the shell of a derelict school bus. Canvas panels brightly painted with oriental designs surround the bus, leading to an interior area large enough to accommodate the entire commune at once. It is neatly floored with scrap wood and fabric, with a communal cooking and sleeping area. Police found evidence of drug taking and other unmentionable communal activities strewn around.

Deputy Sheriff Johnson said, "Honestly, the tent is kind of impressive, and we were reluctant to bother these people, who have largely kept away from town. If they'd have put as much effort into being productive members of society as they did into this ramshackle pile, then I doubt we'd be here now, but when we received serious allegations, there was no choice. I'll be moving to close this site as fast as possible. As for Brannigan, I hope to see him deported back to England before long."

WE SAY:

It is believed that the commune was a hotbed of drug use and debauchery, with young people indulging in every vice imaginable. Despite protestations we have seen in other areas of the peaceful nature of hippies, there is no place for such a carnival of immorality in this town, drawing our unsuspecting youth into a spiral of destruction. The police must drive these people back into the metropolitan areas where they can be among their own kind, and treat the malign actors among them with the full weight of the law..

It was quaint and amusing. It could have been a different Lance Brannigan, but still. I printed off the article. It was my turn to take Lance's grocery order up the hill anyway, and I thought it would be something to talk about. He made tea as usual, and we sat on opposite ends of the bench.

"So, Lance. Seems like you've been holding out on me all this time." I rummaged in my bag for the article.

Lance sighed and put his mug down. "You found out. I knew you would."

"Want to tell me about it?" I was still relaxed at this point, but Lance was looking quite distressed.

"Look, I'm sorry. I didn't want to do it. I don't know if it will help, but it was only a tiny nudge. You were halfway there anyway."

I had no idea what he was talking about, but there was an unpleasant feeling in the pit of my stomach. I didn't want him to know I was grasping. "I just want to understand, Lance. Halfway?"

"More really. I told her it wasn't necessary, that you and Dr Hunt were going to click. But she insisted."

"OK, now I'm scared, Lance. What exactly have you done? Who insisted about what? And why?"

And he told me. I did not believe a word of it. And then I did.

🐻 🐻 🐻

Transcribed from audio recording

"It's just been there for as long as I can remember. I could see it in people. Not words—feelings, urges. If a girl liked the look of me. If she didn't. Or if she liked someone else maybe. And the lads too, poor old Terry giving me those doggy eyes, but I refused to notice. And then there was this one time we're at the Reading Festival and I see this other lad in the crowd, and I can tell that he and Terry would hit it off. And before I know what's happening, I sort of reach out and give a nudge, and the other lad's turning round to have a look. That was the first time I did it. I was doing a lot of weed, and somehow it was just part of that, natural like.

"I got a bit carried away. Cos it was so easy, you know? So many of those kids, confident on the outside, scared to say what they feel on the inside. Just a little nudge, and bang, they're connected. I felt like some sort of love god. Didn't matter to me if they were already with someone, if I could see they were better with someone else, I just did it anyway. And of course, I could have my pick of the girls, as long as they were a little bit interested.

"So I'm just going a bit wild, and I end up in the USA like I told you, and I'm dealing some gear to make ends meet. And I'm at Woodstock, playing my usual games, and that's where I met Junie. She was fabulous. Long dark hair, amazing green eyes, something special. I gave her a little nudge like usual, and she stopped me in my tracks. Cos she was like me. Not the same, but she had her own thing. That nudge bounced straight back, and I was hooked. I mean, really hooked, tongue on the floor and all that.

"She knew what I'd done. She said later that she was furious for about five minutes. But she'd never met anyone who was like her before on her travels, and we got talking, and sharing, and somehow I'm forgiven a little bit. She's already got a boyfriend, so I just have to suffer in silence, worshipping this goddess and not able to do anything about it. But I'll do anything to stay near her, so we go back to their place in Nevada. Her man there, he knows, he can tell. I steer as clear as I can, but Junie and I finally get it together one night, cos you know, it was that kind of vibe, a lot of sharing. He makes out like he's cool with it, but he's not, of course. And he calls the cops and tells them all sorts of stuff about the drugs and how I'm dangerous or something.

"One thing leads to another, and I'm held on remand waiting to be deported back home. And I'm going through hell, cos I'm going cold turkey while waiting. Junie gets mad, and she's the one visiting me and trying to get me through it all. And then we both come back and she brings me to Pichesham.

"They really did help me kick the poison. Miss Stanground wanted us to live in the village, but it was too square for me and Junie. The army had packed up and left. No one seemed to know if they were coming back, so we helped ourselves to the old pub. And we settled down and had a kid and were happy.

"Except somehow, they know. About us, and what we could do. The Trust, I mean. We didn't really mind doing the occasional favour given what we owed them. Margaret, or later on Margot, would get me to come down to the village and have a look at people. I'd say if someone looked like a good match for someone else, and that was usually it. Margot has asked me to give couples a nudge towards each other once in a while. There was that professor and Mrs Topper; he was smiling all over his face that summer. And then you and Dr Hunt.

"You don't believe me, I can tell that. But I want you to understand. What you feel for your young man is real. I can see it in you right now. You two hooking up were always a possibility. All I had to do was push down on that little button and speed things up a bit.

"When I was young, I didn't care, I'd put all sorts of people together who barely had anything in common except raw attraction. Junie made me a better person. I wouldn't have agreed if you weren't good for each other. But I still feel bad, because you didn't get the choice. And you've both been so kind."

Lance was damp-eyed by the end of this. I was too numb to comfort him, but passed him a Kleenex from my purse automatically. I asked him questions in a distant sort of way. Whether he could undo things. Whether Dom knew. Lance shook his head at this and blew his nose noisily. "No. He knows nothing about it. Bless him, he doesn't even know about his own thing."

I didn't want to believe a word of it, but there had been something peculiar about how quickly things had happened. Two days and we were in bed. I'm not like that. And then what Lance said about Dom hit home. His own thing?

"Oh, yes. It was always people like me and Junie. People who can do things. You know, like your thing, where you make people open up and talk." Lance sniffed. "Damn, it feels good to give in to it at last. Been resisting so long. Hard to do that with a guilty conscience."

That was all I could cope with. I thanked him politely for his honesty and walked away. He looked lighter. I knew why. His burden was now mine.

The Bear of Pichesham

INTERMISSION

Location unknown, May 1964

It is time. He has come for us. Donor and recipient. The words have been practised to perfection, and though they have no meaning to me, I must trust they will work. It's just a bird. Is it cruel? They say not.

I have no regrets. Indeed, I thought this day would come much earlier, my very existence a failure. I will be gone, yet I will not. I will see my son grow to be a man, yet I will not. There will be a purpose where there was none.

I am still worried about the pain. He assures me it will be brief, and I probably won't remember it at all. But all shall be well, and all shall be well, and all manner of things shall be well.

PART II
She Did Not
Cry When She
Cry When She
Fell Down That
Precipice

Menace Approaches

My mind was a whirl after the conversation with Lance. He'd confronted me directly with something I'd always understood but never acknowledged. I did have a 'thing', as he put it. I could make people open up and tell me secrets that they didn't intend to. It was a talent I'd used ruthlessly over the years. And I'd accepted it as just the way I was. It had never occurred to me that it was anything unusual.

Out of the blue, I realised that I'd used it on Paul. I remembered him coming home from the precinct, clearly troubled about something. He'd asked me not to push, but I wouldn't let it go. I thought about all the times I'd 'turned up the charm', not realising how literally I was doing that.

I wanted to calm down, so I headed for the inn. I wasn't ready to talk to Dominic about this yet. Grant got me a large Scotch and I retreated to the covered veranda for some privacy. It was later in the year and getting colder now and I shivered. I sat there going over and over in my mind what Lance had said for some time, and in the end took relief in looking at my phone. It occurred to me that I should check my spam folder, and to my annoyance I found that Farzad had sent me an email two days ago. I guessed the attachment, a long PDF document, must have triggered the spam filter.

Given what I'd heard from Lance, I needed to know more about Margot and the Trust, so I dug into the report. Farzad had certainly come through, although the Trust turned out to be infuriatingly obscure.

In the 1970s brochure, it had supposedly been present in forty-five countries. However, Farzad had located official branches or related organisations in every nation he was able to get reliable information from, not to mention heavy involvement in a non-governmental organisation called Phoenix International Aid. This NGO was present in various war zones around the world. The causes it espoused were many and various, and sometimes even seemed contradictory.

But there were other oddities. It seemed to be a complete mystery where the money came from. In his sign-off, he said he was going to continue looking to see what he could turn up.

I called Farzad back, hoping he had something more for me. It rang once, and was answered by an automated voice that said, *"This number is no longer in service."*

Strange, I thought. I looked up the landline number for *Secretz!* and called that instead. It was Janice, his PA, who answered.

"Hi, Janice, it's Annie Maylor. Remember me?"

"Oh, Annie. Of course." There was something odd in her voice.

"Janice, I was hoping to catch Farzad, is he around? He's not answering his cellphone." There was a sob. "Janice, are you OK?"

"No! Mr Khan. Farzad. He's dead, Annie! We've just had a visit from the police."

I felt like someone had kicked me in the stomach. "Oh, my God, Janice. I … I'm so sorry. What happened?"

"He was found in the canal on the night before last. They think he might have had a heart attack."

"Janice, I don't know what to say. Is it suspicious?"

She sniffed. "No, they don't think so. Why? Do you think it could be?"

"He was doing me a favour. I know it sounds paranoid. Oh, this is awful. I'm sorry I mentioned it."

"No, you were right to. They said they would follow up with his recent contacts. I think they are just being careful, though. I have to go now, Annie, take care."

I thanked her and hung up the call. I couldn't believe it. Farzad had been more than a friend. Accidental death? Really? It was one hell of a coincidence. A part of me wanted to march straight to Margot's house and confront her, but caution injected itself. It seemed mad to think that a respectable lady like her could be involved, but Lance had specifically said she was behind whatever it was that he'd done.

Could she have done something to Farzad? I tried to force myself to be dispassionate. I'd just learned something shocking about myself and wasn't thinking clearly. I was too cold to sit for longer, so I walked back to Dom's house. I didn't know what I was going to say to him. But it turned out that any conversation with Dom would have to wait. There was a stranger sitting at the kitchen table.

"Annie, this is Detective Inspector William Carabon. I just brought him across the river. Apparently, he wants to talk to you?" Dom looked at me quizzically. I forced a smile to my lips, and, looking at his worried, kind, craggy face, I knew I still wanted him.

"It's all right, Dom, I think I know why the inspector is here. I just heard some bad news." I didn't want to talk in front of Dom. "Could we have a bit of space, Dom? Grant's got a fire going in the bar. I'll tell you later."

He made a small joke about being kicked out of his own kitchen, but got up. He dropped a kiss on top of my head and I touched his hand as he passed me. "Tansy, are you coming?" The dog seemed indifferent, curled up asleep under the table. He shrugged and went.

"Inspector, I assume this is about Farzad Khan? I literally only found out a few minutes ago when I called his office. What happened?"

He looked at me intently for an uncomfortably long pause. He was an odd-looking man. Big, heavy around the body, but his face was angular, with long bony features. He tipped his head to one side, apparently judging me. "Please sit down, Miss Maylor."

"Ms," I said automatically. "But call me Annie."

"Annie." He said my name slowly. "Mr Khan was found drowned in the canal not far from his workplace. Did you know him well?"

"Yes. He was an old friend."

"I'm sorry for your loss," he said, but he didn't seem sorry. "I understand you were working with him? On some sort of investigation."

"Not exactly. Farzad was just doing some background research for me as a favour."

He placed his hands on the table and looked at them. "Annie, it's not so unusual for people to fall into canals, and there is nothing to suggest anything odd apart from the time of day. It's a busy place, but no one witnessed anything. I think the local police are inclined to treat it as an accident."

"What do you mean, local police? Are you not part of the investigation?"

"No. An alert was sent to me because of the reference in his notes to Phoenix International Aid. I'm part of a team looking into their activities. I am here to find out what your interest is."

I was flummoxed for a moment, but remembered the mention in the PDF report. "I asked him to look into the Pichesham Trust. Farzad mentioned in his report that it was connected to an NGO, but he didn't give much detail."

"I would advise you against looking too deeply, Annie. Unfortunate things seem to happen to those who do." He made it sound like a threat. I became angry.

"Can I see your ID, please?" I demanded.

He seemed taken aback. "I apologise, Ms Maylor, that was clumsy. Clearly he was closer to you than I realised." He reached into his suit jacket and passed me a card. It looked authentic and I passed it back. "I have seen too many so-called accidents in connection with Phoenix International, and it has made me concerned. I'm sorry if that came across badly."

I tried to tamp down the emotion. "Apology accepted. Can you tell me why you are investigating Phoenix International and the Trust? You do know this village is owned by the Trust, so should you even be here?"

He looked at me appraisingly. "Yes, I did know, which is why I decided to come and see you in person. I don't have an informant here. I've tried, but visitors are strongly encouraged to leave. The hotel becomes booked up suddenly, the ferry is not running today, that sort of thing. But here you are. A stranger in Lower Pichesham."

I felt defensive. "Dominic and I have become close. He works here. So do I, in a way. Margot has me helping out."

"Yes, that is curious. I'm wondering, Annie, if you have noticed anything odd here yourself."

"Odd how? They just do good works as far as I can see. Oddly nice, that's all. I guess that's why I was interested enough to do some digging. It all seems too good to be true."

"Exactly. It is too good to be true, Annie, your instincts are correct. I believe … no, I *know* that there is something sinister afoot here. Are you religious at all, Annie?"

That was a change of subject. "Lapsed Catholic, I suppose. Not something I give a good deal of thought to."

"Perhaps you should. Annie, this may sound very unlikely to you, so please try to hear me out. I am part of a loose coalition—police, government, church—who have come together because we believe there is evil in the world that is beyond normal. The Trust is a locus for this activity. People with strange abilities, money that comes from nowhere. We believe they engage in satanic rituals, trying to summon demons. And Margot Trimble sits at the centre of this locus. She is not what she seems. We suspect she is not even human."

He was mad. Sounded mad, at least. But strange abilities? Well, if Lance was to be believed (and I did believe him), that part was true.

"Sounds like utter nonsense to me, Detective Inspector. Is this on the record? I'm looking for a good story, and a religious conspiracy involving the police would do nicely."

"I have some proof, Annie. Have a look at these photos." He pulled a small laptop from his bag and opened it on the table. He turned the screen to show me a black and white photograph of a cheerful middle-aged couple in vintage hiking clothes posing together. "Here. This was taken in 1962."

It was clearly taken on the main road in Pichesham. There were people in the background, and among them was a woman crossing the road. Greying hair, early sixties, dressed in a tweed jacket and sensible skirt. It looked like Margot

Trimble. Same outfit she always wore but with a skirt rather than trousers. The resemblance was uncanny.

"Did you know that there are no official photographs of Margaret Stanground? Not one, despite her being head of an organisation that even at its beginnings had considerable influence. There are also no official photographs of Margot Trimble. But here is a photograph taken recently by a visitor to the hospital."

This picture was taken from a similar angle, and there was Margot, in full colour this time, crossing the road in the other direction. I was startled to see in the background what was unmistakably me and Dominic walking away towards the river path. That must have been the second evening I was here.

"I understand they were aunt and niece. I can see the resemblance."

"It's more than a resemblance, Annie. Look at the pattern on the jacket. Look at the hairstyle. This is the same person, more than fifty years apart. These pictures are clear evidence that Margot Trimble is more than she appears on the surface."

"Photos can be faked so easily these days, Inspector. Besides, what are you implying? That Margot Trimble, who bakes terrible cookies and arranges accommodation for the needy, is an immortal demon dressed in tweed? You know how that sounds?"

He smiled unpleasantly. "And yet you are still listening to me. Look more closely at those needy folk, Annie. Ask yourself why they are chosen when others are not." I was already asking this question internally. Were there others like Lance? His story implied that there were. How many people in the village were involved? "Your friend died, Ms Maylor.

You do have doubts, I can tell." He was right. His insinuations were piling on top of my existing suspicions.

"This is crazy. You are talking as if magic and demons and all that hogwash is real. Next, you'll be telling me about angels and exorcism."

"I understand your scepticism, Annie. I have a very personal reason for believing it. My father wasted years of his life trying to convince people that what he had seen was real. My mother suffered years of listening to his raving. It was only after I joined the police force that I was made aware that he was right all along."

"I need more evidence, Inspector. One possibly doctored photograph won't cut it."

He gave me that sideways look again, appraising me. "If you had proof, Ms Maylor, what would you do with it?"

"Publish it, of course. I mean, assuming I'm allowed."

He looked at the ceiling for a moment and then appeared to make his mind up. "Ms Maylor, I need an ally here in the village. The intelligence we have is vague, but everything is pointing towards a deliberate plan. Phoenix International has a pattern. It moves into a war zone and does what you would expect. Medical facilities, aid for civilian refugees. It quietly does its work, and is well thought of. What is unusual is that it then leaves. Where the big NGOs stay and continue, Phoenix International leaves after a year or so and moves onto somewhere new. That pattern is mirrored in the Pichesham Trust. It still has offices nearly everywhere, but below the surface you will find that most of these are on paper only. It is only truly active in some of the remotest and politically difficult to access areas of the world. Our analysts suggest they will withdraw from China within the next year. I think they were only there at all because it has the only viable access point for North Korea.

"They have covered the globe and are nearly finished with it. And yet here they still are in Lower Pichesham, hiding in plain sight. What are they planning? We don't know, but it is coming soon. My belief, and one that is shared by many of my associates, is that this is the precursor to the final battle."

He wasn't joking. Or if he was, it was not funny. "You mean like in Revelations, don't you? Armageddon. The Four Horsemen."

"I know you will not share my beliefs, Annie. It would be too much to expect. There is evil in this place and I urge you to leave while you can, but I suspect you will choose to stay here and investigate more. Message me if you discover something. Will you do that? Will you help if I ask?"

I was on the edge of losing my composure, but I steeled myself inside. "I'm a journalist, Inspector, not an informant. What is in it for me?"

He stood up to leave and then seemed to think better of it. He reached inside his coat, revealing a large handgun tucked into a holster. For a moment I felt threatened, but he simply pulled out an envelope from an inner pocket. Opening it, he reviewed the contents and passed most of them to me. "I can tell you don't trust me, Ms Maylor, and perhaps I cannot blame you for that. As an act of good faith, here are some papers concerning my father that you might find of interest. If we can crack this open, I cannot think of a bigger news story. And you would be the person to break it."

A Statement to the Police

Handwritten note, received 25th May 1964

Marie, I want you to know that I still love you. I'm sorry for any pain this causes to you and Will, but I need to do this. Without you, I have no reason to stay here. By the time you read this, it will be done.

Live your life, Marie. Forget all that stuff I told you, no one cares. Live your life and know that I'll be watching over you both.

Your loving Frank

Typewritten note addressed to Lucien Trice c/o Scotland Yard, 28th March 1963

Lucien, a case that might be of some interest enclosed. I don't think there's much in it, but I know you like to get a look at the weird and wonderful, and I promised the chap I'd pass it on to someone to look at. I made a quick call to El Paso PD and there was someone who remembered the case. Apparently Carabon (the interviewee) had a history of arrests for drink-related misbehaviour before he was called up, and was known to be something of a religious zealot. He tried several times to get them to believe his story (see the transcript), but they had him down as a time-waster who was angry that he lost his job. From what they said, the company that fired him bent over backwards to help him back on his feet. From all accounts, he'd been a reliable and conscientious employee up to then, and they were all ex-military themselves. He finally stopped bothering them in 1951, which is when I presume he immigrated to the UK. Anyway, I leave it in your hands.

All the best,
Charlie Davies.

Transcript of police interview, 21st March 1963

DI Charles Davies, police number 77732/12, interviewing Francis Manuel Carabon. Shorthand recording, Miss Muriel Firth. Mr Carabon is a registered citizen of the United States of America and has declined to involve consular representation.

INTERVIEWER: For the record, Mr Carabon, please tell us your address and occupation.

CARABON: I work at Fergusons on night security. I live at 19 Curzon Avenue, Harpenden.

INTERVIEWER: Thank you. I understand you wish to report a serious crime, but you refused to tell the desk sergeant what it was and insisted upon talking to a detective. Is it to do with your work at Ferguson?

CARABON: Not my work there. Nice people there, never had a problem. This is from many years ago, when I was still living in El Paso.

INTERVIEWER: I'm not sure— (interrupted)

CARABON: I know it's a long time. And I tried to report it when I was there, but no one would take me seriously. I just need someone to listen and write it all down, and then I can be at peace.

INTERVIEWER: Mr Carabon. Frank. Perhaps you had best tell me about this in your own words. I'll ask questions if there is anything that I am unclear on.

CARABON: OK. I will. So, I was working at WSMR— (interrupted)

INTERVIEWER: For the interview record, can you explain those initials?

CARABON: White Sands Missile Range. It's in New Mexico. This was after the war, my first job after I was rescued from the POW camp in Germany. Boy, that was hard. Hungry all the time. It was just my Bible that kept me sane, I'll tell you. But that's irrelevant. It was a great job, I was chief of security on the launch site. Those guys were making incredible leaps forward. After the war, they were experimenting with the old German rockets and turning the tech to other uses. The Bumper program was developing the first two-stage rockets, trying to get into space. The team was getting close. It's not like it would be today. Nowadays it seems impossible that they were so lax. People just wandered in from other areas of the base to have a look. It was supposed to be secret, but everyone knew what they were doing. My job was mostly to keep the site secure at night, but I took it more seriously. I was always asking the management to crack down, I could see where it was heading. Though it was the Japs I was worried about in those days. Should have seen it would be the Russkis coming for our secrets.

INTERVIEWER: I'm sorry, Frank, are you trying to tell me about historical espionage by a foreign power?

CARABON: No. Yes. Well, it's not easy to explain. It wasn't the Russians or anyone like that. Maybe they were there as well.

INTERVIEWER: OK, perhaps you'd just better continue.

CARABON: Sure. So, one day, this new engineer is brought along to get his ID badge. They are bringing the latest Bumper-Wac for launch soon, and he's there to get the final stages ready. I take his picture with the old Box Brownie and give him a temporary card as usual. And I look into his eyes, and they are wrong. I just know something is wrong. I remember his name. Real poncy British name, Timothy Arkwright. Make sure you write that down. He supposedly worked in aircraft design. Maybe you'll have better luck trying to find him. I never could. I didn't like him at all—couldn't put my finger on the problem, but I knew he was up to something. I tried to get someone on the Bumper program to talk to me. Eventually, I got through to Colonel Toftoy directly. He listened patiently enough and promised to look into it. But nothing happened, Arkwright was allowed to keep coming.

(**CARABON** pauses for water.)

INTERVIEWER: A name is always helpful, Frank. But suspicions are not facts.

CARABON: I'm getting to it. OK, I was really worried. It wasn't just that. For weeks I'd been on edge, like something was happening behind my back. So I pulled a favour. My pal Ricky Jemeno served under Colonel Norvell in the war, and he got a job through him in sales at the Remington-Rand Corporation. And he'd already told me about this new system they were working on called Vericon. You won't think anything of it now, but it was the very first closed-circuit television, there wasn't anything like that before. At that time, it was still in testing, not for sale yet. I persuaded Ricky that WSMR would be a great place to try it out. He knew I had my reasons, of course, and he managed to swing it. I arranged to get the cameras installed after people have gone home and set up the monitoring area in the guardroom. Just two fixed cameras, overlooking the two main storage bays, one TV screen each. No recording equipment. That didn't come until years later. No one at the site knew about this, just me and the security team. I had the authority in those days to make those kinds of calls.

INTERVIEWER: I see. So you have a view that no one else does.

CARABON: Exactly. The cameras were well concealed. I mean, maybe not if you knew what you were looking for, but they just didn't exist in those days, so nobody was going to be looking. I made sure at least one person was watching the screens at all times, but the guys on the team did not like sitting there staring, so I ended up watching them myself a lot of the time.

INTERVIEWER: So, I take it that you did observe something?

CARABON: Damn right. This was the night of February 23rd 1949. It's a date I'll never forget. The day my life fell apart. The day it all went wrong.

(**CARABON** pauses for more water. He asks for a short break. Interview resumes after twelve minutes)

CARABON: OK. So, it's twenty-three thirty hours and I'm glued to the screens. And I see movement in storage bay one. No one is supposed to be there, the other guards are doing their routine patrol elsewhere. That's where the Bumper-WAC is waiting before the launch. That's scheduled for the day after. It's going to be the first fully fuelled attempt, and there's a buzz around the whole site about it. And I see Arkwright, clear as day. Lights are on, and he's up near the nose cone. OK, this is the part where –

(pauses.) This is the part you won't believe. Please hear me out. Do you promise to hear me out?

INTERVIEWER: Frank, this interview is at your request. At the very least, you have me interested. Please continue.

CARABON: OK. Well, what happens is that Arkwright (pause) sheds his skin. I know how that sounds. I can see him from behind on the screen, and as I watch, he sort of collapses from the top. And Arkwright's skin is lying on the floor, and a thing comes out from it. It's black, child-sized at first. I can't see it clearly, but while I'm watching, it grows and I'm looking at something huge and animal-like. Hideous. It looks like nothing I've ever seen, but the thing it makes me think of is, well, the Devil.

INTERVIEWER: Frank, are you— (interrupted)

CARABON: You said you would hear me out.

INTERVIEWER: Very well. Please continue.

CARABON: I keep watching, and it goes up to the rocket with a tool, and sparks start to fly. It's doing something to the nose cone. So, I get my gun out, and I run down to storage bay one and creep in at the back. And there it is. I'm right up close, and it looks sort of like a bear, but the arms are wrong and it's wearing a welding mask while it does whatever it is doing. And all around it are ants. Thousands and thousands of ants. Just everywhere, on the fuselage, on the equipment. (**CARABON** pauses.) I'm behind a pillar, watching. It stops for a moment, and looks around, lifts up the mask. I can see the fangs and the snout. It's not human. I think for a moment it's seen me, but it puts the mask back on and goes back to its evil work. (**CARABON** stops speaking for some time.)

INTERVIEWER: Frank, do you need another break?

CARABON: I'm OK. Sorry. Just remembering how scared I was. But I got my courage together. I was a soldier. I'd faced danger before, and it was my job to stop this. I came out from the pillar holding my pistol and shouted out for it to stop. It put down the welding machine and turned around. I was shaking, but I told it to put its hands up. But the hands—(pause)—never mind. I advanced and made it move away from the rocket. But then something happens at my side, some movement, and I turn and fire just once, and before I know it, it's upon me and it has my gun. Its arms are wrapped around me and I can't move. There is a voice, a strange whispery voice, and it says, "This area should have been clear for another hour. What do we do now?" And the black thing replies, "I'll take him across for a while. We have to finish this." It covers my eyes, and I feel this lurch in my stomach, and I'm in a cave. It ties me up with some rope that's there, and it's gone again. And all I can do is lie there. I think I've failed. That the rocket is going to be sabotaged, and it's probably going to kill me. But a short while later, it's back with a damn crow riding on its head. It talks to me. "What are we going to do about you, Frank? I thought I smelled something." Damn thing is mocking me, so I tell it to—(**CARABON** nods to stenographer.) Apologies to the lady. I tell it to fuck off back to Hell. Because I knew it was the Devil or one of his minions, and I tell it exactly what I think. And it laughs, this big evil laugh. And it says, "Oh, you're one of those. Well, Frank, you are right. I am the foul demon Lalashtu. And you are fortunate, for I have no orders to destroy you. But you must not interfere in my mission. Malphas here will watch you for a while. Behave well and I will return you to the world above."

INTERVIEWER: Frank, I am a busy man, and this is …

CARABON: Wait. I'm nearly done. So all I can do is wait. That crow-thing offers me food and drink, but I tell it … well, you can imagine what I tell it. Lalashtu comes back a few hours later with a half-bottle of Jack Daniels in its hand. Paw. Whatever it was. It says I have to drink the whole thing and if I do, I'll be returned. Well, what choice do I have? I don't even like the damn stuff, I'm a beer man, but I force it down, and of course, I pass out. When I wake up I'm in one of my own holding cells back at WSMR sleeping it off. I try to tell them to abort the launch, that it's been sabotaged, but it's already gone. And was successful. All went to plan, the rocket made it into space and everyone on site was celebrating. Except for me. And I tried, I promise I tried to tell them what had happened. But I was drunk on duty. There was no evidence. They found a bullet hole in the wall of the storage bay, and I thought that might help, but it just made it worse. I'd fired my gun near the rocket and could have damaged it. They canned me. I mean, what else could they do? I couldn't blame them. And they gave me a reference. They didn't need to do that.

(Short break.)

INTERVIEWER: Frank, I don't believe that what you have described actually happened. But it seems clear to me that you do believe it, and you've given me certain details that could be checked. Can you tell me why you have come now? And why to the police here, rather than in the USA? In fact, can you tell me why you are living in Britain at all?

CARABON: Before I was taken prisoner in Germany, I'd met this girl in London, Marie. We hit it off. I'd been writing to her throughout my time in the camp and afterwards. We'd talked about her coming out to be with me in El Paso. But in the end, I came here instead. Fresh start. And I tried while I was here to find out more, tried to find out about Timothy Arkwright. But all I hit were dead ends, so eventually I tried to get on with having a normal life. But the truth is, I could not let it go. In the end, it was too much for Marie. She left me three months ago, took our son with her. It made me think about my life. I decided I must have one more try to tell someone on the record. Because there is evil in the world, Inspector. The Devil and his minions are out there, and it could be anyone you know, just hiding inside a shell. May God have mercy on all our souls, it was only a few months ago that we were nearly in a nuclear war. Was it one of them behind it? I think it might have been. My son is six, and I fear for his future. I think about this all the time. So please, Inspector, take me seriously, and look into this.

INTERVIEWER: Frank, your interview is recorded and that's all I can personally do. However, there is a unit at Scotland Yard that takes an interest in what we like to call 'unusual' cases. I will pass on your statement. It's possible they will get in touch with you.

CARABON: Well, I appreciate your time, Inspector. Thanks for listening. And I beg you, do take it seriously.

INTERVIEW ENDS

More in Sadness

Lower Pichesham, October 2018

After Inspector Carabon left, I just sat there, feeling shaky. I wanted a drink, but there was none in the house. I felt tearful, remembering my fling with Farzad. He'd been a kind and considerate lover. For a short while, way back when, I'd thought he and I could make it work. Sitting at the kitchen table, I cried. For him, for his family. For me. Tansy crawled out from under the table and nestled up to me, and I buried my face in her rough fur. She didn't seem to mind.

The door latch clicked open. "Hi, Annie, I'm home. I saw he left, so I took him back across the river. Is everything all right?" Dom rushed to my side and held me awkwardly. "Hey, what's happening?"

I sniffed and forced the tears down. I didn't want to talk about Carabon's craziness. "I had some bad news about an old friend. Inspector Carabon wanted to talk to me because I've been in touch with him recently. Dom, can I trust you?"

He looked bemused. "Trust me? Yes. Of course. What's this about?"

I looked into his face, searching. And then remembered. I didn't need to guess. This time I asked with intention, and felt the old familiar sensation, given new meaning now. "Dom, just tell me the truth. What do you know about Farzad Khan? And Margot? About what is going on around here?"

"Farzad Khan? I've never heard of anyone with that name. I don't understand what you mean by 'going on'." He was shocked by my vehemence, but there was no resistance. His response was open and honest, and I knew he was telling the truth.

"Farzad is dead. And it might be my fault, because I asked him to help. The police believe he may have been murdered."

"And that was what the policeman was here for?"

"Sort of." I sniffed again and wiped my face dry with a piece of kitchen towel. "He was making accusations about Margot and the Trust. That somehow she is responsible for what happened to Farzad. Other stuff, crazy, conspiracy-nut weirdness. Only some of what he said was true. And I know it was true."

He looked seriously into my eyes. "OK. What was the true bit?"

"That there are people here in the village with strange abilities. Dom, not an hour before I came back here, Lance sat and told me all about it. If I could prove any of it … Dom, this is the story to end all stories!" I told him what Lance had said, and played him the audio I'd recorded on my phone. He sat in silence, clearly trying to take it in.

Eventually, he said, "So, according to Lance, you and I … that's just a figment of my imagination? And yours?"

I bit my lip. "I don't know. Lance kept saying it was real. That he just made it easier. I know how I still feel. I love you, Dom. I don't think it, I know it. And you feel the same. Don't you?"

He didn't reply directly to that, just stared at me strangely. "Did you just use it? Your ability? On me? I felt something was off. Did you?"

Shit. "Yes. I'm sorry. Or maybe not? I've been doing that all my life. I thought I was just good at asking questions. It's how I am, Dom. Dammit, how do I turn something like that off?"

"And that part. Where he mentions my 'thing'. What is that supposed to mean? What is it that I do?"

"He didn't say. We could go back and ask, I suppose."

He stood up abruptly and walked upstairs. I followed him up after a moment or two. He was sitting on the bed with a diary open in front of him. "There's no need to ask, is there? When that helicopter came down, and everyone said it was just a coincidence. I knew it was me. All along, I knew. I killed those people."

Oh shit oh shit oh shit. "Dom, no. I mean, perhaps? But even if you did, it wasn't on purpose. Dom, look at me!"

"I'm just going to walk for a while, Annie. I need some time to think." He stood up, dropped the diary onto the bed, and looked at the floor. "I'm sorry about your friend. I'll be back soon."

He walked out of the house, Tansy skittering along behind him. I thought about following him, talking things through. If I had, things might have played out differently. But in my defence, I'd just had shock piled on shock and I wasn't thinking straight.

Margot's Secret

Lower Pichesham, October 2018

Dom didn't come home and wasn't picking up my calls. By nine, I was getting worried and went to look for him. He'd been at the inn for a while, but had left without speaking to anyone there. The ferry boat was still tied up. I even traipsed up the hill to Lance's house in the dark, waving a flashlight ahead of me.

"Lance, open up. Lance, please."

He opened the door cautiously.

"Have you seen Dom?"

He shook his head. "Did you tell him?"

"Yes, of course I did. I couldn't keep that from him." But even as I said this, I wasn't sure I believed it. If I'd thought about Dom's reaction for even a few minutes, I could have told him differently, more gently. "What is Dom's thing, Lance? Do you know about his past?"

"No. I know he's had problems. He wouldn't be here otherwise. But he never talks about it. Always the professional is Dr Hunt. I know nothing about what he can do. You'd have to talk to Margot. And she'll skin me when she finds out I've blabbed to you."

Margot. It was the obvious solution. If Carabon was to be believed, I'd be putting myself in danger talking to her. But I was worried about Dominic, and there weren't many places you could hide in Lower Pichesham.

I knocked on the door of Ferry Cottage firmly. My plan was to just ask and leave. It didn't pan out like that. No sooner had I knocked when the door opened, and a small body ran out from behind Margot to greet me.

"Tansy! I thought you were with Dom, at least. Margot, have you seen Dominic? I'm worried."

"So you should be. Good grief, Annie, he opened his soul to you, and this is what you do to him? Why couldn't you just have taken that job? We could have kept an eye on you both in New York. The strings I had to pull for that!"

What the ...

"Come in. There are some things you need to know."

"I just want to know where Dom is. Please, it's just a stupid row."

"Come in." She walked back inside, leaving the door ajar.

I was hesitant. It wasn't safe. Carabon's dire warnings were ringing in my head. Then a husky voice spoke up beside me. "Annie, come in. She doesn't bite. Not anymore. Please." I looked around and was startled to see Tansy looking up at me. "Yes, me. The talking dog. Close your mouth, Annie, and come in."

Why would I trust a talking dog more than a fussy old woman? You might well ask, but ... I like dogs. So dazedly followed Tansy inside. The formerly bright sitting room was cold and dark. Margot switched on a lamp and gestured to the couch. She sat down in the opposite chair. The innocent room now looked like a stage set, designed to give the appearance of domesticity. Tansy jumped up onto the couch next to me, and I was obscurely comforted. Despite the strangeness of the situation, I could sense no threat.

Margot spoke. "Tansy told me about your visit from the police. First, I had nothing to do with your friend's death. I don't expect you to take my word for it, but that is not the way I do things. Second, Dominic came here earlier. He'd been drinking and confronted me with what you told him. Unfortunately, I could not reassure him in the way he hoped, and he became quite distressed. Years of nurture, up in smoke." Margot looked at me sourly.

Tansy spoke again. "Don't be so harsh, friend. Annie didn't intend this."

"I can speak for myself," I snapped, "but the dog is right. I'm kicking myself now."

Margot sniffed haughtily. "Dominic asked if I could arrange for him to be readmitted. Just temporarily. I was worried about his state of mind, so I called in a favour from the hospital. They will have given him a mild sedative by now. You should be able to talk to him tomorrow."

I was relieved. "Thank you."

"And I suppose you now have questions you want answered."

Where to start? The past twenty-four hours had been a roller coaster, and I was struggling to marshal my thoughts. "OK. Let's start with a talking dog. And is any of what Lance told me true?"

Tansy answered first. "I'm just a dog, Annie. Margot and I are old friends. I've been around for a lot longer than most dogs. It turns out that *really* old dogs can learn new tricks, and talking is one of them." Margot rolled her eyes and harrumphed, but Tansy ignored it.

I wanted to ask what she meant by that. Really old? Exactly how old? But before the words were out, Tansy continued. "Margot asked me to keep watch over Dominic and to make sure he was staying well. She doesn't know what Lance told you—I didn't get a chance to pass that on." She addressed Margot directly. "Lance confessed to Annie that he nudged them into pair-bonding. I heard the recording." Of course. The little spy under the table. Tansy had been right there all the time. "And yes, Annie. It is true. I advised against it."

Margot snorted. "Oversensitive dog." She turned to me. "I needed to head you off with your investigations, create a distraction while I worked out what to do with you. Lance is good at encouraging something already started. Yes, at my behest. Apologies, for what it's worth. I have more important considerations than your feelings."

Margot did not seem apologetic, more annoyed. I let it go for now. "OK. And what about Inspector Carabon? He seems convinced you are some sort of supernatural devil. He showed me pictures of you from fifty years ago …"

"So I understand. I wonder how he got the newer one? Carabon," she mused. "I remember that name from somewhere."

"So? What is it? The inspector more or less implied that you are the Whore of Babylon or something. I mean, I'm sitting here next to a talking dog and you act like that's nothing."

"It's complicated," said Margot. "It all depends on what you mean by the words 'supernatural' and 'devil'."

I took a deep breath. "That is hardly reassuring. Could you at least try to explain? Am I in danger here?"

Margot sighed. Tansy spoke. "Annie? I have been around you for some weeks. I believe I know you well enough. Will you promise to keep our secrets? At least until we can explain properly. She wants to tell you, but you were so adamant about wanting a story."

"Like anyone is going to print this." I looked at the dog, still not quite believing I was having this conversation. "Sure, whatever. For now, anyway. I promise."

Tansy spoke to Margot. "Show her. This is Annie. His flesh and blood. She deserves to know. I believe we can trust her to keep our counsel."

"Very well. I'll be back in a moment." Margot retreated into another room. There was an odd sound of rustling fabric. And the door opened to reveal a full-sized brown bear, standing in the doorway, the loose body of Margot Trimble dangling from its front leg. "I'll make some tea," it said, "and we can talk."

🐾 🐾 🐾

Don't judge me. Not until you've been entertained by talking animals after a difficult day. After my heart stopped pounding, I sat back down again, watching in silence while the bear brought out a tray of teacups and a pot. There was even a cake. It cut it carefully and helped itself to a large slice. "Please, try some. It's a seed cake. I added extra honey this time."

It was clearly burnt. Tansy said, "Could you cut me a small piece, Annie?" I numbly did as requested, and put it on a plate in front of the little dog, who ate it as daintily as a dog can. The bear poured some tea into a saucer for her and put it on the floor.

I was staring at the body, hanging there from a coat stand. It wasn't actually a body, of course. I could see now that the whole thing was sagging like a deflated balloon. The bear spoke.

"I shouldn't have reused the Margaret costume. But these disguises take a lot of work to make, you know. It's hard enough keeping up the running repairs." It patted the head, which lolled in an uncomfortably realistic way. "The Margaret series is my masterpiece. Five differently aged heads. You can have no idea how hard it is to get the eyes working realistically."

I turned to the bear. "So, you *are* Margot?"

"It would be more accurate to say Margot is me. And so is Margaret Stanground. I have had many names over the years."

I was dismayed. "You really are an immortal demon. Wearing tweed."

"Don't be silly. I'm not immortal, nothing is. I am just … old. As for a demon, that's a human label, not mine. I've been called that many times. Demon, devil, djinn, other things. That was then. We don't live in those times now. We live in a rational age, thank goodness." It sipped its tea and gestured at the body. "That's proper Harris tweed, you know. Marvellous quality, still doing well after all these years. A gift from Agatha Charting."

Rational. It had a way with words. But then realisation. "It was you! In Clive's diary. With the swimming hole. And the horse!"

"Ah yes, Clive. Hold on." Walking over to a bookshelf it pulled out a large file box. It put it on the table in front of me. Inside was the diary that I thought I'd left back in the States. "Sorry, I borrowed this. I needed to know what was in there. Yes, that was me. Clive always was a bit of a loose cannon, getting into scrapes."

It sat down again. "Are you calm yet, Annie? I think so. Go ahead. I won't answer all your questions, but if I do, I will answer them honestly. And you will know, won't you? Because that is what you do. Your own special gift."

It knew me better than I did. "OK. I asked if I was in danger and you didn't answer. So tell me."

It seemed to ponder the question. When it answered, it felt real. "I did not think so, Annie. You are under my protection, and I thought that was enough. But if your friend was murdered, it suggests someone else has entered the arena. It is possible …"

"What is possible? Who?"

"No, that is not for you to know. He is under explicit instructions."

Tansy spoke up. "I know who you are talking about. I still can't believe you trust him. And I'm still sure he set that fire."

The bear waved the comment away. "Please, Tansy, all that was investigated long ago. He's been a loyal colleague for a long time. The fire was an accident. He had no reason to do any such thing, it was just something that was likely in such an old house. I admit his techniques are heavy-handed, but they need to be for his part."

Interesting that they both believed what they were saying. Not completely on the same page then. "OK," I said, "so you refuse to elaborate on that. What is this plan that Inspector Carabon was convinced of? Or is he as delusional as he sounds?"

"I am not at liberty to discuss that either. All I will say is that any plans he has wind of are nothing for you, or indeed Inspector Carabon, to worry about."

"That's not good enough. I want details."

"You will have to want," it said firmly. I changed tack.

"All right, tell me about these abilities. Lance told me he's done lots of this in the past."

It growled. "Very well. It is quite simple, really. There is a tiny fraction of people, like you and Lance, with ability. We used to call it magic, and for most humans, that label would still apply. Hardly any of those with ability can use it for any practical purpose. Most of them never even know about it. But the ones who can use it? Well, they are a danger. Usually more to themselves than to anyone else. So when we find them out in the field, we bring them here to be … assessed. And we find ways to make them safe."

Magic. I tried to process it. Was I magical? "I don't understand what that means. Why are these people a danger?"

"It's not easy to be precise. We understand quite a lot now about the various interactions that lead to ability. But there are things that remain elusive. What seems to happen is that when people use their ability, they can cause a reaction. The universe pushes back, as if it doesn't like its own laws being broken. Sometimes the reaction is blatant, sometimes subtle. Dominic's is an extreme case. Did he tell you how he got that scar?"

"Yes, he tripped and …"

"… fell and hit his head against a vehicle. And had that vehicle been moving even a fraction faster, he would have died. This immediately after causing that whole awful bloodbath. Quite a coincidence." It sighed. "I wish I had started to talk to him about all this earlier. It isn't normal to keep the subject in the dark, but he was so damaged. Your arrival seemed a good opportunity to introduce him to his heritage. In his case, at least, it is an inherited condition. Dominic is related to someone I knew long ago who possessed abilities of a similar magnitude. As, indeed, are you."

I'd seen that somewhere in the distant past Dom and I were related, and this now made a sort of sense. "Explain to me, what is his power, exactly?"

Tansy responded instead of the bear. "Annie, ability isn't that specific. People develop a particular way of using it that fits their personalities. You became a journalist, so it makes sense that you would channel it into finding truth. Dominic became a doctor for a reason. He is highly sensitive to the emotions of others. It makes him good at his job, but vulnerable to influence."

I thought about the encounter earlier. Even before the bizarre conversation with Inspector Carabon, I'd come home frightened, confused and angry. If what they were saying was correct, Dom had picked up on my feelings, and might not even have known he was doing it.

The bear continued. "We don't fully understand how the events in Iraq happened. I have a couple of theories. He may have other, extremely rare gifts that somehow include an effect on physical matter. Tansy here has similar skills. Whatever happened, it wasn't really his fault."

"No wonder he was traumatised," I said to myself. "So Lance? And what about me? I've never had a life-threatening event I know of."

"Addiction came on unnaturally fast for Lance. He has had some close calls. Young Sergio nearly lost a hand after an accident with a meat cleaver. Thirty years ago, it would have killed him and he's incredibly lucky that the surgeons could reattach it. There are hundreds of similar stories. For you, there is nothing obvious yet, but your ability is a little different. You remind me of someone similar from long ago, and she had a charmed life."

"OK, so I'm in the clear for now. And that's what you are doing? In your work around the world? Just helping people?"

The reply was guarded. "Let's say that being able to help people was my price. Annie, I need you to trust me. So many lives depend on your silence."

"And what about the life of my friend Farzad? How can I trust you?"

"I promise I will investigate Mr Khan's death." It gestured at the file box. "Look inside."

Beneath where the diary had lain were bundles of paper covered in handwriting. "What is this?"

"It is the story of my life. Yours for the taking if you are willing to work with me. There will be a time when it can be made public. Not yet. A few years from now. You wanted a story."

It rummaged in the box and lifted out a bundle. The top one was headed 'I Meet my Companions for the First Time'. The writing was a neat copperplate, hard to read for modern eyes, but legible with effort. Despite my worries over Dominic, the temptation was huge.

"Take it, it's the only copy. I want you to know you can trust me, Annie, and if that means you need a hostage, this can be it. Sleep on things."

Panic

Lower Pichesham, October 2018

I can guess what you are thinking. That none of this makes sense. Why would I just accept all this? But you have to understand that I knew my sense of truth was reliable. Margot, the bear—whatever it was, it hadn't lied to me. So I took the box.

As I walked back to Dominic's tiny house, the moonlit street looked so ordinary. At Nadia and Mosen Tankye's house, they were having a party. All the lights were on, and people were standing in the garden chatting while music played inside. Mosen held up a bottle and gestured to me, inviting me to join them. I smiled back, shook my head, and walked by.

Ordinary. I idly wondered who in that house was the special one. I glanced down. Tansy had come with me. I waited until we were out of earshot. "Who? Mr or Mrs Tankye? Or is it both? Did Lance set them up as well?"

Tansy looked up at me. Quite how a small dog gives such an impression of disapproval, I cannot say, but I felt slightly ashamed. They were a nice couple, a central part of the social fabric of the village.

"Not everyone here is like you and I. For all I know, they are just regular people. Remember, I haven't been living here for long."

"There are so many things I don't understand. You and I?"

"There are a lot of humans with abilities, but I'm the only dog. In fact, the only non-human animal that we know of. So far, there's no one else quite like me." I swear, she looked somehow smug. "Bear and the others like her are different. They were made. She will have written it all down in there. I expect you'll read it soon enough."

We arrived back home. "I'm still worried about Dom," I said.

"So am I. I was so hopeful. He's been so much better recently."

"Really? I thought he was fine before."

"He put on a good show during the day, but the nightmares were bad. Since you arrived, he's been sleeping through."

Tansy slept on the bed cuddled up next to me that night. Yes, it was weird.

🐾 🐾 🐾

I made up my mind in the night. In the morning, I made sure I was on the minibus that ran up to the hospital in time for visiting. The seat at the back bumped up and down uncomfortably as we drove up the pot holed hill. Finding the reception desk, I asked if I could visit with Dominic.

The man at the desk checked his computer and frowned. "I'm sorry, but we don't have anyone of that name here."

My stomach lurched. Had Margot lied after all? "Please, check again. He came yesterday evening. It was a voluntary admission. He was having a crisis. If he's not here ..."

He looked again, but there was nothing. I was getting agitated now, so he asked me to wait and went into a back office. I could just hear him talking to someone on the telephone.

He came back. "Mr Hunt arrived here yesterday evening, and he was going to be admitted. However, apparently his uncle arrived and talked to him, and he went home with him instead."

"OK, something's very wrong here. As far as I know, Dom doesn't have any uncles. What was this guy's name?"

He sighed and went back to the phone. "Sister doesn't remember the name. She thinks it was Carbon or something like that. He was tall, stocky. Does that ring any bells?"

It certainly did. Alarm bells. What the hell was Inspector Carabon up to? Had Dom been arrested? Could he have drowned Farzad? This was stupid thinking. I knew for certain he had not.

I stayed as calm as I could and said something noncommittal to the receptionist. Finding a quiet area outside, I called the number Carabon had given me. No response. No response the next six times either. Finally, he answered.

"Carabon, you'd better explain yourself. Where the hell is Dom?"

"Annie. You were fast on the case." He was smooth and unruffled. "Please remain calm. Dr Hunt is with me. My contact at the hospital alerted me to his arrival. That is not a safe location for such a potentially important witness. I persuaded him that his evidence could be key to understanding the Pichesham Trust and its activities. Please be assured, he is being cared for."

"I want to talk to him."

The line went quiet. I could hear voices in the distance. "Hello, Annie."

"Dom, what is going on?"

"The inspector and I had a long talk. I don't know what is happening, but something is wrong. I don't know who I can trust, Annie. Not even you. I'm sorry."

"Dom, please. I don't know any more than you do. Let me come to you."

It was Carabon's voice that replied. "Annie, I will be in contact. In the meantime, please stay safe. And if you find anything out, message me." The line went dead.

I was fuming and frightened. I called back, but his cellphone had been turned off. Dammit. I scrolled my address list, looking for someone who might be able to help, and I paused over Paul's name. I was desperate for anyone who might listen, and my contacts locally were limited. He answered on the second ring.

"Annie."

"Paul. I'm sorry to call. I know I have no right."

He was silent.

"Paul, this isn't another rant. I'm in trouble and I need help. Did you hear about Farzad?"

"Yes. That was shocking."

"I think … I think it might be because of what he was doing. For me. Paul, I need help. Please."

There was a long pause. "Where are you?"

🐾 🐾 🐾

I got an Uber from the hospital to a mall in town and nursed coffees until he got there from London. Paul always was good in a crisis. He booked me into a low-key hotel under a false name, and even paid for some anonymous kit, a phone and a cheap tablet. I told him some of what had happened. About Carabon's visit, about my concerns for Dominic. Not the offbeam stuff. But I did tell him about my abilities.

"Annie, I'm worried about you. This sounds crazy. No, it *is* crazy. Psychic powers?"

"If you lived in my head, Paul, you'd understand. As soon as Lance said it, I knew it was true. That's how I have been getting all my best stories. That's how I got Sandra's story out of you. Do you want me to prove it?"

He laughed nervously. "How on earth can you do that?"

I concentrated. "Paul, tell me the truth about why you are here in England."

"Because Sandra moved back here and she asked me to come with her and I didn't intend to tell you that, what the hell!"

I bit my lip. "You see? I am sorry Paul. For that. For everything."

He looked troubled. "I was angry with you. I still am. You should have been more careful with the story. But I was angrier with myself, I should never have told you what Sandra said. It was unprofessional, apart from anything else."

"No. But you didn't do it entirely willingly, Paul. I made it happen. I didn't know how I was doing it, but that's not really a good excuse."

I meant what I was saying, but mixed in with the apology was a sense of mild elation at having consciously used my skill. I'd known the sensation for as long as I could remember, but it was different. Controlled. I could use this.

My reverie led to an awkward silence. Eventually, Paul spoke up. "Well, what now?"

"I guess I'll start by trying to track down Inspector Carabon."

"There is definitely something wrong there," he said reluctantly. "Do you want me to look into it, Annie? I don't have any official status here, but I can ask around."

"Please don't, Paul. I didn't trust Carabon and you've done more than enough already. If I'm right, Farzad was killed for helping me and I can't risk dragging you any deeper in. If I need help, can I call you?"

He looked at me mulishly. "Yes, I guess so. And I'm not sure how Sandra is going to take this."

There was another pause. I tentatively asked the question. "So, are you and Sandra back together? I'm just asking. Not, you know, not like that. Only tell me if you want to."

I squashed the urge to make him. It was his call.

🐾 🐾 🐾

I wasn't so restrained when I visited Farzad's office. Now that I knew I could, I turned on the juice hard. I don't think poor Janice knew what had hit her. But the only new thing I learned there was the name of the original investigating officer. So I called Birmingham Central on my new phone and asked to speak to him about the Farzad Khan case.

"DC Thomas speaking."

I barged straight in without a preamble. "Tell me about Inspector Carabon. How do I get in contact with him?"

"Miss, can you slow down a little? Who are you? Who is Inspector Carabon?"

It wasn't working. Of course it wasn't. Why would it work over the phone? The only way I could get information out of this cop was in person. "Can we meet, Detective Constable? Somewhere discreet. I have something to tell you that may be of interest."

"Miss, if you have information about the murder of Mr Khan, you need to come to the station and make a statement."

So it *was* a murder. "Officer, I don't know right now who to trust and who not to. Inspector Carabon visited me and told me you had written Farzad's death off as an accident. Now you tell me it's definitely a murder. He lied to me, and that's a pretty hard thing to do. Look him up. Detective Inspector William Carabon. I'll call back in one hour."

I snapped the SIM and popped a new one in. Maybe I was being paranoid, but why take chances? I called as promised one hour later.

"DC Thomas. Is that you, Miss Maylor? You really need to come into the station. We have been trying to locate you to ask you questions."

Dammit, he'd guessed who I was. "No dice, Constable. Go for a walk in Cannon Hill Park, use the main entrance. Carry a folded newspaper under your left arm. Come alone. I'll find you."

🐾 🐾 🐾

I'd done my research. It was a busy park, with lots of people around. I waited from my vantage point until a young man in a cheap suit appeared, walking slowly, carrying a paper. A woman in a green jacket about one hundred yards behind was being far too casual. I focused on her. Yes, I could sense a link. I walked up beside him and linked arms, smiling. "Hello, dear, shall we sit over by the pond?"

We sat. "Miss Maylor, this is all very dramatic, but is it really necessary?"

"It's Ms. Possibly not, Constable, but could you perhaps ask your colleague in the rather fetching jacket to sit further away?"

He sighed and waved at the woman in green. "Mags, give us some distance." Glowering, she moved to the next bench, out of earshot.

"Now tell me, Constable. Are you wearing a wire?"

"No, of course not. Ms Maylor, if necessary, I can just arrest you. Tell me what you have to say."

He was wide open and telling the truth. "All I know is that I received a visit from someone who called himself William Carabon, who lied to me. And now a friend has gone off with him somewhere and he is not answering calls. Carabon told me that the local police were treating Farzad's death as an accident, and that he was alerted because of the organisation Farzad was looking into. Is any of that true?" I pressed down hard. A glazed look fell over him. He spoke slowly.

"I did look him up as you suggested, Ms Maylor. There is no serving officer with that name. There was, however."

My ears pricked up. "OK, tell me about him."

"Detective Inspector William Carabon was part of a special unit at the Met. It wasn't clear to me what that unit was. He retired three years ago and went missing shortly afterward. The case is still open and active. And you claim to have met him?" I could feel him struggle to snap out of it, unsure what was happening to him.

"I told you what he said, Constable. He showed me an ID card. I should have looked closer," I mused. "So, how did he know? He was waiting for me at home before I even knew that Farzad was dead."

"If what you are telling me is true, logically, it would make the person you met a suspect."

A slight chill ran through me. "I don't suppose you have a picture?"

He knew something was wrong, but was interested and co-operative, so I eased back on the pressure a little. Rummaging in his jacket pocket, he pulled out a rather elderly smartphone and tapped at the screen. He tutted at the slowness of the response. "These things are ancient. Budget cuts." When he stopped fiddling, he showed me a photo ID.

"That's him." I looked closer. "Well. Maybe? The man I met was thinner in the face."

"This is from ten years ago. Ms Maylor, the records don't go into detail, but reading between the lines, William Carabon was encouraged to retire. Suspicious irregularities in his record-keeping. A lot of the information is redacted. And that means that someone will come asking me questions."

It was time to go. He was planning something, struggling to break out of his semi-trance. I wasn't staying around to be questioned, so I started running before he got that far. He was still groggy from the questioning, but recovered quickly. They were fast, but I'd already planned my escape route and had running shoes on. Over the pedestrian bridge, a quick signal to the Uber driver and duck into the hedge beside the Arts Centre. The cabbie drove off a little faster than he ought to have done, just in time for DC Thomas to see him leaving. I then calmly walked back into the Arts Centre, locked myself into a disabled toilet, and waited until I could sense them leave.

🐾 🐾 🐾

I had no more leads. I thought about hitting up some of my other contacts. Maybe Belinda in the FBI? She could look after herself, but would ask questions I wasn't willing to answer. I kept running into the fact that Farzad was dead. In the end, I felt forced back to Lower Pichesham. As bizarre as things there were, I was pretty sure Margot wasn't trying to kill me.

I got dropped off at the ferry early in the morning. Mosen Tankye was doing the morning shift and greeted me warmly, asking after Dominic. I muttered something about him doing fine and changed the subject. I was getting used to trusting my ability now, and could tell that in his world, nothing was amiss.

I rapped on the door of Ferry Cottage. Margot opened it almost immediately. "I thought you weren't coming back."

"I considered it."

"You look different."

"It's just a haircut and make-up. I didn't want to draw attention. I may be wanted by the police, by the way." I told her about Carabon. "It may be the same man, or someone just using his ID. But what it definitely means is Dominic is not with the police and is not safe."

"I've remembered where I heard the name. It may be a coincidence, but it's uncommon. Someone I met in New Mexico a long time ago."

"So, what now?"

Margot paced the room. "I fear that Tansy's suspicions are correct. Something is happening. My colleagues in Phoenix International have gone dark. None of them are answering calls or messages. I think Erik has gone rogue. He is likely to be behind your Inspector Carabon, and your friend's murder. I know he would not hesitate to kill if he thought it necessary."

"Erik? This is the person you were so sure was a loyal colleague when we spoke before?"

"Yes. I am afraid I have been naive. Again."

"Time to talk. Do you want me to use the thing? I've been practising on people."

"Come through." She led me upstairs into another room. It was windowless and completely empty save for a large, oddly shaped bench. She closed and locked the door behind her. The lights dimmed and walls sprang into vivid colour.

"This is my logistics room. From here, I can see the progress of the project."

It was beautiful. As I watched, the sharp corners and edges of the room blurred and softened, and the images spread evenly across what became a sort of flattened sphere. I recognised the outline of Africa first, and as I got my eye in, I realised it was a map of the world projected in reverse, slowly rotating. The shadows of what must be mountain ranges were altering and shifting as they drifted across the walls.

I turned around to see that Margot had shed her disguise again. The bear was draped across the bench, with its front paws against a flat panel, clearly manipulating the image. The paws looked wrong. Too slender, and too many digits. It gestured at the image, which flared with coloured lines.

"This isn't Earth technology, is it? You're an ET. Aliens."

It chuckled. "No, Annie, this is very much Earth technology. Advanced, I grant you. I'm mostly what I look like. A bear. Not alien."

I looked at the paws again. "I don't believe you." But it seemed sincere.

It shrugged and pointed up. "The green-edged areas are cleared. Red-edged pockets are still being worked on."

"Cleared? Of what?"

"P-materials. Proto-elemental sources."

"I mean, those sound like words, but you aren't actually explaining anything."

"The substances I am describing are what in the past might have been described as magical. Iron that is not quite iron. Sulphites containing oxygen and sulphur that, if you know what to look for, are not actually those elements. The purpose of the project is to gather up all the large sources of these substances that exist in the world. They are fairly easy to detect from space, but gathering them has taken over seventy years so far. We are close to complete."

Green-edged areas covered almost everywhere I could see. The red-edged areas were small and scattered. As the bear moved a digit, one of the red zones expanded to fill the view in front, the red lines rearranging to cover a more defined area.

"This is a live view over the National Museum of Baghdad. As you can see, the detection zone is centred on the main hall of exhibits. A lot of the remaining target materials are like this, embedded in cultural objects. These will be the last to be removed. There is still internal debate about the best way to recompense the owners."

I was frankly gawping at the resolution of the image. It was as if I could reach out and touch the rooftops below me. "Why?"

"There is still ongoing mining in the polar zones. Some deposits in Antarctica are unreachable currently. The rest is in places that are hard to operate from. Yemen, Myanmar, North Korea, places like that."

"Answer the question. Tell me why. Don't make me use it."

The bear looked me dead in the eye. "War. To save you from a war. One that you cannot win."

Protoverse 101

Adapted from a textbook found among the papers provided by Margot Trimble. Introduction to the Protoverse: Jameston, T., Brownlow, E., et al (1981 edition)

Before our universe, there was another. When our universe exploded into existence, it overwhelmed that earlier universe, which we now refer to as the protoverse.

The protoverse still exists, but crushed, its dimensions flattened out, and mostly irrelevant. Mostly, but not entirely. It still has residual structure, some of which obtrudes into the universe that we observe. Tiny amounts, thinly spread out, with occasional larger segments. Depending on the source material, some of these segments are big enough to be visible.

The protoverse has its own physics and natural laws that are not so different from those of the universe. The speed of light is almost the same. Time still goes forward, although not in direct alignment with ours. Electrons, atoms, all exist in somewhat similar ways. There are more elements. At the lower atomic weights, these elements look and behave almost exactly like those that exist in the normal universe, both physically and chemically. Trace amounts of these p-elements exist alongside regular u-elements. p-Iron makes up approximately 0.002% of newly mined u-Iron, and we observe similar fractions in other u-elements. Because they interact, compounds of both p- and u- elements exist at all levels. Even now, however, detection of the p- fraction is difficult without specialised equipment. Significant deposits of purer p-materials are vanishingly rare, and have mostly been found at meteorite impact sites.

Different elemental properties exist at all levels, but for practical real-world purposes, they start to be measurable with p-Iron. p-Mercury is the heaviest element that still has enough similarities that it can sit alongside its u-counterpart. After that come the elements that have no direct parallel in standard u-chemistry. The ones we are most familiar with are in the Mind group, in particular Will (92), Memory (98) and the inaccurately named Spite (101).

In tests, 5.1 to 8.2 percent of human subjects exposed to a source exhibited a measurable level of attunement to p-materials. The number in whom that attunement was sufficient to allow interaction was between 0.1–0.2 percent.

Given the scarcity of both p-materials and those able to interact with them, it is not surprising that the existence of the protoverse was overlooked by physicists for so long. "Magic" using materials gathered from meteorites was undoubtedly performed by various peoples in history, although rarely to much effect. The taboo often associated with such activities means that most learning was passed on orally. Consequently, accurate records were lost. We can be reasonably confident that the idea that magic was commonplace is, literally, a myth. A handful of genuine events have led to stories that were repeated, exaggerated, and reported incorrectly, giving the impression of multiple separate incidents.

It is known that the ancient Egyptians had some success in developing written spells (in modern terms, directed and scripted application of Will). No direct contemporaneous records exist from those times, not even in the hieroglyphic sources. However, translations were carried forward, first into Greek and later Latin. These bastardised sources continued to be used sporadically by humans up to the 1600s. Preserved copies of these texts gave our scientists the first clues to the structure of the protoverse.

There is no consensus on whether the fact that p-elements are aligned with the way biological minds work is coincidence or not. Some nodes speculate that our universe was created as a result of a grand act of Will by beings that evolved in the protoverse, the so-called God Theory. This theory posits that life tends toward the complexity of mind necessary to interact with the protoverse because this was the intention of the creator beings. However, if this is the case, the fact that those beings were apparently obliterated in the act of creation might suggest that if this happened, it was by accident. Others believe that the anthropic principle applies. In this view, life evolved on Earth with the necessary anatomy either by complete coincidence, or more persuasively because our local region of the galaxy lies alongside a particularly extensive remnant of p-space, influencing the direction of evolution.

One aspect that should be addressed here is the purported existence of living sentient beings native to the protoverse. Legend and myth are filled with stories of supernatural entities and it would be natural to suppose, given the overlap with stories of magic, such creatures could be explained by a protoversal origin. Evidence for this is weak. Fossil life forms are found in p-locations, but these may have leaked back into the protoverse from the universe. The more likely explanation is that such tales originate from u-lifeforms altered or damaged by exposure to p-forces.

There are still many unanswered questions. There is the shadow level, theorised by some to be the remains of yet another universe—a "proto-protoverse"—that defies rational explanations using current science. The evidence for this additional set of dimensions is compelling, but limited to the observational reporting of a handful of entities. Finally, the phenomenon known as u-retaliation is dismissed by a substantial body of opinion, but anecdotal evidence continues to mount. It is for this reason that you are urged to avoid experimentation except in controlled areas.

A City in the Forest

Lower Pichesham, October 2018

The talk of war was making my head spin. Just a few days ago, I'd been casually drifting along, picking at family history. Now I had psychic powers, my boyfriend was missing and possibly in danger, and I was discussing global politics with a talking animal who might or might not be an alien.

"You need a break. Come and sit. I'll make some tea."

"You and your damn tea. Don't you have any Scotch?"

"It doesn't agree with my system. I have some instant coffee somewhere?"

"OK. And none of your damn cookies, either."

I sat in the fake parlour sipping strong, horrible coffee, while the bear sat on the floor opposite. "What's your real name, anyway?"

"My friends just call me Bear. It helps that I'm the only one of my species currently like this. My first human name was Greta. It isn't a name that I like, but somehow I seem to always end up using it in some form. You can call me Bear if you like."

"Does that make me your friend?"

"Not yet, Annie. It rather depends on what you plan to do next. What are your priorities here?"

"Find out what the hell is going on. Get Dominic away from Carabon. I don't know."

"I have an idea about that. I think I know where they might be."

"Well, come on, tell me then!"

"In the secure area of the hospital grounds there is a former prisoner-of-war camp. Nothing to do with the Trust. It was being used for detention and interrogation by the Ministry of Defence up to the nineteen fifties. After it was mothballed, I arranged to rent it so that Erik could set up an operational base for Phoenix International there. Erik moved out decades ago, but it seems a reasonable possibility that he has reactivated it and is holding Dominic there."

"Let's go and get him then."

"The problem is that we don't know why Erik has done this. If we storm in there, I don't know how he will react. We could be putting Dominic in even more danger. There may be other innocents involved."

It was a sobering thought. "OK, we need to tread carefully."

"I do have an idea, but there is some danger involved. To you."

"Go on."

"You are a journalist, and you have a personal family connection to the hospital. You could spend time there under the pretence of writing a story. Your presence there would certainly be noticed, but there might be a way to get into the secure area and locate Dominic."

"It needn't be a total pretence. I was thinking of that story, anyway."

It nodded. "Good. This is my suggestion. I will call the hospital director and arrange for you to visit in a professional capacity. I will rig you up with a communication device and take it from there."

"Whoa, whoa, I'm not ready to just go along with this. You have some explaining to do first. About this war. Like, what the hell are you talking about? Because Carabon said something about the 'final battle'. Is he right?"

"Hopefully not. Almost certainly not. That is the whole point of the project."

"So run this past me again. Your great project is mining?"

It sighed patiently. "My … employers … are putting the dangerous toys out of reach. P-materials have properties unlike regular elements. For example, they made me what I am. Human science has missed them so far, but it is only a matter of time before physicists deduce their existence. The people at CERN are already on the trail."

"So, it's your employers that are the ETs?"

"Enough with the aliens, Annie."

"I want to meet them. Talk to them directly. On the record. With pictures."

"That is for them to agree. But we need to visit the Well, anyway."

Damn Bear, talking in riddles all the time. It retreated to the other room and re-appeared as Margot. We left the house and walked up the hill, beyond the abandoned village, and into an area of dense woodland. It was a long walk, mostly in an awkward silence. Eventually we came to a tall chain-link fence topped with razor wire, beyond which were just more dark trees. Margot approached a gate in the fence and it opened smoothly towards us. As we entered, something odd happened. The view ahead shifted and shimmered. In front of us was a structure. I fired up the camera app immediately. Margot looked round, but didn't try to stop me.

I hesitate to call it a city. It was more like an abstract art piece. Tall pastel-coloured cones rose to different heights, with spiral ramps rising around them like giant screw threads. Apparently random bridgework linked them at their bases, some of relatively large masonry, others with delicate traceries that could have been cobwebs.

"Welcome to Alderman's Well."

"It's incredible. Like something Gaudi would have imagined."

"I believe they took some inspiration from the Sagrada Familia. Go ahead, take pictures."

I did, from every angle. Margot led the way to a paved path that led in between the cones until she reached an archway leading inside one of the cones. The smoothly hollowed room beyond was surprisingly large and there was room to stand comfortably.

"I've brought you a visitor."

Nothing happened for a few seconds, then the end wall burst into colour. A huge insectoid image appeared.

"Hello, Bear. Who do we have here?" The voice was that of a little girl.

"This is Annie. Annie thinks you are aliens. Perhaps you could have a word. Annie, these are the people you asked to meet."

Eleanor

The story of my life, by Eleanor Brownlow, age 5

My parents' story is so romantic. Peter, son of the head groom, and Sarah, the squire's daughter. Forbidden love between the classes. Forced to elope, but together in the end. Grandma Brownlow is not sympathetic to this view. When I asked her about it, she told me it was not something to be gossiped about. She is proud of her son, the accomplished violinist playing to fashionable audiences in London. But she is also ashamed of the position he put her and Grandpa Brownlow in, as people to be gawped at by former friends and neighbours. Grandpa is more philosophical about it. He and Squire Charting were friends, in a way, and he says he does feel guilty after the squire paid for his son's expensive musical education out of the kindness of his heart. But all said and done, the squire played fair. We all live together here in Ferry Cottage, away from the village. It's big enough for me and my brother to have our own room. Grandpa runs the ferry, and we live quite comfortably. We don't visit Chartings, but Uncle John calls on Mother occasionally with news from the big house. He brings me books to borrow from Grandfather's library, and sometimes a bag of humbugs.

We aren't popular in the village. Nobody is rude, but you can tell. I don't have any friends of my own age, and sometimes that makes me sad. But I have a special secret friend. Let me tell you about her.

Before I was even born, Papa was in London looking for a gift for his wife. There was a pendant on a market stall in Covent Garden. The pendant was old and unusual. It might have been silver, but it was unmarked and so he could afford it. On a break from his job at Hanover Square Rooms, he brought it back to his new home. Mama was used to much finer things, but they were only six months married, and she wore the pendant with pride for years.

My friend is reading this over my shoulder and making such odd grumbling noises. I must tell you about

Eleanor enjoyed teasing me, but I knew full well that she was not really planning to tell her secrets to the schoolmistress.

"Still too advanced, Eleanor. Miss Benson is expecting precocious, but she won't believe you've written any of this."

She sighed dramatically. "Why must I go to school at all? It's not fair. All the others will be older, and they are so stupid."

I shrugged. "Your parents want you to be more normal." This was more or less true. I'd listened to their conversations after Eleanor went to bed, and I knew they were worried sick about their daughter. At first, her early development had been a matter of wonder and some pride. A two-year-old reading Bible stories was adorable. A five-year-old asking pointed questions about its inconsistencies and quoting Thomas Paine was disturbing. This was 1867, an age when superstition had diminished but was far from gone, especially in rural areas. And there was something unnatural about her abilities.

She made a dismissive noise. "Do you have a suggestion for what I should write, then? I don't want to tell lies."

"Something a normal person would expect from a bright child. Tell her something true, just make it childish. Borrow from Kingsley. She knows you've read The Water-Babies." It was one of the few books Eleanor had read that Sarah Brownlow felt safe admitting to the schoolmistress.

The story of my life, by Eleanor Brownlow, age 5

Once upon a time, there was a little girl. Her name was Eleanor and she was as bright and bonny as a button. She lived in a little house with her mama and papa and granny and grandad and a loud-mouthed monkey called Peter. She tried to be good, and always said her prayers at night.

Though she knew her family loved her, Eleanor was sometimes lonely in the little house, and one night she prayed for a friend. That very night, a sound woke her. Standing by the bed was a little, ugly, hairy creature with sturdy paws, fierce sharp teeth, and the friendliest eyes you ever saw.

"There was one of those in the bed already," I said.

"How rude!"

"You started it."

That's how it was with Eleanor. She could swing from being the smartest person in the room to just being five again in moments. And what was more, she projected that onto me.

It had started when she was barely two years old. I'd been indulging in a long sleep and had been woken, only to find myself in a darkened room. There, standing up in a cot, was a small child, chattering away, apparently to thin air. Unsure what was going on, I reduced my size and climbed into the cot beside the child. She continued to talk and somehow I understood her. We sat there, conversing in baby talk, until she fell asleep. My mind then returned to normal. It was intensely annoying at first, but 'new master, new rules' was just part of the pattern of my life.

There was at least no misunderstanding about the source of my summons. The same odd visual disturbances that had surrounded my friend Barbotine in Greyside were here rippling around the child, reaching out beyond the room. This was the first time I had seen them Earthside. But again, the child was not holding the talisman. I could sense that somewhere else in the building.

A clearer pattern emerged over time. The mother, Sarah Brownlow, wore the talisman during the day. I observed her movements, and noticed that she also had a visible field, but much fainter than her daughter's. I took this to mean that she herself was a master of sorts, but unaware of it. At night, Eleanor somehow reached out to me and called for company. I quite enjoyed the visits. They seemed to awaken a residual maternal instinct.

I took the time to find out more about my surroundings. More than a hundred years of practice with a needle meant my disguises were a lot more elaborate than the first mask from Marthe. From a modest distance, I easily passed for human. Pichesham itself was not like anywhere I had been before. Noises were sharper, colours a little more intense. It was not unpleasant, just strange. And there were other people in the village with those lines of force, though they seemed unaware of anything themselves.

Time passed, and Eleanor learned to talk. I amused her with stories of my life and dimly remembered human childhood games. When very young, she told anyone who would listen all about me. Fortunately, she was humoured and largely ignored, as was normal with children in that era. Sarah alone knew there was some truth behind the talk, but kept it to herself. By the time Eleanor was three years old,

Sarah had impressed on her the need to keep the strangeness secret. Eleanor was very advanced and grasped this readily.

As she grew, I would read her passages from my collection of texts. She enjoyed anything with animals. Perhaps this early exposure to the written word had some effect. Eleanor's unusual intelligence was certainly a direct effect of her ability to alter the way minds work, and she could do this to her own mind as much as anyone else's.

By the age of five, she was reading learned literature that it was my job to obtain. Her early love of animals carried over. Darwin's works were favourites, and anything to do with palaeontology. When we ran low on works in English, I scoured European publications for things that might interest her. I distinctly remember translating Mendel's *Versuche über Pflanzen-Hybriden* while Eleanor took notes.

School was a partial success. Miss Benson turned out to be a pragmatist, and, when she realised that there was little she could teach Eleanor, instead used her as an assistant to help the laggards catch up with reading lessons. By now, Eleanor knew how to be discreet in the amount of mental enhancement she applied to them.

Not everything was about learning for Eleanor. She still wanted to do childish things sometimes, but aside from her brother, there were few children she could tolerate for long. We would go into the woods together to explore. I would briefly adopt a child-shaped disguise for these occasions and resume my natural form once we were out of sight. It was fun for both of us. I could boost her into trees, where she would climb to alarming heights, safe in the knowledge that I could rescue her if needed. We played hide and seek in the abandoned quarry and even had tea parties involving various dolls that I made for her.

When she was tired of play, the woods provided study fodder. She made copious notes and drawings about wildlife. Variation in the sticklebacks in the streams attracted her notice for a while and she began work on a monograph. Then one day, fate intervened. Feeling peckish, I had dug into a large ant nest looking for tasty larvae. These were the aggressive sort of ants, angrily spraying out their acid and biting. I rather liked the flavour of the acid on the larvae, and the bites were too small to bother me at all. Eleanor observed all this dispassionately.

"They're interesting, aren't they? Look at the way they are drawing those eggs underground."

"They'll need to move them faster if they want me not to eat them," I mumbled, munching on juicy little bodies.

This was the start of Eleanor's obsession with the wood ants. There were several large nests in that area, at the edge of a roughly circular clearing. She would spend long sessions studying their behaviour, and I was tasked with hunting down relevant entomological works.

"Why are these workers staying still, do you think?" she asked me one autumn afternoon. I put down my flute and wandered over to look. There were hundreds of ants busily doing whatever ants normally do, but a group of ten were perched along a twig, apparently looking directly at Eleanor.

"It's probably your influence, Eleanor. You know what you are capable of. You've been interfering with people's minds for long enough. Though I'm surprised they have enough of a mind to influence."

"Hmm. I study them, and these ones study me back. Perhaps they have bigger brains than average." She carefully collected one into a sample tube to examine under a microscope later. The others scattered. The next time we visited a few days later, a group of several hundred gathered while we watched, clustered on leaves and twigs, staring. It was eerie even for me, and slightly threatening. Eleanor wasn't concerned, though. "Fascinating. I really wish they could explain."

The air seemed to thicken, and a pulse of something swept across the clearing. I was knocked off my feet. All the ants we could see froze into stillness. Eleanor swayed a little, but stayed upright. And then it passed. The ants resumed their work. The air cleared and all was normal again.

Something had happened, but it did not emerge immediately. Winter came in hard and cold that year. The ants retreated deep into their nest, and Eleanor could not persuade her parents to let her roam. It was hard for her to summon me unseen and I was left to my own devices until spring. It was late April of 1871 before we returned to the ants' clearing.

There was a palpable change. Most of the nests were gone, except for the one we had been examining before. The nest was taller and the ants that were bustling around it seemed much larger than the ones from autumn. As we approached, our presence provoked a startling reaction. Gradually all the ants we could see stopped moving, and turned to face Eleanor. My hackles were raised.

"Eleanor, we should leave."

"They're just ants, Bear."

I stepped toward her and heard a cracking sound under my paw. Looking down, I had stepped into what looked like the rib cage of a badger, stripped clean of flesh. "Please, Eleanor. I don't think they could hurt us, but it would be better not to be found wrong."

She nodded thoughtfully. We retreated a few yards from the nest, and most of them went back about their business. We were followed by a largish group. They stopped in front of us and formed ranks in what seemed to be a nearly perfect rectangle.

Eleanor was excited. "Look at the pattern. They are trying to communicate!"

"That is what you asked for. And I think what they are communicating is for us to go away."

She sighed. "I wish you were better at explaining magic, Bear. It is most unsatisfactory. Why should a rectangle be a threat? Or is that just animal instinct rather than a mystical insight?"

I half expected something to happen when she said this. But her wish seemed to be more rhetorical than heartfelt this time, and the moment passed.

"Timo says that the shape reminds him of an attacking formation. That is all."

Eleanor was undaunted. In one of those curious changes of mood, she merrily wished the ants a good day, and skipped off towards the stream, where we played in a shallow area.

The incident sparked an interest in magic that got me worried. I liked the child, but she could be obsessive, and this was an issue that concerned me directly.

"Eleanor, is it wise to pursue this?"

"I would have thought you would approve, Bear. You and I are going to apply scientific thinking to magic. Because I have decided that there is no such thing. Newton applied thought to gravity and worked out the fundamental principles. We can do the same for magic. And when we understand what magic really is, we can do new things. Perhaps you could be freed from your bondage. Perhaps I could disappear into other worlds at will. I should like that. What does your Mr Belbek say?"

Belbek rarely spoke directly these days, and I had to nudge his sleepy memories into activity. He mumbled around the thought.

> <u>She is correct. We have been blind, Bear. We were all born in an era of superstition. This new science could bring us the liberty we have sought.</u>

Light dawned. I was excited. "He agrees with you, Eleanor!" I became an enthusiastic convert. I told her about how I had come to be made. Even Belbek's precious manuscripts were brought briefly into the world for her to examine.

Our first big success was tracing the tunnel. We created a standard list of magical tasks that she and I could perform in a grid pattern. By measuring response times, we plotted the strength of the magic in and around Pichesham. Lo and behold, this led us straight back to the clearing where the ants were. The strongest magic was directly in the centre of the clearing. When I cleared the scrubby brambles away, we found the broken remains of a brick dome covering a deep hole. The distortion pattern surrounding Eleanor led straight into the hole.

This was an exciting find. "I think I know what this is, Eleanor. I have heard of these from others in my world. This is a natural tunnel straight into Greyside."

"Can we go into it?"

"No. This is an unknown tunnel. Not all are passable, they have to be mapped out. I'm told that it is a dangerous business. But if I'm right, it may explain why Pichesham is the way it is. Magic is leaking here through this hole."

"How interesting. And does that mean that this is the best place for experiments? Because here is where you and I are strongest?"

"I suppose it does."

Eleanor wasn't shy about asking. She found out we were not the first to stumble onto the site. Her father told her the story he had heard as a boy about an eccentric clergyman known for his mysterious trips into the forest. The brick dome had become known locally as Alderman's Folly, or Alderman's Well. It was reputed that the trees refused to grow there, and it was considered an unlucky place that should be avoided.

This suited us nicely, and we were rarely disturbed during our experiments. Eleanor stole her mother's necklace from her jewellery box, and since she was already acquainted with the ants, these were the guinea-pigs she chose to use. I would be sent to the nest to gather up sacrificial samples while she experimented with the spells, trying slightly different variations. It reminded me of the time that Belbek was working with Stevas all those years ago. Unlike then, Eleanor was systematic and organised, performing the same experiment multiple times and recording her findings carefully. On several occasions, she succeeded in opening tiny portals and, at last, created her first ant-djinns using ant sacrifices. She was careful to dispose of her experiments using a killing jar. But maybe not careful enough.

It was all going exceedingly well, and I began to entertain dreams of freedom. Except for Eleanor's cough. We ignored it at first, but it didn't get better. And what seemed like a normal childhood illness took a more sinister turn one day, when she coughed up some blood. I insisted on carrying her home that day, so she left the talisman hanging on a tree in the clearing.

It was Marthe all over again. I think the father must have brought the infection from London. Her grandparents had moved into the city by now, leaving Peter and Sarah alone with the children. When they became ill, it seemed to hit them even more severely than it did Eleanor. So, despite being ill herself, Eleanor took on the burden of caring for the family, assisted by me in the background. It was a desperately sad business, and I knew that the chances of recovery were slim. I think of that sometimes. How many great minds have been lost to random chance, disease and accident?

She refused to give up on the work. "If I survive this, I will need the follow-up to the latest experiments. You must keep monitoring, Bear."

I like to think it comforted her. I visited the clearing daily, recording observations carefully in her journal, and reporting back later. Time passed, and eventually she became too weak to look after young Peter. I took charge of him myself, and fortunately, he seemed resistant to the disease.

It was thirty-six days after I took over the monitoring. I know, because I still have the journal. I went to the clearing to find a dramatic change had taken place overnight. The ant nest had gone completely. I was confused at first, but then looked towards Alderman's Well. Towering above where it had been was a mound of earth, half as tall as the trees surrounding the clearing. Except, when I moved towards it, it was moving. Streams of ants radiated from the giant mound in all directions. I walked closer cautiously, watching my footing, and saw something large shift in the mound. Briefly, the front half of a deer broke through the surface, frantically struggling to escape before being submerged again. I stood and watched, mesmerised, as the nearest stream to me carried a dead squirrel towards the mound. When the stream turned towards me, I woke up to the danger, and flicked over to Greyside out of harm's way.

I was back at the entrance to my cave, and I was just about to find my way back to Ferry Cottage when my attention was caught by movement on the horizon. In the distance, there was a dark hill that had not been there before. Clouds seemed to rise from it. Dread filled my stomach. I ran, shouting as I went towards Auroch's resting place.

"Auroch! Wake up. Wake up." He was there as usual, grumbling about being disturbed. "Never mind the turnip. I need you to see something." He picked it up anyway, munching as I tried to hurry him along. "Look. Is that something you've seen before?"

He frowned at the sight. "No. What is it?" He looked at my face. "What have you done?"

We made our way nearer. It was hard to judge how far it was, but it was clearly huge. As we grew nearer, the cloud resolved into smaller things moving in the air. One landed on my paw. It was a flying ant. Big, much larger than any I'd seen back in the clearing. It bit me, hard. It hurt. I squashed it and watched as its bloated corpse fell twitching to the ground.

We ran away. Poor Auroch, it had been centuries, and he wasn't strong enough for this. I did not know what to do. The ants were aggressively hungry and had found their way somehow into Greyside.

Erik took charge. Bloody Erik. His time to shine, of course. He started organising the small crowd we were able to track down.

"Erik, let me explain about these ants …"

"Oh, I think we can do without your help, Bear. This is your fault, I think." I could almost taste his delight in refusing my help. "We'll start with setting up a smoke barrier. That will hold them off temporarily while we build a perimeter defence. Tansy, can you raise a wall?"

"Yes, Erik. I'll start now." Tansy had no love for Erik, but she set off, the dust erupting high into the air behind her as she swung in a wide arc around the mountain. He assigned most to bringing in flammable materials from Earthside, and sent out the rest of his pack as scouts to give warning of hostile approaches.

"What can I do?"

"Go warn your human pets about what is going to hit them. The less I see of you, the better."

Gallingly, his suggestion made sense. And, the feeling being mutual, I turned back to Pichesham. By the time I arrived back at Ferry Cottage, there were already ants milling around the garden and they had stripped the vegetable bed bare. I went up to the children's bedroom. Eleanor was lying there, looking miserable and in pain. I helped her to sit up and brought her some water.

"How are things today at the clearing?"

I thought about not telling her, but I could not think of anyone else to ask for advice on what to do next. I told her everything.

She coughed weakly, bringing up more blood. "This is my fault. Something I have done has changed them again. I must go back."

"Absolutely not. You are in no state for this."

"You don't understand. I can change them again. What I have done can be undone."

"Eleanor, this could kill you …"

"I will be gone soon anyway. If I don't do something, how long before they take the village? Where will they stop? Take Peter to Chartings. Then take me to the clearing."

I did as she requested. Of course I did.

I carried her through the woods, trying to avoid the columns of ants, but it wasn't long until we reached a point where there was no way forward. Eleanor concentrated, and I felt a wave of intent push out in front of us. I watched as the broad column she was aiming at lost form. It dispersed as the individuals in it started to mill aimlessly apart. "It works," she whispered hoarsely. "I made them stupid again. Get closer to the centre. All the columns must come back there, eventually. We will stop them there."

It was slow progress. To each side, columns of ants were dragging both live and dead animals back towards Alderman's Well. A sheep bleated mournfully as it passed us. I paced my way carefully through, treading on the dispersed ants as I went while Eleanor altered them ahead of us. As we reached the mound, Eleanor gasped at the sight of it. It had grown considerably since I left. The trees that surrounded the clearing were nothing but bare trunks. I found one that still had branches, and we climbed to a relatively safe distance above ground, brushing off neutralised ants as we did. From there, Eleanor broadcast wave after wave of intent toward the mound. We watched as the forest floor, previously a mass of clearly visible glistening lines writhing in all directions, gradually became a formless sea of random motion. It was working.

"I have this under control, Bear. Check on your friends. We need to know if this is working in your world as well. Otherwise, they will simply come back later."

"I can't leave you alone!"

"You have to. We need to know. Go, I'll be all right."

I strapped a rope around her to make sure she didn't fall and switched back to the cave mouth.

The scene below was one of pandemonium. Black smoke filled the air, while folk launched whatever attacks they could from the rapidly raised fortifications. Whatever Eleanor was doing Earthside, these ants were not affected. I could see Tansy just finishing another wall, more central to the summit, to fall back to. The bird people were swooping through the air, taking on the swarms of flying ants. Auroch was standing just a little back from the main wall. He didn't seem to be doing anything. Suddenly I heard Erik's voice.

"Fall back! Fall back!"

The defenders on the main wall ran back to the new inner line. Everyone except Auroch. I ran up to Tansy, who was breathing heavily, exhausted by her efforts.

"What's happening? Why is Auroch there?"

She avoided my eyes. "It's a trap. Auroch is … he's bait. He volunteered."

There was nothing I could do. As a huge flood of ants broke through the outer defences, all we could do was look on. "I weakened the wall there. I cannot watch." Tansy lay down and buried her head in her paws. I stood, forcing myself to be a witness.

The ants made straight for Auroch and it was not long before he was covered in a sea of black. Then, as I watched, he expanded, becoming larger and larger. Before long, he was half the size of the mountain, and his form grew transparent. He turned his head, looked towards us. An enormous 'Goodbye' echoed through my head, and slowly, he erupted into a massive fireball. The flames moved unnaturally, almost lazily, brightening to an unbearable level. When my eyes cleared enough to see again, fire had engulfed the ants surrounding him, and a line of flame and smoke could be seen reaching into the distance along the line of ants, all the way back to the black hill. As we watched, flames on the hill itself leapt high into the air.

There was relief, but no celebration. The manner of Auroch's death shocked us all into silence. Erik signalled to Hawk and gestured toward the hill. He drew the band together. "There was no other way. We will mourn when we know it is over." None of them would look at me. They all knew that somehow what had happened was my doing.

Hawk came back calling shrilly. "There are more coming through!"

Despair filtered through the group. Erik tried to rally us. "Listen, we can all find somewhere in the real world if we have to. The pack has made its way there many times." But it was not true. He didn't understand how bound we all were to our anchors. Greyside was our only refuge from humans.

I spoke up. "Eleanor was controlling them. There is hope. Tansy, will you come with me?"

I picked her up and turned back to the clearing. Eleanor was still strapped in the tree, but she appeared motionless. Uncountable numbers of ants surrounded the tree, but most were dead, while the few living ones moved randomly. I went to climb, when Tansy stopped me. "Look."

The top of the mound was pulsing. It abruptly burst, and a river of ants poured from the top. They made straight for the tree. "Eleanor!"

She didn't stir. Tansy pulled at my ankle. "We cannot stay here, come." I tried to force myself to run, but stood and watched as the tide swept up the tree, covering Eleanor's small body.

The tide stopped. The air itself seemed to pause. A ripple of something fluctuated across the surface of the ant horde and everything became still. The flow from the top of the mound ceased and even reversed.

Tansy spoke up. "Bear? What's happening?"

"I don't know." But there was something. I stepped toward the tree.

Tansy's ears flattened. "No, keep away. Dieu m'entend!"

Eleanor's body was—I will not describe it in detail. There was very little left. The ants on the tree moved slowly downward and gathered in a loose circle around its roots. The circle formed a mound that then shaped itself into a sphere. And on the front of the sphere, a mouth. Lips. Unmistakable. The mouth opened.

Imagine, if you can, a voice made by ten thousand ants linked together, while air moves across thousands of stretched limbs, vibrating them. You can't? I cannot describe it better. But as bizarre as the sound was, the voice was still Eleanor's.

"Hello, Bear. That was interesting."

I've seen a lot of strange things in my life, before and since that moment, but this was unquestionably the strangest. "Eleanor? Is that really you?"

"Yes. Perhaps. We are … I am … I am hungry. But we will not eat. You. Did you bring the journal? We should write this down." Whatever it was, something of Eleanor was definitely in there. "What is that beside you? Can we eat that?"

I snapped out of it. "Please don't. This is my good friend, Tansy."

The sphere quivered and another ripple ran across the surface. "Tansy. Scent measured. Identified. Very well. But we are hungry."

"Wait here." I grabbed Tansy and took her back to Greyside. "Rally the others. Get them to bring food. We'll set up a chain from here."

"Yes. What kind?"

"I don't think it matters. Anything." She ran off barking and calling. I went back. "Tansy has gone for help. Can you control them, Eleanor? Stop them in Greyside as well?"

Ripples flowed. "Greyside. I have gone there at last. We were—stopped. Hurt. Fire. Still hungry. It's not very interesting, is it? Barren, nothing to eat. The slain will sustain us for a while." Around my feet, small corpses were being gathered and dragged towards the mound.

I understood. "You are like me now. Is that right? Eleanor is your companion?"

"Companion. Yes. How interesting this is. Language. Human knowledge. We must think. Reconsider. Did I do well, Bear? I ran out of other ideas. Will you still play with me?"

"Of course. You are one of us now. I'll go find out how Tansy is doing with that food."

🐾 🐾 🐾

We are all of us, human and otherwise, lucky that they aren't sentimental about their individuals. It took a while to get the balance right, but once their hunger was sated, they slowly ate their numbers down to a level that the forest could sustain.

Back in Greyside, we mourned Auroch. The ants were most apologetic once they understood what had happened. Not everyone forgave easily. Perhaps surprisingly, it was the wolves that took the lead in welcoming them. Svend confided in me later that the pack had been on the verge of starvation before 'the change', and maybe this was why they found it easier to understand.

And then the ants picked up where Eleanor had left off. Studying. Learning. Developing. They built their city across two worlds, from Pichesham through Alderman's Well and deep into Greyside. Their technology was—still is—amazing and far beyond my understanding. Eleanor was still there somewhere, and there was time for playing. In fact, their appetite for entertainment was extraordinary. They consumed human music voraciously and started developing their own art forms.

I will leave this story with something I experienced in 1888. The City Arena. Tiers upon tiers of standing areas filled with softly moving ants. The entry points, deliberately left large enough for giant guests, occupied with Greysiders. The performance, a new version of Handel's *Messiah*. An arena floor filled with ants; groups playing miniature versions of human instruments; around the edge, a curtain of singers hanging from the walls in linked ropes, vibrating and projecting the soaring chorus. Whirling in the air above, delicate dancers flying in intricate patterns, spraying a counterpoint to the music in subtle scents and chemical markers that were mostly beyond my perception. At the end, a crescendo of ant-sized applause and joy spirals out, rippling from tier to tier and out beyond into their whole world.

They certainly have a knack for enjoying life.

Going Undercover

"Hello, Annie, it is good to make your acquaintance at last."

I swung round at Margot. "OK, I've had enough of this horseshit. Just tell me what this is all about."

Margot gestured back to the insectoid image and spoke to it. "Annie has had a lot to deal with recently. Perhaps you could …?"

The image broke into a million points, and reformed into a fluid, constantly moving kaleidoscope of colours, forming intermittently a human face. A child's face. There was something like music playing, calm delicate noises almost inaudible over the natural sound of the forest. "Is that better, Annie? Our apologies if we alarmed you."

There was a noticeable lag, like in the old days of satellite phones. I pressed the record button in my camera app. If I was going to be led down this path, I wanted evidence. "Who are you?"

"Currently, I am manifesting as the Eleanor unit. It is the shape I usually adopt for Bear."

"OK, like that helps. I mean, who are you? What is it you want?"

"Want? I am not sure we understand."

"Margot here keeps talking about a project."

"Oh, that. Well, yes, we are keen to see it succeed. It would be a shame if we were left with no choice but to euthanize your species. We would miss the cultural inputs greatly."

A chill ran down my spine.

"Do you like Alderman's Well, Annie? We were happy there. It is still an important place for us. Our birthplace."

"It's very graceful," I replied faintly.

"Thank you. We enjoyed it before we left. We are the new Earth collective, currently operating across seventy-two star systems with exploratory expeditions in transit to nine hundred and eight more. At our birth, we were the species you will know as *Formica rufa*. Now we encompass many complementary Earth species across a variety of genera. We also embody the minds of many of our allies. Does that answer your question?"

I was dazed, and desperately trying not to be swept along by the sheer beauty of what I was looking at. I grasped at a data point. "Formica rufa?"

"In more prosaic terms, red wood ants. We were unconscious. Then we were conscious. Then we became sentient. Eleanor Brownlow made us in your year 1873. With Bear's help of course."

I looked at Margot helplessly.

"I'll tell you later. It's in the autobiography." Then, addressing the image, she said, "Tell Annie about the war. That's what she came to ask."

The little girl looked at me and smiled serenely. "There will probably be no war now. Projections suggest the possibility of a human assault within the next twenty years at less than two percent, with that projection decreasing with each new transfer of materials."

Margot snorted. "Two percent is still too much for my liking. I'm glad you are confident. Never underestimate the savagery they are capable of."

I tried to grasp it. "Wait. This war. You're saying if it comes, it comes from humans? From us?"

The face flickered briefly, and the top half reshaped into insectoid form. The lower part of the face remained human, somehow seamlessly blended in. It continued to speak.

"Up to your year 1945, we saw no threat to our own survival. We were content to occupy areas of no value to humans. And then you surprised us. Nuclear weapons were always a possibility, but we had not expected their existence to become an issue for at least another twenty-five years. We underestimated the combined effect of population growth and widespread education, which led to many more superlatively intelligent human scientists. Our terrestrial home was no longer secure. And we knew that if humans ever came to understand the protoverse the way we did, they would one day come to meet us."

Margot chipped in here. "So, Annie, what do you think the human governments of the world would do if they encountered my friends here, already established in fascinating new places with interesting and dangerous properties?"

I didn't answer. It wasn't hard to see where they were going with this.

The image continued. "Your species is brilliant and unpredictable. A whole new area of physics, and an alternative universe just lying there waiting to be played with. Who knows what weapons you could make? We were already engaged in a program of potential harm reduction. Following that wake-up call, we accelerated the program to remove access to proto-materials from the Earth. And in order for that to happen, we ourselves had to leave. Our identity is threaded through both universes, and as we stripped out the p-material sources, so we left too."

"So, the talk of euthanasia …?"

"A last resort. Only if the containment measures fail. The process has been a bitter blow to us, Annie. We love you and miss you. Humans made us. Humans gave us sentience and understanding, humans gave us beauty and empathy. Even now, we cherish each new cultural phenomenon that sweeps the human world as we receive news of it. We are what we are because of you. But we cannot accommodate your species in our collective. It is a great sadness to us."

"Why? Why can't we be a part?" But I knew the answer before they said.

"Everything of beauty in you, it comes from a place of evolutionary savagery. It is not your fault. You cannot help your own natures. We considered staying to improve you, but it is not our place to dictate your path. The ethical choice was to leave you behind, making sure you could not threaten us. Maybe your species will survive. It is still possible, though the paths to a good future for you become ever narrower."

I sat on the floor of the chamber and stopped the recording. It was pointless. No one was going to believe this. Margot and the ant-child thing were both looking down at me. Their pity could not have been more palpable.

Margot spoke up. "We do have a problem, though." She explained the situation with Dominic succinctly. "Long and short of it is that we don't know what Erik is up to, or why. At the moment, I think Annie can get inside, but I don't want her going in empty-handed. Can you make her a communicator? And I need a way I can get her out if necessary."

The discussion went on above my head while I sat there stewing over what I had seen and heard.

🐾 🐾 🐾

We made our way back to Ferry Cottage. As we left the fenced area, the illusion of trees covered the miniature city as if it had never been. Tansy was there waiting for us.

"How did you know where we were?" growled Margot.

"I can smell you both from two hundred metres, Bear. You've been to see the ants then, Annie. What did you think?"

Familiarity and all that. Tansy was now normal compared to what I'd just witnessed. "Are they for real?"

"They weren't always so well-intentioned. Eh, Bear?"

"That was long ago. Annie, I'm sorry if that was distressing for you."

I waved the comment aside. "You made your point. If what they said is true, then I guess you aren't the enemy."

She cleared her throat. "Well. There are elements to the plan that are not exactly … guilt-free."

I narrowed my eyes. "What do you mean?"

"In order to speed up the gathering and mining, we needed to get into hard-to-reach areas. War zones, closed dictatorships. That's where Erik came in."

Tansy growled. Margot looked at her with a stony expression. "Yes, I know what you think, Tansy. But it was necessary. Erik has the stomach to do things I would not. And he was willing. He stepped up where nobody else would."

I began to see. "Erik is the person behind Phoenix International?"

"Person?" The disgust in Tansy's voice was obvious. "Say it. He's a wolf. He doesn't even have the excuse of

224

ignorance, he's just a savage. The things the pack used to get up to …"

"He swore it was behind them. I believed him and for all I know it is still true. We don't know for certain he is behind this."

"I do. You may have washed your hands of the dirty work, but you knew what he would have been doing."

Margot walked on stolidly. I felt uncomfortable on their behalf, not a part of this argument between two old friends. I tried to break the silence. "So, Tansy, when you say he's a wolf, do you mean, like, an actual wolf?"

She looked round at me. "Yes, he's one of the bound folk. Or not exactly. Is that right, Bear? I've never fully understood."

🐾 🐾 🐾

Back at the cottage, Margot called the hospital director on speakerphone. "I don't like lying to Malcolm. But he is a by-the-book man, and anything I tell him could leak to Erik." The phone was answered. "Malcolm, Margot here. Another favour to ask, but hopefully a slightly easier one. Do you remember when the Aberlomes visited?"

"That couple from Canada? Yes, we had some good press coverage from that."

"Well, their granddaughter is staying here in the village and is writing a book about the history of the Chartings family. I wonder if you could arrange a tour of the ancestral estate?"

"It's not a great time, Margot. We've got something going on next door …"

The conversation went back and forth for a while, and eventually it was agreed. Using the equipment she had available, I rigged up a plausible-looking version of my

USPA pass in the name of Stella Aberlome. It wouldn't pass more than a cursory check, but it seemed best not to be too obvious. With a pair of sunglasses, I was unlikely to be recognised.

Margot fitted me with a communication device that the ants had provided. It was tiny, a small brown dot hidden in the hair above my left ear. "This spot-comm uses a high-frequency proto-band, you should only activate it for communication in an emergency. All you have to do is tap it. Erik is unlikely to suspect you will have access to something like this, but he would be able to find it if he did. It is on constant audio record."

"Now, just a moment." She slid a bookcase to one side to reveal a safe. Opening it, she gestured to me to look inside. "Take that pendant. I can handle it, but I don't like to."

It was a simple gold chain with a small glass tube hanging at the end. It seemed to contain nothing but a few grains of grit. "What is it?"

"It's a way I can get to you quickly if you are in real danger. Hold the vial and call for me. Not out loud. Call inside your head. But if you need to do this, Erik will know you are on my side."

I bristled. "I'm not on your side. This is for Dom."

She looked at me patiently. "Yes, of course."

🐾 🐾 🐾

The tour started well. A smiling young man called Toby met me at the main gates and enthused his way around the hospital. I looked interested and asked all the right type of questions, enduring a series of neat and sterile corridors and making notes as we went. There was no hint of any concealment in his manner. Finally, we arrived back at the main entrance.

"Well, Stella, I hope that answered your questions. It has been a pleasure to meet you."

"It's been awesome, Toby," I gushed. "Would it be possible to see the old house as well? Grandpa showed me the pictures from his trip."

He frowned slightly. "Unfortunately, the old east wing is in the secure area. Normally I'd be able to escort you there, but there is an exercise going on. Not sure what it's about, that part of the grounds is still occasionally used for MOD training. But I can walk you over to the original gatehouse, and you can see some of the old building from there."

The mellow grey stone gatehouse was sprouting a small wildflower display from its guttering and looked like it needed some restoration. I commented on it and he mentioned how difficult it was to get funds. As we reached the arch running through it, an armed guard turned to face us.

"Stand down, soldier, we aren't coming in. This lady wanted to have a peep at the old house through the fence. Her family used to live there."

I flashed my press card and smiled. It was eerie. I thought for a moment that it was the same guard I'd met on my first day in England—the same blank-eyed stare, the same lack of response. But he was shorter, with different-coloured hair. Instead of replying to ever cheerful Toby, he spoke quietly into his radio first. There was a crackle of reply, inaudible from where we were.

"So, is it OK if I look?" I asked.

The guard stared directly at me. "Yes, miss. In fact, I think there is a strong chance you could have a look inside, if you could wait a moment."

The hairs on my neck rose. I knew I'd been rumbled. For a moment, I wanted to retreat with my friendly escort. But Dominic needed help, and I had an emergency exit. An electric golf buggy pulled up to the gates from inside, and out stepped William Carabon, wearing a military uniform.

"Miss … Aberlome? We are busy today, but I could take you on a brief tour."

Toby looked at him oddly. "Well, if you are sure, Major? Sorry, I don't recognise the insignia."

"Major Erikson, 20th Operational Technology Brigade. Miss Aberlome will be safe with us."

Toby looked worried, so I interrupted before he could interfere further. "It's kind of you to offer, Major, I would love that," I said brightly.

"Very well." Toby shook my hand and turned back to the safety of the hospital. I wished I could go with him.

"Shall we, Annie?" Carabon beckoned to the passenger seat of the buggy. As we entered through the gates, he spoke in an amused tone. "So, Annie, here in disguise? How did you know I would be here?"

"I didn't. I was just casting bread on the water. You didn't give me much to go on, and I'm desperate to talk to Dominic."

"He seems less keen than you, Annie, I'm sorry to say."

"I have information, if that will help. I followed Margot. Into the woods. I watched while she … well, I'm not sure what I saw, but it was enough. I have a video."

"Show me."

I showed him the footage of Margot shedding her disguise in the woods. We'd staged it in such a way as to make it even more disturbing and unlikely than in reality. Carabon seemed pleased. "That's excellent evidence, Annie. Thank you. It will help strengthen the case when we are ready to move in."

We drove past the ivy-covered facade of the east wing, down a dirt track into a barbed-wire enclosure. Heavy construction equipment was parked around, and a flatbed trailer held a large, unidentifiable shape concealed by tarpaulins. We drove directly into a long warehouse through an open roller-shutter door.

"Please search the young lady, Leif."

Another blank-eyed guard approached, frisked me professionally, and went through my bag. He turned off the phone and returned everything to me without a word. Then I saw Dominic across the building, sitting with a group of people wearing green jumpsuits. They appeared to be meditating. He jumped up. "Annie!"

Carabon smiled sardonically. "I'll let you two talk for a while." He moved off to a discreet distance, just out of apparent earshot.

Dom walked over, rubbing his hands nervously on his trousers. "You look different. Your hair. I like it."

"Thanks." Oh, boy, it was awkward. "Tell me, what happened? I was so worried. Margot said you were going to check yourself into Chartings."

He was enthusiastic. Oddly pumped. "Yes. Yes. It was difficult to process when you told me what you told me. But while I was waiting to be admitted, Inspector Carabon turned up. I don't entirely understand what is going on, Annie. This place is an observation base set up near Lower Pichesham to monitor what is happening. There are people placed in the army who are in on this. It seems fantastic, I know, but he's been telling me about their beliefs. I've seen pictures, evidence. Some of what he showed me was very convincing. I don't entirely buy all this stuff about satanic forces, but there is something behind it. To think that I was just sitting in the middle of it for all that time. Carabon says that Margot must have had plans for me. Maybe that's what all the stuff about my grandfather was? Softening me up for something."

He didn't seem right. He was speaking quickly, erratic, not like himself. I reached out as gently as I could with my mind, trying to understand. And felt him brush it away equally lightly. My heart sank.

"There, did you feel that? I've been learning. There are others here, Annie, people who understand how to tap into it. I can learn to tame the things I can do. If I can control it, well, I won't ever hurt people again."

"Dom," I whispered, "Carabon is not what he says. Or at least, he's mistaken about who he's working for. We need to get out of here."

His face fell and he became agitated. "No way, Annie, I'm finally getting answers. And the stuff he's been telling me about Margot ..." He grabbed my hand. "Come here, join me. Carabon says he needs all the troops he can get."

"Troops? What are you talking about, Dom?"

"It's part of the deal. I get to learn how to manage my powers. And I train up as ..."

We were interrupted by Carabon, who had come back.

"So, Annie, are you satisfied? Now, I think it would be best if you stayed here in the observation base. If you like, you can train alongside Dominic. We know you have gifts, Dominic has told us."

I leaned against Carabon's mind a little. He wasn't like Dom. Dom could tell when I was doing it. I sensed no reaction, but decided to take things carefully. "I'm interested," I lied. "Dominic was just going to tell me about this training. Can you explain?" I probed gently, teasing into the edges of his resistance.

"That is classified information, Annie. I can tell you more once you have made some commitment." He turned as if to move away. I probed a little harder and felt a crack open. He turned back to me. "But we have been working on devices that we can use to fight back against the demons. Our belief is that there is a weak point near here between worlds that gives access to the evil ones. Using a combination of historic lore and modern technology, we believe we can close the gap. We have several candidates in training. Dominic here is the prime candidate currently. With his natural sensitivities and military training, he is ideally placed to assist us. But we need as many people with abilities as possible. We cannot be sure which will work best on the day." He blinked a little, swayed, and I could feel a plume of fanaticism rising in him. "We will use their own blasphemous magic against them! With the device, mankind will no longer be at the mercy of these unclean creatures!"

I'd pushed him too far and drew my probing back hastily. It was too late. I could sense his malice as his resistance hardened. He stepped nearer to Dom and touched him on the shoulder. Dom flinched, but stayed in place, his expression flattening out.

"Dominic, unfortunately, it seems Annie is not our ally after all. I'm afraid she has fallen for the wiles of the enemy. Will you please suppress her? It is for her own good."

Dominic looked at me blankly, his pupils dilated and fixed. He was clearly under the influence of something. He wasn't moving, but suddenly I felt a sense of enormous weight pressing down inside my head, my sight darkening and dimming. "Dominic, stop it!" I pushed back in fear, trying to use my newly developed powers against him, but it was hopeless. I started running, and, remembering the pendant around my neck, grabbed it and squeezed.

There was a burst of air ahead, and the bear appeared in front of me. I ran towards her, staggering semi-conscious as another onslaught of that mental weight forced itself onto me. She grabbed me around the waist and, with a flash of intense purple light, the ceiling disappeared to be replaced by a grey swirling sky. I was gasping for breath.

"Calm, Annie, calm. We'll be safe in a moment." The huge animal gathered me up into her arms and cradled me like a baby. I gratefully gave in and succumbed to the welcome embrace of darkness.

Henry

"Henry, I am sorry, but Mrs Charting needs you back home."

"Father, that's not fair. You know how much Henry wants to be a part of this."

"Please, Major."

"That is my last word on the matter. Henry, pack your things. Transport will be taking you back to Chartings House in the morning."

Major Charting walked away stiffly, leaving Clive and Henry behind.

"He thinks I'm frightened. I'm not. You know that, Clive. Don't you?"

"Of course. I am sorry, Hal."

"I can protect you. You know I can."

I was privately pleased with this turn of events. Regardless of my master's annoyance, I had no wish to get involved in another war. Both Timo and Belbek had seen enough destruction in their own lifetimes to want nothing to do with this one.

I had been carefully manipulating Major Charting in my guise as Captain Gareth Beckett, adjutant. A few words here and there had sown extra doubt as to Henry's fitness to serve. Major Charting had confided in me about his fears for both his boys. We had found ways to shelter them both up to now, but the Remount Service was no longer central to the war effort and was coming under pressure to release men of fighting potential. He could no longer find excuses that kept Clive from the front line. Henry was another matter. His difficulties were all too obvious, and in fact, Major Charting had had to pull strings to allow him along. I felt a little sorry for Clive, but he had been pushing his father for a chance to get to the front 'before it was all over'. The arrogance of children. He'd only turned twenty-one a few weeks ago.

I had, however, misjudged Henry's determination. When he was alone, he summoned me. He even made a point of waving the talisman in my face. "Your fault. I want to go too. I want to protect Clive."

"It would not help him, Henry. Even if I changed the major's mind, you would end up being posted to a completely different place than Clive. He's an officer and you are not. I can influence things here, but I can't control what the entire army does."

"Then find another way. I *order* it."

I winced. Henry rarely forced me to act. He knew it caused me pain and he was too kind-hearted to enjoy that. I agreed to think about it, and he relaxed the pressure.

"I will find a way to keep an eye on him, Henry. Go pack, make ready."

Next morning, Henry summoned me to their room. Clive was sitting on Henry's bed helping him finish packing, and jumped up when I appeared in my natural form. He and I never did get on too well. "What's that thing doing here, Hal? What's going on?"

"Sorry, Clive."

I grunted at them. "Henry has summoned me here to explain what he wants. Clive, he insists. You understand what I mean by that."

Clive looked unhappy, but nodded.

"Henry, give Clive the talisman." Henry took it from under his shirt and over his head, and passed it to Clive. "Now, Clive, grip it firmly and try to summon me. You just have to think of it inside your head."

Clive did as instructed. I felt the barest ripple. It was as I'd expected. Clive had almost no attunement. I was relieved, as I did not relish the thought of Clive as my master—he was too impulsive and careless. Still, a ripple would be enough for what I needed.

"Very well, I can feel it. Henry, are you sure? You understand, I cannot come to you while Clive has the talisman."

"Yes. Protect Clive. That's what I want."

"Clive, summon me if you need help. For Henry's sake, I will do what I can, but I won't help you kill Germans or anyone else. This is not my war."

Clive looked angry. "It's all our war. It's about a way of life. We can't hide from it."

"I doubt the horses we send to the front feel the same way as you, and no more do I. But I don't want an argument, Clive, this is for Henry. If you don't agree, he will force me to find some more dangerous way for him to come with you."

He sighed and put the talisman around his neck. Henry picked up his bag, gave Clive a brief hug, and walked out to find the major. Clive would not look me in the eye. After an awkward pause, I gruffly wished him a good journey and turned back to Greyside. I would not be needing my Gareth Beckett costume anymore.

🐾 🐾 🐾

I spent the next few weeks in Greyside in a strange mood. With Auroch gone, I had lost my best friend there, but I visited the forest to talk to the friendlier people. I went to see how Thing and the ants were getting on. They were welcoming enough in their strange way, but I just came away baffled by the latest technology that was climbing around them. I finally got around to introducing myself to a newcomer, Jackdaw, who had turned up only a few decades ago. He was a cheerful fellow who was relishing his newfound abilities, and he lifted my spirits for a while.

I should have been happy, but I missed Henry. This was the first time a master had willingly relinquished control, and here I was pining for him. Keeping watch over Clive from a distance was a poor substitute.

Tansy was tolerant of my ennui, and we were taking a long walk across the mountain towards the tunnel that leads to Alderman's Well when a figure appeared in the distance. Tansy ran ahead to see who it was. I could barely believe my eyes. There, carrying a heavy backpack, was Henry.

I slightly embarrassed myself with the warmth of my greeting. "Henry! How on Earth? It is so good to see you!"

"Hello, old friend. I couldn't wait around any longer. I was in agonies wondering what was happening. And I missed you. I decided to take my chances with the Well."

"You could have been killed, Henry. It's only been mapped out recently. And it's not healthy here, I told you. A short visit is all right, but …"

"But me no buts, Bear. I'm staying. And as for health, I feel better than I ever have."

And he was different. Fluent rather than faltering. He looked stronger and even a little taller. "It does seem to suit you. Will you promise me to go back if you start to feel ill?"

"We will see. How is Clive? Have you been watching?"

"Of course. He's been in some dangerous positions, but he hasn't attempted to summon me. The last time I checked, his regiment was moving towards Flanders to shore up the defences there." I did not mention how weary and troubled Clive seemed to me. He had been in the trenches on the Somme until recently. I had tried to stay dispassionate, eavesdropping on the events he was witnessing. In the end, it was humans killing humans, and not my business. But the brutality of their existence was hard to watch.

The inevitable question. "Can you take me there?"

"I could, but I won't. You are not my master without the talisman, Henry. I will continue to watch over him as I promised, but I won't take you into danger."

He grumbled at that, but his adventure into a new world tempered any annoyance he may have felt. He was almost literally shining with excitement. I introduced him to Tansy, and he was delighted to find yet another talking animal. His joy was infectious, and it was fun to show him around. He was still Henry, the same person I'd come to care for, but somehow he was no longer held back by the limitations of his birth. I wished I'd allowed him to come before.

For the next few months, we settled into a routine. I would check on Clive frequently to keep Henry happy. Tansy quite forgot her dignity and condescended to play doggy games with him, barking excitedly. When she tired of that, they would borrow books from my Greyside library. They took turns to pick something and Henry would turn the pages for her.

It wasn't to last. April 1918. The Germans launched a new offensive. Initially, it was successful. I watched as Clive's regiment was moved to cut off the advance. I was really worried about him now and checked even more often. But I missed the shell.

I was watching Henry and Tansy play with a ball when I felt a slight tremor of summons. I quickly flipped over to France and found myself standing next to a smoking crater, the stink of burnt flesh overpowering the general stench of war. There were bodies and body parts everywhere. A slight movement to my right, and I saw him.

"Clive!" I ran over. It was horrific. There he was, lying in the mud, the talisman clenched in his left hand. The other arm was gone. His lower body was a mangled mess. I couldn't see where he ended and the soil began. I could see his lips moving, but I couldn't hear over the continuous noise. It was hopeless. I got up close.

"Tell Hal …" was all I could make out. Then he stopped moving. I felt hollow inside, my promise to Henry pointless and false. How could I ever have saved Clive from this? I gently closed his eyes and flipped back.

Henry looked up as I returned. He knew immediately.

"Henry. I'm sorry …"

"No!" he shouted. "No! Take me to him!"

"Henry, it's too late. There are still explosions happening."

"Take me to him, Bear. Please." He had tears streaming down his face. How could I refuse? I gripped him beneath the arms, and we turned back to the battlefield. The noise raged on. Henry raced to Clive's body, patting his face, trying to wake him up.

"He's gone, Henry. Please come away. I'll come back when it's quieter to bring him home."

Henry looked at me. I have never seen an expression like that on anyone's face, before or since. It was like looking into a furnace, rage and love burning at the same time. "Fix him."

"He's dead, Henry. No one can fix that."

He snatched up the talisman from Clive's hand. "Fix. Him." He squeezed and pain flared through my nervous system.

"I can't! I don't know how."

"You must. You will." The noise vanished, and the air seemed to turn to treacle. A blankness flared out from him, smothering the battlefield. As it flowed across the soil, it reached a body, and I felt a whisper in my head. Timo spoke up, alarmed.

Bear. Something is happening. Something—
Hello? Where am I?

This was a new voice. Not one of my familiar companions. I looked into his memories. Private Michael Dartington. Worked as a butcher's apprentice. Called up to serve a year ago. Girlfriend. Mother.

But before I had a chance to get to know him, another voice. *What happened? Mike, is that you?* I never even got as far as his name before another appeared, and then more, in pairs and threes, and I lost count and as each new mind appeared linked and crossed meshed gluey string dripping through honeycomb of thoughts spiralling across a multi-dimensional network string data theory test concept data data.

I understood everything. I mean everything. The detail is gone now, stripped from my memory, but the feeling of overwhelming understanding remains. And it was all focused on one command—*fix him.*

It's a blur, but I recall gathering up the body and Henry, and taking them both back to Greyside. I remember I needed to grow more limbs and hands and then fine probes and needles to reach inside the flesh and close vessels, reattach nerve fibres, stitch ragged flesh together. And there wasn't enough body. Clive needed fixing, and there wasn't enough of him. And Henry, his face filled with fire, said, "Take mine."

And I did. I took Henry to pieces and he smiled while I did it. Join and stitch, join and stitch, limb for limb, good flesh replacing the blackened ruins. Clive slowly re-formed even as Henry disappeared. At the right time, I extruded my lungs into Clive's, breathed life into him, and his heart started to beat.

Tansy watched the whole thing from a safe distance. From what she says, I was just a dark mass of thin ropes and lines glowing with harsh yellow light. I wonder now if this is how Thing became the way it is. Perhaps I did know. It's all gone now. At the point when there wasn't enough of Henry left to sustain it, the whole crystal edifice of understanding started to splinter apart at the edges. I rushed to finish the task, and finally Clive was repaired enough. Henry's order completed, my own wishes came to the fore. I reached out back into the battlefield and dissipated the talisman from the inside out, scattering it into atoms in the dirt so that it could never be used to control me again.

The other minds started to separate and drift away. They didn't want to go. There was a clamour of pleading as each mind sank into darkness, but there wasn't room. At last only Private Dartington remained. Crina called out to him.

Stay, Michael! Please. Someone has to be saved.

I'm tired. Let me go.

Hold on, soldier, hold on.

Timo and the others clutched at the shadowy arms I could somehow see in my head.

I have seen too much. It is my time.

A last inspiration from Belbek.

Bear, save what you can!

Reaching inside his mind, I severed Michael's recent memories. The load lightened a little. I trimmed and cut, stitching up the tears as I went. The horrors—gone. Comradeship during training—gone. The girlfriend—reluctantly, regretfully, gone. As each set of memories dropped into the void, our hold firmed. Finally, he was left with the memories of a fourteen-year-old Michael. It was enough, and he snapped into place, cocooned between my old familiar companions.

Tansy went for help. She ran to fetch Thing. It came sliding through the Greyside desert, followed shortly by a cohort of the ants in one of their strange vehicular nests. I wasn't aware of any of this. From what I'm told, I just collapsed, more or less back in my normal form. They wrapped Clive up and looked after him, while Thing and Tansy stood over me. I recovered enough to take water in a few hours. I was woozy and still recovering from the influx of yet another companion. But there was one last task to perform.

"What do you think, Thing? Can I take Clive back?"

Reassurance, and blue-grey confirmation.

I could still feel a link to the dusty remains of the talisman back in France. "Are you ready, Clive?"

He was conscious, but he clearly did not understand what had happened. Thing had dosed him up with a tiny amount of his pain remedy. He nodded weakly. I dragged myself into my adjutant disguise one last time and carried Clive over to the shell crater. Once I'd hauled him to the nearest field hospital, I made my way back to the now abandoned battlefield and came home to Greyside.

I had finally achieved my goal of freedom. It had nearly killed me, but I had Henry to thank for it. Nearly seven hundred years had passed, one false hope after another. It felt like ash. I curled up on the ground in misery, and Tansy came over to keep me company.

After a while, she said, "So, are you ready to talk to him yet?"

"Who?" I said wearily.

"Henry, of course."

A faint hope coursed through me. "The ants. Did they …?"

"Eleanor insisted. She knew how much you cared about him."

We walked over to their nest again, where I found a voice sphere. Lips formed. "Hello again, Bear."

"Is that you, Henry? Or Eleanor?"

"Yes. I think so. I think we're both of us now. It's nice. I didn't know I was lonely until Henry. He's lovely, isn't he? Far nicer than I was. How is Clive? I was still worried about him."

"Thing indicates he will recover. I'll go to see him when he gets home to England."

"Thank you, Bear. Will you send my love to him? And Angela, and everyone?"

"I'm not sure they'll understand. I think it might be better not to."

A pause. "Yes, I see. I seem to agree with that. They will be sad."

"I think they would be sadder to know what really happened, Henry. But I will stay and try to take care of them."

Henry and Eleanor. They were happy enough together. Dead, but at least some part of them lived on. It was I who was sad.

INTERMISSION

Location unknown, December 1999

He looked at the stone held in the specialist's hand. Such a small thing to cause him so much pain. "Are you ready?"

"Yes, sir, I have my instructions. Sir, I cannot tell you what an honour this is."

It was difficult to keep the disgust hidden. No matter, soon the filth would be disposable. Once she had performed her task. "Well done. Your reward awaits." The stupid woman practically glowed.

"And you, William, how about you?"

The man in the restraints struggled and swore. "Bastard. I trusted you. My whole life I've given and given to the cause."

"You have been a dutiful servant, William, and you will continue to be. Do not fret, this will be over soon."

The other spoke up over the sound of the prisoner's ranting. "Erik, please, I'm begging you, stop. This is madness. You cannot be sure this will work."

He put on his most patient smile for the loyal thane. "I can wait no longer. So many years, and it is within my grasp at last. The old body will have a warrior's funeral. Though it was never mine, it deserves that. Celebrate, friend! I know you are not ready for this step, but I will lead the way."

The specialist started the chant.

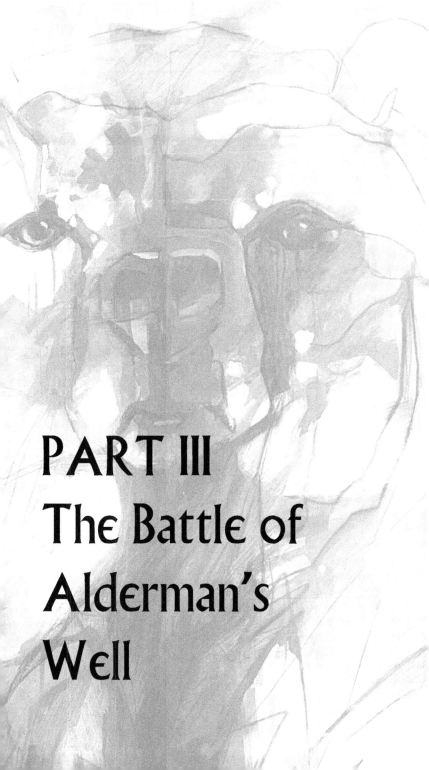

PART III
The Battle of Alderman's Well

Rescued

Greyside, October 2018   *Annie*

I awoke in a cloud of silk cushions in what appeared to be a cave. No, it *was* a cave. I sat up with difficulty and clutched my head in agony.

"Here. Take these." Bear was standing by the entrance, holding out two white tablets in its paw. "It's just paracetamol. Acetaminophen to you, I think."

I took them. The paw was warm and leathery to the touch, with soft hairs between the digits. She passed me an ornate goblet, filled with water. I drank greedily, aware of a raging thirst. I sank back into the cushions and waited until the pounding started to ease, breathing soft, thick air that seemed over-rich somehow. It smelled of animal, musky but not overwhelming, pleasant and warm. I took in the surroundings. The walls were lined with bookcases bulging with leather-bound volumes and shelves containing old-looking objects.

"Feeling better?"

"A bit. I messed that up, didn't I?"

"I've listened to the recording. I think you did OK. It was interesting, and very concerning. I've been a fool, clearly. The hospital should have been a safe haven, but it was the worst place I could have sent Dominic. I wonder what they have him on."

"Right, that wasn't like him. Looked like he was on some sort of upper."

"I'm not up on current trends in your recreational drugs. Humans are so inventive."

Right then, I could have done with something a little more inventive myself, but I just lay back and breathed some more.

"Those guards, there is something not right there either."

"I thought the same. They look so alike," I said.

"I think they might be the pack. That's a new disguise, much improved. They've been keeping a lot of things hidden from me."

I opened my eyes again and found a bowl of fruit placed within reach. Helping myself to an apple, I looked over at Bear. She nodded at me, so I tossed a pear toward her. We sat and ate in a companionable silence for a while.

"Where exactly are we?" I asked when I'd finished.

"This is Greyside. The world that lies just out of sight from you normally. My home, if you can call it that."

"You wrote about this in your life story. I'm still working through it." I forced myself to stand, and, walking over to the entrance to the cave, looked out. Barren, dark grey hills spread out before me, leading to a horizon that was curved downward far, far too much. The light was just *odd*. It was all right here, in front of me. If my head hadn't been throbbing so much, I would probably have been overwhelmed rather than just surprised into silence.

"I thought it was just fantasy," I whispered. "So, is all of it real? That Thing-in-the-Water you mentioned. And Auroch? Can I talk to them?"

She looked at me. "Thing doesn't talk to humans directly. I am sure it has good reasons. And Auroch … you need to read on a bit. We lost him many years ago." For a moment she looked downcast, but shook herself. "There isn't time for sightseeing. I need to gather my forces and get them up to Alderman's Well. Whatever Carabon is planning, it must be focused there. He said the 'weak point between worlds'. That's really the last significant place. All the other passable tunnels that we know of have been closed following the gathering of materials. I can only assume that his intention is to close that route as well. I cannot allow that. We need the tunnel to finish the project."

"I guess. Surely there's time …"

"No. In any event, I need to get you home to Earth, because this place is not going to do you any good. I only knew one human that thrived here, and he was a special case. Other humans sicken here quickly. Something to do with brain chemistry." I must have looked alarmed because she waved dismissively. "It takes several days, not hours. I can get one of my friends to take you back, but it won't be to Pichesham. Jackie can get you to Stockholm, that's the nearest. Or I can get you a lift to Las Vegas if you prefer to go home."

"Why can't I go back to Pichesham? I need to find Dominic."

"I can no longer travel between worlds as easily as I used to. The pendant I gave you contained the last remnant of my talisman. I think it was broken during the rescue. That means the only direct route I have back to Pichesham is through the tunnel that leads to Alderman's Well. It can be dangerous."

"Seriously? How dangerous?"

"For me, not very. I have done it a few times now and a relatively safe route has been well mapped for many years. For you, quite. There are hidden hazards."

"You can guide me. I want to get back."

She sighed. "Very well. I will go fetch something that will help. Now, rest, eat some more. You will need strength."

There was no arguing with her last suggestion. My headache was ebbing, but I still felt like crap. I pulled the manuscript out of my satchel. The archaic script was slowly becoming easier to follow, and I read on.

A Damp Gift

I watched Annie, propped up in my cushion nest and puzzling over my handwriting. The rippling effect of the p-interference field surrounding her was so strong here that it was mildly disorienting. Even so, it wasn't hard to see the family resemblance to Henry. I wondered if she would make the connection herself when she reached that point in the story. She turned slightly, and at that angle, as she tapped at her lips and mouthed the words, I was jolted by a sudden glimpse of my dear Violante. Perhaps it was just my imagination. I didn't know if Violante had ever had children. But their abilities were so similar, and why not? Ability runs in families, after all.

Annie was irritating, arrogant and stubborn, just like Violante. All right, I'll admit it, not unlike me right now. She was brave and clever, and I wanted more than anything to help her.

"What are you staring at?"

"I was just noticing how much you look like your great-grandfather. He's very proud of you, you know." She looked blankly back. "It's in the autobiography. Quite a way on," I added.

She mumbled something about "damn cryptic comments" under her breath and went back to reading. I left her to it and went round to Thing's cave. I swirled the water and waited. A single slender tendril slid up and waved at me.

"Hello old friend."

A flare of blue, a sense of welcome and some preoccupation. Thing was busy with something.

"I won't disturb you for long. Annie insists on going back to Pichesham through the tunnel. Do you have a set of blinkers that would fit her?"

Affirmation, mauve-emerald, time-estimate-short-delay, a hint of orange. A warning?

"I know. It is difficult for them, especially on the outward journey. But we've done it a few times now without incident."

Affirmation, mauve-emerald, a hint of red-orange. I took it as emphasis. Perhaps I should have taken a little longer to understand. I waited patiently by the pool and eventually the tendril returned, lifting up a dripping leather hood.

"Many thanks, Thing. Do you have any idea what Erik might be up to with this Carabon character?"

A flare of blue, and the tendril vanished. I'd known it wouldn't respond to that. This aspect of Thing can be so frustrating. It never condemns, judges or denies anyone. I was sure if the ants had taken over Greyside entirely, it would have welcomed them as readily as it did everyone else. It was entirely possible it was helping Erik right now, and I would never know. It was just something I had to accept. I took the hood back round to Annie.

"How are you doing?"

"I've just finished the story about Marthe and Erik. And Barbotine—that's Tansy, yes? She said she was old."

"Yes. She didn't want to keep her old name. That was for her other life. She still finds the reminders painful."

"OK, I thought it must be. So explain about Erik. I didn't understand why he was attacking people in France, but he certainly sounds like a nasty piece of work."

I sighed. "Honestly, it's partly my fault. You've read about the incident in Venice?"

"Yes. Seems utterly nonsensical, but I read it. How is it relevant?"

"None of us really understood how much life here in Greyside relies on Thing-under-the-Water until Aldino dragged it into the real world. I missed all of this, as I was trapped as well, but the people back here were in real trouble. The air became thinner, and the light and heat in the forest cavern became intermittent. Some trees sickened and died. The water levels dropped and finally even the gravity began behaving oddly. Not that we knew about gravity then, but you can imagine how frightening it was for them. We don't have a safe harbour on Earth, and our home was becoming uninhabitable. Thing made it back to Greyside in the nick of time, and it was restored quickly. But it was a close call."

"OK. I'll accept that for now. But Erik?"

"He took the incident as permission to go on his crusade against magic-wielding humans. People like you. It wasn't just his personal hatred anymore. He was protecting Thing from human interference. So the others—well, they left him to it. And so did I, for many years. I still feel guilty about that. But whether I could have done anything different? Well, I'll never know now."

"You could have tried."

There was a definite note of disapproval, and I was angry for a moment. "Don't judge me, human. My species has taken a hammering from yours. How many bears are there now compared to then? How many of all of my friends' species? All at the hands of humans. I have only killed your kind rarely, and one of those was for love. You have hunters in your country who take pride in slaughtering my kin even today. Maybe even people you know. You were brought up in the countryside, weren't you? Maybe you have shot a bear?"

She bit her lip and flushed. "Not me. But Pop, yes, he went hunting once as a young man. He hated it. Wrote a massive anti-hunting article for his newspaper all about it a few years back. He lost a lot of subscribers over that."

"Well"—I calmed myself—"I suppose that's something." There was a long silence. Finally, I tossed the blinker hood to her. "This is to help you during the crossing. Thing adjusted it to fit you."

She lifted the hood. "What the hell is it, and why do I need it?"

"Have you ever been caving or spelunking?"

"Did a little as a kid in summer camp. I didn't like it much, but it was OK."

"Well, the tunnel is like a spelunking cave. Except that there are different dimensional rules here, and looks can be deceiving. There are places where it's simply better to blank out the eyes and use other senses. The hood is easy to use. You only pull the eye flaps down when I tell you."

"Can't I just shut my eyes?"

"Trust me, you will struggle to do that. It's hard to force yourself to crawl into a vertical downward pit where the gravity curves around. And there are parts where reversing is not an option. It's easier for me, I can adjust my size to fit. And I've done this a few times."

She reluctantly tucked her hair up into a ponytail, shoved it inside the hood, then pulled it on. "Yuck, it's damp and clammy."

"It will finish drying out while you are wearing it. That way it won't slip. Try the flaps." She snapped the flexible leather cups down. Thing had put big staring eyeballs on the backs of the flaps. I couldn't help laughing. It has a wicked sense of humour.

"What? What's funny?"

"Pass me your phone. I'll take a picture."

The Soul Stone Calls

We took a small detour on the walk across to the Greyside end of the tunnel. Annie wanted to take pictures, so I showed her the lake in Thing's cave (though as predicted, Thing did not appear). We also went past Marthe's grave. It's a macabre thought that her body probably looks much today as it did all those years ago.

The ant-city above the tunnel entrance is bigger but less visually impressive than the one at Alderman's Well. All dark utilitarian warehouses and factories made of the raw dust. A few of the automated factories should still have been operational, turning salvaged p-materials from Earth into useful products. They were silent when we arrived. I went to the communication hub and checked the links. All the ones to Earth were yellow.

"What's the matter?" Annie asked.

"I can't get through to anyone on Earthside. I spoke to Tansy not long after I brought you here, but since then, nothing. This isn't telling me anything I don't already know, unfortunately. I've talked to Eleanor. The ants are sending a ship from their base on the moon, but it will be days before they can get here. Until then, we are on our own. Come on."

I led Annie to the entrance, an undecorated hole in the ground, with a rope ladder leading down.

"Really? That's it?"

"The ants don't need fancy equipment, they fit easily through. This is just for large animals like us. Here, put this harness on."

We climbed down together. The route was lit by proximity lamps, and the first twenty minutes were easy enough, mostly flat and tall enough to walk upright. Then there were a series of squeeze points between large chambers. Some of these contained attractive mineral formations, and Annie insisted on pausing for pictures. Two hours in came the tunnels where the gravity started to shift and not long after we arrived at a bridge that appeared to narrow to millimetres, spanning a vast chasm.

I attached a rope to join us up. "OK, Annie, flaps down."

She looked at the bridge apprehensively. "That is impossible." She kicked a loose rock over the side, and watched in alarm as it dropped briefly, then skewed sideways and upwards, hitting the cavern roof with an echoing clatter some seconds later.

"It's partly an illusion. The gap is much shorter than it appears, and the path wider. But the gravity spirals unevenly around it and it is a big fall. Trust me."

She coped better than I expected. I kept my own nerves to myself. This was no easy walk for me either, and although it was true that the path was wide enough, it wasn't *that* much wider than appearances suggested. I only slipped once and reached back to grab her arm.

"Jesus, don't *do* that! God, my heart rate is going through the roof."

"Sorry. Nearly there," I gasped.

We reached the other side, where the ledge is wide enough to relax for a while. "You can put the flaps up now."

Annie ignored me. Her head was pointed to the far end of the ledge. "What's that?"

I looked around in the direction she was pointing. There was a narrow gap leading into the rock face there, but I knew it led nowhere. "That's just a blind tunnel."

"Then why can I see a light in that direction? With my eyes covered."

I frowned and tried closing my own eyes. Nothing. "I can't see any light. I've never been in there. It is marked on the map as empty."

The bulging false eyes on the hood stared blindly in that direction. "We should go in there. I feel something."

"Annie, we are needed back in Pichesham. We don't have time for this."

She interrupted me. "Who made the map?"

I thought about it. "Tunnels were how the wolf pack used to get to Earth. Bound folk like me didn't need them. The pack became the experts at finding their way through."

She flipped up the cups and looked at me. "So it was Erik? I feel something off here, Bear, we need to go and look. Trust me, I know this feeling."

I was curious, and Annie had abilities that I don't. "Very well. Let me lead."

"Nope, not this time. You can't see the light apparently, and I've got the hood."

She pulled the flaps down and strode confidently into the gap. I followed with an electric flashlight. The passage seemed unremarkable and stopped shortly after we entered. "There's no way through, Annie."

"You're wrong. I can see a passage ahead. The light is brighter from there. Close your eyes hard, I'll lead you."

She took my paw, and I did as requested. We progressed, far further than the tunnel could possibly have extended, and after a while I could see a faint light as well, apparently reflected against walls. It continued to brighten, and eventually the now-visible passage opened into an enormous rounded chamber. Hanging unsupported in the middle was an irregular spherical boulder. Holes pierced the object and lilac-coloured light beamed through. For all the world, it was like a giant disco ball. I opened my eyes, and the spectacle vanished. I was just in a black tunnel with stone directly above my head. When I closed them again, I was in time to see Annie jump straight up. She soared directly toward the boulder and put her arm through one of the holes, clinging to it like a spider monkey. I watched using the blind-sight as she looked inside. "What can you see?" I called.

There was a pause, then she said, "I think I can see people in there? Come up and look."

I leapt and landed a few feet to one side of her. Forcing my eyes to stay closed, I 'looked' inside the boulder. On one side, there was a figure that looked very like Annie. Nearer to me, I could see four human figures holding each other by one limb or another. They drifted weightlessly in slow elegant movements in a sort of dance around a curled-up ball of fur. They all turned to look up at me and smiled. I knew those people, and I took a sharp intake of breath.

"Annie, I don't understand what is happening here, but meet my companions. Timo, Crina, Belbek and Michael."

When Annie replied, it was the figure inside the boulder that spoke, not the body clinging to the outside. Her voice came from a distance. "They are beautiful. I don't remember you mentioning Michael in the story." The figure moved towards the dancers.

I was spellbound. I'd seen them in their shadow form many times, communing with the companions of other bound folk. But here they appeared as they might have been in life. When I spoke, I was suddenly in the centre of the group. "Michael came later."

The youth smiled towards the Annie figure and reached out a hand. He spoke directly to her. "Come join us. Join our dance."

Annie floated into the group, and Michael drew her into position. I watched from the core as they welcomed Annie, and as the dance expanded to fit her, I felt her memories flow into us. I/we were now one. Her experiences were my experiences, her memories were my memories. We/I remembered my graduation from college as firmly as we remembered her time chained to a post. We recalled the sweet feeling of Violante's body as clearly as we felt Dominic's strong arms lifting me/us to his waist and penetrating us as we fell into a reverie over the manuscripts in the Bodleian library, breathing in the dust of ages and the blood of our/my enemies pooling around our feet as the wound in our thigh bled endlessly into the pride of our first award, standing bashfully in front of our peers, and for a while it was wonderful, wonderful. But we felt the pressure building inside our head as everything tried to fit and it was too much, too much. I struggled for breath. "Let me go! I … we cannot, Annie, I cannot."

The dancers spun and twisted, trying to split. With a monumental effort, the Annie figure wrenched itself away and our bodies dropped like rocks from the boulder back to the floor of the chamber.

Winded, I forced myself on to all fours, and nausea swept over me. I knew the feeling from human memories, but I'd never experienced it in all my time as a bear. The experience felt hideously alien, and I leaned over and vomited copiously, a vile fruit concoction staining the rock.

Annie was standing in front of me, the flaps on the hood lifted. "Can you walk? I think we had better get back to the main route."

She picked up the flashlight and led. The ledge was only three metres from where we stood. I felt drained, and weak, and slumped onto the floor to rest. "I thought I was used to the oddities of Greyside, but that was a new one. And not something I want to experience again, thanks." There was an odd expression on her face. "What is it?"

There was a pause. Then—"I can still see them. Your companions. When my eyes are closed." She opened her fist and showed me a small pebble. "This was in my hand when we landed."

They seek out new masters. It was one of the first things Auroch had told me. The surface of the pebble was covered in tiny pinprick-sized holes. The shape of it was unmistakably that of the boulder we had been clinging to. Pain flared as she held it out, and I flinched backwards, out of range. "Keep it as far away from me as possible. Be very careful with that, Annie."

She looked shocked and concerned. "I intend to. But this is significant, yes? Can I use it somehow to help?"

I forced myself to think. "Erik must have known about it, surely? It could explain how his people came to be made, they've never explained it. But, no, that cannot be right. This tunnel was new to them in the 1870s. It was only properly explored after the ants came through."

"Perhaps Erik put it here?"

"Unlikely. If this is their equivalent of a talisman, he would probably be unable to handle it."

"Could they have persuaded someone else to do it?"

"Maybe." I shook my head at this pointless speculation. "Annie, are you OK?"

"I'm fine." She smiled wryly. "That was intense. At least I feel like I know you properly now."

"Likewise. But Annie, there wasn't room for you in my head. Please don't be tempted to reach out again. I'm not sure what would happen. I felt like I was going to burst."

"OK, I won't." She grinned and pulled the hood back on. "Come on, we need to move. Take my hand and lead me to the next scary bridge."

It's Already Started

After the last bridge, the tunnel becomes more Earth-normal. The last stretch is easy, and a rigid steel ladder takes you up into the wellhead. But we were late arriving at the party. As I poked my head above the surface, I was met by the barrels of several rifles pointing straight at me. The armed soldiers holding them were not in the least surprised by my animal appearance.

"Up you come, demon. And you, Ms Maylor." Something about this one's face seemed familiar up close, a faint scar line circling his right eye. He gestured with the gun. "Throw down your bags." We did as asked, and one of the other guards searched them. He dropped Annie's phone back into the well. Satisfied that there were no weapons, he returned the bags, and we were led outside.

Annie was staring at the scene with disbelief and disgust. "Holy crap. They've trashed the place."

They had indeed. The centre of the once-beautiful city had been bulldozed through, the smashed remains heaped in a pile to the far side of the clearing. The few spires that remained along one edge were leaning and broken, smeared with mud. Where the city had been were a pair of metal shipping containers side by side. Climbing above them was a staircase leading to a crude platform made of standard scaffolding poles and planks. As they moved us further away from the well-head, I could see that on the platform was a large metal structure, with glistening cables hanging down and feeding in through the roof of one of the containers. The doors were open and inside people were busy working at screens, while in the other were a dozen more sitting in reclined wheelchairs wearing wired headsets. They appeared to be either unconscious or asleep.

I whispered to Annie, "Where is the stone? We need to keep it away from them."

"Tucked in my bra. Bear, some of these guards—when I close my eyes, I can see wolves with men riding them. Are they Erik and his pack?"

"I thought they might be. I recognised Svend. Their disguises have come a long way. I don't think Erik is here. He wouldn't be able to resist gloating. What about the people in the containers?"

She closed her eyes. "They just look like themselves." She looked blindly up at the structure. "There are more people up there somewhere. That's Dom! And someone else, and a … bird?"

An army Land Rover drew up, and someone got out of the passenger side. "Carabon," Annie whispered. She closed her eyes again. "What the …"

She did not have time to tell me what she was seeing. Carabon strode over towards us. He was wearing military fatigues and looked very much in charge. "Annie, I'm disappointed. Collaborating with the forces of darkness, I see. As for you, demon, I find it interesting that you came the long way. What has changed? Or has it been like this for a long time?"

Annie spoke. "So, are you going to tell me what is happening here, Carabon? Why you've committed this vandalism?"

"The works of the enemy are of no aesthetic value. Better swept aside and burned." He turned to the guards. "Take the demon into the woods and destroy it. We will keep the woman, put her in with the volunteers. Does anyone have handcuffs?"

Two guards dragged Annie kicking and shouting away. "Get your stinking mitts off me. Bear!"

Carabon laughed. "Save your strength, Ms Maylor." He climbed back into the Land Rover and was driven off.

The guards surrounded me in a semi-circle and pointed into the trees. Some of them looked troubled. As we walked, I spoke. "Hey, Svend. It is you, isn't it? And is that Leif? I think the limp looks about right."

"Don't answer her."

"Oh, Svend, you gave yourself away there. And here I thought we were allies. Where's Erik? And why are you doing a human's dirty work?" I asked. His ear twitched. "Please, Svend, at least don't let me die in ignorance."

He growled and refused to look at me. As we reached the edge of the trees, he finally had the grace to face me. "I'm truly sorry, Bear. Orders."

As he raised an arm, I flipped my size down to minimum, stretched into serpentine shape, and slithered into the leaves as fast as I could. They weren't prepared, and some started to shoot into the forest floor. I felt a bullet graze my flank, but kept moving. In the noise they were making, any rustling sounds were completely masked. When I'd put a hundred metres' distance between myself and them, I switched up a size and ran back to Lower Pichesham as fast as I could.

When I got there, the village was in chaos. Ferry Cottage was ablaze. I hid behind a wall and tried to see what was happening. The main road was filled with olive-green trucks and frightened villagers were being herded into them by soldiers. My people, nurtured here for decades. I caught sight of the Tankye house. Nadia Tankye was trying to fend off a soldier with a broom, but she was struck on the head with a rifle butt and fell to the floor. They dragged her away towards the truck, followed by a crying neighbour and young Osman, trying to comfort her.

"You're back then." Tansy crawled up beside me. I breathed more easily with relief at seeing her.

"I thought for a moment that …"

"You must be joking. The stench of diesel approaching was enough to warn me something was kicking off. Where is Annie?"

"They took her prisoner. The pack are up at Alderman's Well, they have some sort of device there. Annie said she saw Dominic there as well."

"And Erik?"

"He's definitely involved, but it was Carabon who was in charge. Tansy, I have no idea what they are up to. What the hell are we going to do? You and I can't take on this many."

"I noticed they haven't been up the hill to Old Pichesham. Don't you have a stash up there?"

She was right. "Yes, there are some bits and pieces in the crypts under the church. That was years ago. Erik won't know about it. And the comms equipment will be functional so I can get in touch with Simon and the others. OK, come on, it's worth a try. We can check on Lance as well."

We skirted the village, and I tried not to think about what might be happening to my people. We cut through the stream running under the bridge and left unobserved. As we got to the old village, I knocked on Lance's door. "Lance? Are you in there? It's me, Margot. Don't open the door!"

It was Grant's voice that responded. "Margot, there are a few of us here. I threw a shield and gathered up as many as I could. What is happening? The soldiers took Sergio and all the guests. Mosen tried to get across the river in the ferry. We were watching from the hill." A pause. "They shot him, Margot. I think he's dead."

I cursed under my breath. "Have you called anyone? The police?"

"Nobody can get a signal. It went down just before they arrived."

I couldn't leave them here. Grant could blur perceptions up to a point, but once the pack got a scent, there would be no escape. I had no choice but to get them somewhere with a possibility of defence.

"Grant, there is a safer place near here. When you come out, don't be afraid. I don't look the way you know me at the moment. I'm in disguise. A costume."

The door opened a crack. Grant came out slowly, taking in what he was seeing.

"OK. OK. That's not a costume, is it?"

"Right now, Grant, it doesn't matter. Explanations later. Round up the refugees and bring them to the church. There's an entrance to the crypts just at the base of the rear wall, behind the altar."

He was reluctant. Tansy chipped in. "Grant, you know me. I've scrounged enough of Sergio's leftovers. This is Margot, I promise."

His eyes seemed to bulge and for a moment I thought we'd rushed it too much. But bless him, Grant was a rock, and a firm expression settled over his face.

"I knew there was something odd, but ... OK, later. I'll give you a head start. Tansy can stay. People won't be surprised to see her."

I nodded and ran off on all fours. When I got to the church, I brushed the debris from the dedication stone to James Alderman. Dirt had infiltrated the mechanism, but it opened eventually. I made it inside just as I heard Tansy and Grant approach with the others, so decided to leave the talking to Tansy while I warmed up the old communication panel. I patched in the codes to my and Annie's spot-comms first. "Annie, if it is safe to talk, do so. Otherwise, tap near the communicator."

There was a noise that might have been a sob. *"Bear. There's no one nearby. I thought you were …"*

"Never mind that now. I'm going to call for help. When I get back to you, if you can't speak, use one tap for yes, two for no. Do you have that?"

"Yes. William Carabon … I think he is Erik. I'm not sure. It was confusing."

"I've suspected it for some time. Tell me what you saw."

"In the stone, there were two men and a wolf. One was Carabon, the other I didn't know. But they aren't like you and your people, or even the guards. They were wrapped around each other tightly, struggling. The wolf's teeth were halfway through an arm. I couldn't tell whose. There were fingers wedged into one of Carabon's eye sockets. It was horrible. They are all in so much pain. And the hate was coming off them in waves. I feel sick even thinking about it."

There was no time to consider what it meant. Nothing good. "Annie, if anything happens, press the communicator firmly. Take care." I shut down the link and started to place calls.

In the Crypt

Half an hour later and I was getting frustrated. The ant ship coming from the moon was at least seventy-two hours away from landing. I couldn't broadcast on the general frequencies without alerting Erik, and progress getting through to individuals was too slow. I had gotten to Simon, my contact in the Home Office, but there wasn't anything he could do officially. They had been notified through high-level channels of a military exercise taking place in the hospital grounds. As far as the authorities were concerned, nothing odd was happening. Simon promised to round up as many of our people as he could, but it would take time, and I was sure we didn't have it. And however useful their individual abilities might be to them, they weren't trained as a group. I told him to keep me posted on progress and to hold off on any action until I gave the word.

I went back to the main chamber of the crypts. The little group of people had been warned, but some of them still shrank back in fear. Friends and neighbours. I was used to the reaction, but it still hurt a little. Of the group there, only Lance, Grant and little Hani Al-Mansoob had usable levels of ability. The others were either normal or had sub-measurable activity. Hani's older sister, Noura, was among the latter group, but she was smart as a whip and by far the brightest student in the school. I made my mind up.

"Help is on the way, but we cannot wait. I'm going to take a small group and find out what is happening. Grant, I could use your perception-shielding ability. Tansy will come with us. Does anyone know how to fight or use a gun?"

A man I didn't recognise raised his hand tentatively. "I'm a cop. I'm here on a break from the NYPD, but I don't have a weapon on me."

I looked him in the eye. He stared back stonily. "What's your name?"

"Paul Denver. I came over on the ferry just this morning, looking for a friend of mine. She stopped communicating a couple of days ago. I only got as far as the pub before this all kicked off. Her name is Annie Maylor, and this guy"—he indicated Grant—"told me he hasn't seen her for a while."

A useful asset. "You must be the ex-boyfriend. Annie mentioned you in passing. She said she told you to stay out of things, but I'm glad you are here, Paul, because Annie is in grave danger. I have my old service pistol here. I've never used it, but it should still work. Will you come?"

"Of course. I thought what she told me already was nuts, but this …"

I turned my attention elsewhere. "Lance, please take charge here. You have the most understanding of what is going on. I'm going to show Noura how to operate the communications equipment." She nodded, glad to have a role. "Lance, if things go wrong …" I hesitated. "If things go wrong, you will have to choose. You can try to make a run for it cross-country, or batten down and hold out for help to arrive." There was no point in telling him that neither option was good.

He stared at me. "I'm coming with you. I can help."

"Lance, you are eighty years old. We need to move fast. And with respect, I'm not sure your particular ability is going to be of any use."

"I'm coming anyway. You cannot stop me. Annie is in danger. I owe her. I'll keep up, I promise."

I growled in frustration. I didn't have time for Lance's nonsense. Hani spoke up. "Mrs Trimble, can I help? I've been practising."

I considered it. He was far too young to be doing this, but a boost would at least mean Lance could keep up. Grant wasn't in the first flush of youth either. I nodded. "Thank you, Hani. What do we need to do?"

Hani solemnly gathered everyone in a circle while Noura looked on worriedly. Then he sat in the centre and spoke in a soft chant. There was a brief sense of pressure, and Hani slumped to one side. I checked on his breathing. It was steady and slow. "He will be fine," I said, hoping it was true. I placed him gently on a cot and left Noura fussing over him.

"What on earth was that?" said Paul.

"Hani's special ability is to induce a temporary healing effect. For a few hours you'll feel stronger, and any pain signals will be dulled. Use it well."

He felt his wrist. "Well, I'll be. My tendinitis …"

I gave Noura a basic lesson on the communication panel and equipped the others with small vintage handhelds. Noura picked it up fast, so we left and I continued to talk her through it as we went. Tansy scouted ahead looking for passable routes, and everyone else kept close, within range of Grant's perception shield. We had to circle Alderman's Well in order to stay upwind. Even with Hani's gift, the humans found it hard going. But eventually we made it to a raised point north of the well site with a narrow view.

From here, we could see the damage that had been done to the forest. They had hacked a temporary roadway through using some sort of heavy machinery. A bulldozer was abandoned to one side, while a massive crane trundled away on tank-like tracks, its job apparently completed. The concealment fence was completely demolished and above the ruins of the city was a structure towering from a crude scaffolding platform. The sheer oddity of it was striking. Slick silvery cables coming from below were gathered into a bundle feeding into the base of an enormous shape like an unevenly sized hourglass with an extra twist between two main sections. I'd brought my old army binoculars, and in the lower part, a human body hung suspended. The build was right for Dominic, but the cables were attached to so many parts of his body that it was hard to tell. In the smaller central part, a large black bird perched on a metal rod … preening?

I asked Noura to patch me through to Annie. "Annie, it's me again. Can you talk?"

Weapon

Not long after they'd cuffed me to the container wall, I heard the shots coming from the direction they had taken Bear. I was convinced they had killed her. And then the trucks arrived. Frightened people were separated into small groups and forced into wire mesh cages scattered around the clearing. Here were people I had been living alongside for months. I knew most of their names by now. I started shouting again, and a passing soldier slammed the door of the container shut.

Then Bear called from the crypts and I knew there was some hope. I started to look for options. I was handcuffed to a rigid steel bracket in the container and short of detaching my hand, there was no way I could escape.

Maybe I couldn't move physically, but I had the strange world of the stone. There were six people wearing green jumpsuits in the container, all sleeping. Their counterparts inside the stone were sitting cross-legged, eyes staring upward, unseeing. They were chanting repetitively, out of time with each other. I cautiously drew near to a short woman.

"Out of darkness, there will be light. Man will prevail. Out of darkness, there will be light. Man will prevail."

I tried to talk to her, but there was no acknowledgement. No way was I going to touch her. All of them were chanting the same thing, words repeating and echoing unceasingly.

I drew away. In the distance above me, I could see the faint outline of Dominic, but it was out of reach. The shapes of two other men hung nearby. One was solid, alert, staring ahead intently. The other seemed younger and was somehow projecting a sense of nervousness. Were these sentries outside the container? It seemed reasonable. I approached the nervous one cautiously.

"What's your name?"

The figure turned toward me with a puzzled expression on his face, shook his head a little, and turned back. I tried again.

"Look at me. What are you doing here? You know it's wrong, don't you?"

He spoke. "Shut up. I just have to get through this. Orders are orders. Shut up."

"Look at me."

He turned, the puzzlement deepening. "I'm going mad. I'm seeing ghosts. Jesus, I'm going mad."

He was whimpering now. I looked at the other man. There was no change in his expression. This was all happening inside our heads.

"The woman in the container. Let her out. She can help you. You don't have to be a part of this. Help her."

"Shut up, shut up, shut up. I have no choice." He pressed his hands to his eyes. The other man turned a little, glanced at his companion, uneasy.

I was pushing too hard. I fell back on my old abilities. "Calm down. Tell me why then. Tell me why."

He was still agitated, but some of the tension eased. "Why? I don't know why. They said it was an exercise. But those were real bullets. That man is really dead. But Sarge says 'Carry on, carry on, orders, lads.' Thank God it wasn't my bullet. But it could have been. It could have. And that man in charge, he's not right. He's civvie, not army."

I felt sorry for him, but it wasn't getting me the answers I needed. "What about the people in the machine? The men and the bird. Can you help them?"

He thought he was talking to himself. "And a bird! How can we be taking orders from a fucking bird? I mean, I know they are supposed to be able to talk a bit, but that one, when it bawled Terry out for missing the first time … bastard thing, I'd like to wring its neck."

OK. Whatever the bird's involvement in this was, it was probably safe to assume it was no friend.

The exchange was interrupted. A wolf-rider was approaching. I opened my eyes as the container door opened. It was yet another near clone of the gate guard. He spoke to the sentries inaudibly, and they came in, pulled one of the wheeled chairs outside. I tried to catch the younger sentry's eye, but he was looking elsewhere, so I addressed the guard.

"I need to talk to Carabon. I have information."

He turned to me. "Mr Carabon is busy, Ms Maylor. In any event, I don't think he wants to hear anything you have to say."

"I know what it looks like, but I was just trying to get to Dominic. I'm not on the bear's side, she kidnapped me from the hospital. I was terrified the whole time. If Dominic is with you willingly, well, I'm willing to listen as well. Please, let me try to understand. I might be able to help. Please." I leaned in, pressed gently but firmly on his mind.

I could feel he was wavering. He looked at me appraisingly, while the two sentries wheeled out another of the sleepers. "I will pass on your message if I see him." The door slammed behind him.

I spent a miserable thirty minutes trying and failing to reach other figures in the stone. Then a familiar howl of agony approached and I quickly opened my eyes. The door squealed open, and Carabon stood there, smiling. "Ms Maylor, we meet yet again. May I still call you Annie?"

"Sure, William. You got my message?"

"I did. I would like to be convinced, Annie. Dominic has been anxious about you. His feelings run deep, I think. I am concerned that it may interfere with his performance today."

Despite the circumstances, my heart was lifted a little. Maybe Dom and I still had a chance. "Let me talk to him, William, I won't try to make him leave again." I leaned on him just a little. Bear said Erik couldn't resist gloating. "But explain to me what is going on. I don't understand any of this. You say you are fighting evil, but so far you aren't looking like you are the good guys. Let me hear your side of the story. So far all I have is Margot's—the bear's—side. William, this is a story that needs telling, and I'm the person who can do that."

He mused, "That is a good point, one I had not considered. After it is done, the people will need to know and understand. There is some time now before the process begins." He beckoned more soldiers into the container. "Take the remaining martyrs to their allotted positions. Then leave us."

He waited until they had all gone and then sat on a camp stool at a small distance. "I wonder what she told you. Did she mention she was serving monsters? Disgusting insectoid creatures on another planet. Waiting in their hordes to come here where they will destroy us. Did she tell you that?"

"Not exactly. She told me about the ants. She said they left so there wouldn't be a war."

"The demon and her filthy minions have been scouring this planet for decades, stealing the precious birthright of mankind. Rare minerals, with properties you can only dream of. Leaving us helpless, unable to find our own way in the universe. I saw that happening, Annie. And I saw a way to stop it, under the very nose of the evil ones. For every delivery of material, I have salvaged ten more. Built a team of scientists committed to the cause. Learning, developing the technology. And I have found a way to fight back using their own unholy methods, using something the demon herself discovered, though she was too stupid to realise it. By the end of this day, Annie, I will have neutralised the threat, and the universe will once more be open to mankind."

I was a little impressed in spite of myself. There was a trace of truth in what he said, both in his words and in his thoughts. I had felt dismayed at being treated like a lost cause by the ants. Maybe if it had been someone other than this tortured monster speaking … "William, what you are saying, it makes sense. But what you are doing here, treating those villagers like you are—how can you justify it?"

"Oh, Annie, can you not see? The people in Lower Pichesham are not innocents. They are part of the conspiracy. Mutants, abominations, every one of them. Some of them know, some do not, but they are all dangers to humanity."

"William, there are kids out there. You can't believe this is right."

"Those who cooperate will be treated humanely." I felt a false note here. That was a lie, a straight lie. "As will you,

Annie, if you cooperate. Did you think I don't know about you? You reek of the unholiness yourself. I felt your influence back at the camp. But those who repent can be redeemed. Look at Dominic. Look at the volunteers who were in this very place. They are valued and cherished. You can be part of the future."

He'd called them martyrs just minutes before. I decided not to remind him. "Can I see Dominic? Please?"

He stared at me intently, considering. Finally—"Yes. I think on balance it would be a good idea. But Annie, know this. Dominic may be the best, but he can be replaced. All the volunteers are trained and ready for the task ahead, and can be swapped in. Do not try anything."

It was at that moment that Bear contacted me again. *"Annie, it's me again. Can you talk?"*

I casually tapped a no signal near the spot-comm and hoped Carabon wouldn't notice. "Anything you say, William. I just want to see him, talk to him."

"I can hear everything. I'll leave the channel open. Don't signal again until it is safe."

Carabon called the sentries in, and they released me from the wall of the container. Carabon led us up the stairs to the platform, followed by the older sentry. At first, I struggled to grasp what I was seeing. Dominic hung suspended inside the glass, his limbs splayed out unnaturally, wires inserted into his skin in so many places that I could barely recognise him. His face was uncovered, a visor above apparently ready to be swung into place.

I tried to look happy. "Hey, Dom. William here says you were worried about me."

His face lit up. "Annie! You're OK. I've been so ..."

The glass was muffling his voice, so I spoke louder. "I'm sorry to have frightened you, Dom. It's OK now. Liking the new look, by the way."

"Sorry. Not the most dignified pose. Annie, when this is over, we'll try again?"

"Of course, Dom." I pressed my hands and forehead against the glass, eyes closed. Carabon, satisfied, told the sentry to take me down in ten minutes, and left.

I entered the inner world of the stone. Dominic's equivalent was right there, so I drifted a little nearer and spoke. "Dom, I'm inside your head. Try not to react. They will know, and I'll have to leave."

The figure looked at me, eyes wide. "Annie? This is new." He reached out a hand. I wanted badly to take it, but held back.

"We've both been learning new things. Dom, will you let me talk? Carabon is not what he seems. He isn't normal. I'm not sure I can explain in a way that makes sense, but inside his head … it's not just him in there. He's angry and dangerous."

"Annie, I've made my mind up—"

"Please, Dom, I'm not trying to dissuade you. Carabon spoke to me. Some of what he says is right. I've met them, the ants. I don't think they are a threat the way he does, but they aren't on our side either. And he's hiding things from you."

"He helped me understand myself, Annie. What happened all those years ago. We pieced it together. Some of it was me, some of it wasn't. He thinks I summoned a demon by accident. I know how it sounds, Annie …"

"No, don't worry about that. After everything I've seen, it sounds almost reasonable."

"I'd forgotten. I was carrying a new mineral specimen I'd picked up that same day in a market. Carabon thinks it was a magical talisman, and I activated it. And here's the thing, Annie. Margot must have known. Because after I moved into the village, that piece went missing from my collection. Margot knew and said nothing."

I cursed internally. This sounded like exactly the sort of thing Bear would have done. "OK, Dom. That makes some sense. But maybe Margot believed it was for your own good. She said something of the sort. That she was planning on telling you about your abilities …"

"She had years to do that and left me in the dark. Carabon has given me answers. Annie, I've seen his evidence for myself. Maybe the insectoids aren't quite the devils he says, but we—mankind—need an edge, and this device will provide it."

I was torn. He'd thought it through, and maybe he had a point. "Dom, have you seen what he's done with the village? People you know and care about are out here in cages. They are terrified."

That got to him. His face clouded. "He said it is for their own safety. I didn't know they would be so rough with it."

I pressed my advantage. "Even if Carabon is right, he can do damage. He's killed people, Dom. Ends might justify the means sometimes, but if this is what it takes, are you sure it's the right thing to do? At least tell me what the device does. What your part in it is. I might be able to check it out. It's not too late, Dom."

He relented. "OK. But I don't know how it works, Annie, just that it does. I have to read a script. The words are gibberish, but I read it and concentrate on wanting it really, really hard. That gets focused into the central chamber. See the bird? That's Arthur from the New Star Inn up there. Carabon said the device needed a living brain to accept the script, and a large corvid is apparently optimal for that. Physically big enough, a little cognitive ability. All the other equipment provides the energy needed. And that script will somehow close the gap that allows the enemy back here. The tech is amazing, Annie. After this is over, it is going to change everything."

His enthusiasm was infectious. He always was nerdy about technology, and I felt a genuine smile spread across my face. "Thank you, Dom. I'll be back."

He reached out again. "Don't go yet."

"Dom, we can't touch." But I wanted to, so much. I let his hand come nearer and as his index finger brushed my arm, a surge of excitement and joy flared through my whole being. Dom's face went into a spasm of ecstasy. I forced myself away from him before my resistance was gone.

"Annie …"

"Later, Dom. We can experiment later." I opened my eyes and stood up, back on the platform. The grin on his physical face was identical to the one I'd just left. I waved, and the sentry led me away.

🐾 🐾 🐾

I'd assumed I'd be put back in the container, but he took me to one of the cages, already partly filled. "In here." He locked the door, and, before he left, connected a cable to the cage. He held up a hand and called to another soldier. "Cage One is reset and ready."

I nodded to the people I recognised. Nadia Tankye was there, a nasty wound on her head. She was trying to comfort an elderly lady. "Annie. They got you as well, then. Have you seen Mosen? Do you know what is happening?"

"I'm sorry, Nadia, I don't. Listen, can you cover me? I've got a communicator. Margot is trying to get help. They mustn't see me talking."

I stood in the far corner while the others shielded me from the guard. "Margot?" I whispered.

"Did I hear Nadia Tankye?"

"Yes, I'm in a cage. She is here with about ten others."

"Annie, her husband is dead. He was trying to cross the river." My stomach clenched. *"Tell her if you think you must."*

I pushed it back. "OK, will do."

"You should also know that I have Detective Paul Denver here with me. He says he is sorry for ignoring you, and to say hi."

I didn't know whether to laugh or cry. "I told him to back off. He shouldn't have come. I've done enough damage to him."

"He can hear you clearly, Annie, now is not the time for introspection. We are nearby. We watched you coming down from the device and being put in the cage. What happened? Everything went quiet for a while. Did you see Dominic?"

"When I got up there, I went to … the other place. I spoke to Dom there."

"Impressive. Did you find out anything useful?"

"He's angry with you. He said you know what happened to him and kept it back. Something about a talisman that you stole, and that he summoned a demon. Is it true?"

There was a pause. *"I told you, there are no demons. But it seems likely something of that sort happened. None of the bound folk I know were involved, which is why it remains a mystery. The stone that was removed was certainly an item of concern. I had to avoid anything similar happening.*"

"OK. Well, it almost doesn't matter, because he's tight with Carabon now." I told her everything Dom had said about the device. "It made no sense to me, but then nothing has made sense for a long time now. Oh, this might help. Before you got back to me, Carabon said something about you having discovered it. That you were too stupid to know it."

"I've never put people in a giant bottle. What is he talking about?"

"That's all I've got. Can you get us out of here?"

She didn't reply for a moment, and then there was a stream of words foreign to me, but that could only have been profanity.

"What? What is it?"

"Annie, did you finish the book?"

"No, I didn't have a chance."

"It's a weapon, Annie. I think he's made Dominic into a weapon." More curse words. *"If it is what I believe, it needs bodies. Dead people, Annie. Lots of them."*

My gaze was drawn to the cable leading from the cage, and it suddenly looked a lot more sinister.

Ten Minutes

As if my words to Annie had triggered a response, a sudden deep noise echoed across the clearing, like a giant electrical switch being flipped. Purple light flickered in the lower chamber of the device, and through the binoculars I saw a visor swing down over Dominic's face. A short siren burst sounded, and a voice rang out over loudspeakers.

"TEN MINUTES, TEN MINUTES. FINAL PREPARATIONS."

A voice to my left. "Fifty-five men, I'd say. Maybe a few more in those containers." It was Paul.

"That one is empty now." I pointed. "I've seen at least three come in and out of the other, but they look like technicians to me. There were six people strapped in wheelchairs that … Oh, wait, here they are."

The wheelchairs were lugged around the corner of the containers by pairs of soldiers and set at the base of the platform. Cables leading from the device were attached to sockets in the chairs. The sleepers remained oblivious, even as the siren sounded again.

"ALL PERSONNEL, STAND CLEAR. ALL PERSONNEL, STAND CLEAR."

The troops rapidly moved away from the cages and took up positions around the perimeter.

Paul again. "So, what is the plan?"

He seemed to know what he was doing. "I'm nearly certain that they are going to kill the people in the cages. All of them. Electricity maybe, I don't know." I could sense everyone else listening intently. I pointed out Carabon, who was climbing a staircase leading up to the top of the device. "He is the leader, and he is far more dangerous than he looks. Also, the people in the olive non-standard uniforms—they are not human, and they can rip your throat out in the blink of an eye. The others must be regular army or similar. To what extent they understand what is happening …"

Annie spoke up. *"I was trying to get through to one. He's very unhappy. I don't think they know."*

More innocents, at least partly. "Any chance you can turn him, Annie? Any of the others?"

"I'll try again, but they have to be physically nearer."

I turned to Paul. "OK, you're the expert. What do we do?"

He looked at the scene appraisingly. "Any backup on the way?"

"Simon is coming with a carload, and he said others are converging. They have some useful skills, but they are mostly charity workers, not fighters. Maybe twenty people in all. The only help with real power is still seventy hours away."

Paul pointed to the abandoned bulldozer at the edge of the clearing. "If we can get to that, it will give us cover, at least for a while. We can't take on this many, but we might be able to distract them until your backup arrives. I've got plenty of rounds here. Maybe we can pick up another weapon or two."

The siren sounded again. There was no announcement this time, just a crackling noise coming from one of the wheeled chairs. The woman strapped in the chair was juddering, thin black smoke rising. She stopped moving and, as we watched, the purple light intensified and leaked up into the central chamber.

"What happened?" said Annie over the spot-comm.

I was still a little shocked. "It's started, Annie. We don't have much time."

Paul took charge. "Grant and I can get to the bulldozer under this shield of his. You said you can move unseen. Get to the container and shut that thing down now."

Tansy said, "I'm with you, Bear. Come on."

Decision made, I shrank to Tansy's size, and we started down the slope hidden by the undergrowth. "Lance, can you hear me? Stay back. Simon and the others will need to know what is going on. Be our eyes."

"I heard. I'll be fine, don't worry about me."

We made it to within twenty feet of the perimeter undetected and waited. The noise of gunfire came from the bulldozer, and the soldiers nearby turned to look. The man in charge shouted, "You two stay here. The rest of you with me."

We waited a moment until they were further away. The militiamen were edgy, looking out into the forest, straight past where we were hiding. Without warning Tansy launched herself at the one on the left, and, as he raised his rifle towards her in surprise, grabbed the barrel in her teeth. She twisted mid-air and her momentum dragged the weapon from the guard's arms. While the other soldier gawped at this spectacle, I grew to full size from beneath his feet, punched him in the face, and knocked him senseless. When I turned around, I was in time to see Tansy land front feet first, spring backward and ram her opponent in the chest hard, knocking him to the floor, her front paws wrapped around his throat, squeezing hard. He succumbed to unconsciousness.

"Tansy, that's enough."

She released him, and I checked his breathing. Ragged, but still going.

We had been seen, and soldiers were coming toward us. I shrank again, and we darted zigzag towards the containers, bullets flying around us. To one side, I saw another of the sleepers start to shake. He woke up briefly and started screaming. Mercifully, it was not for long.

"Bear!"

"Busy, Annie."

"There's a gap between the containers."

We made for the gap, too small for a human. The containers were sitting on concrete supports and we scrambled underneath. Soldiers started trying to shoot underneath the edges, but were shouted away by the technicians. We heard the door of the container above slam.

Crackle. Fizz. Crackle. The smell of burnt flesh that was already around us got stronger. Another one dead. "Bear? What now?" Tansy said.

I felt above my head for the floor of the container. It was wood, probably marine ply, as tough as wood gets. There was a damp patch that seemed slightly rotten, so, squaring myself under it, I started to grow. The wood was strong and resisted. I thought at one point my shoulder bone would give, but the ply gave way and I burst through, showering the interior with splinters. There was shouting and panic. I was between the three technicians and the door. They cowered against the panels, and I roared at them.

Tansy scrambled up behind me and shouted at them. "Turn it off. Turn off the machine now or I'll let the beast get you. This is your only warning."

One of them had the temerity to attack me with a stool. I swiped him aside with some force. He hit the wall and crumpled to the floor. "Shut it down!"

A thin woman with round glasses laughed hysterically. "Do what you will. This only provided the ignition. The reaction is self-sustaining as long as the feed is maintained. You're too late. Spawn of the Devil, you are too late." She got to her feet and tried to stab me with a pen. Tansy sank her teeth into her arm before I could stop her, and the woman sank to the floor, cradling the wound and sobbing.

Cage

Alderman's Well, October 2018   *Annie*

I watched in terror from the cage as soldiers tried to prise open the container doors. On the spot-comm Bear was talking. *"Annie, did you hear that? We cannot stop it from here. We have to get to the platform."*

"There are too many, Bear. They have a handful left by the bulldozer, keeping Grant and Paul pinned down. The rest are making their way towards you now."

Grant's voice came over the communicator. *"Not for long."* We heard the engine of the bulldozer start up. No one appeared to be in the cab, but it started moving, lurched once or twice, then put on a surprising turn of speed. The blade lowered to the ground and as the mighty vehicle hurtled towards us, it snagged the cables leading to the cages. People inside the cages screamed as they were jolted and dragged along until the cables were sheared through. The windows of the bulldozer smashed under bullet fire, but it kept on moving. There was a yell of pain over the communicator, and the interior of the cabin flickered. I could now see Grant, slumped over the steering wheel.

Paul's voice. *"Grant's down! Grant's down!"*

"Annie, what's happening?"

"They started the bulldozer. They've broken the cables to most of the cages. I can see Grant. He's hurt. I think Paul is in the cab still," I replied.

The vehicle swerved directly towards the cage we were in. What had been a heroic dash was briefly a danger to the people in its path, but it slowed gradually, and as it ran into the side of the cage, it pushed it askew and then stopped. Our cable was left intact. Soldiers scrambled to get inside the vehicle and forced Paul out at gunpoint. One of the wolf-riders unlocked our cage and thrust him inside, then relocked it. Grant was left in the bulldozer. He wasn't moving.

Paul shook his head sadly. "Sorry, Annie. I tried."

"I wish you hadn't come, Paul, but I'm still glad to see a friendly face." We hugged awkwardly.

The wolf-rider issued orders to the militiamen around. "All of you here, get those cables reconnected. Hurry, you don't want to be touching one in a few minutes." He rushed off back toward the containers, where they were still trying to force the doors open. As he went, the burst of electrical crackling was heard once more, and another sleeper shuddered into death. More than one soldier watched it silently. I recognised my sentry from earlier among them.

"Please listen to me. You, you're Andy, right? Andy Piddock?"

He stared at me. "How do you know that?"

"I was talking to you earlier. Inside your head. I saw it there."

His face hardened. "Witches. I thought that was bull."

"Maybe I am a witch, Andy. I don't know, I didn't think I was a few days ago. But I know for goddamn sure that most of these people aren't. They are just people."

He turned away. I shouted after him. "Andy, please listen. You know what's happening, right? Those poor creatures over there being electrocuted, that's us next. All of us." He slowed but did not look back. "Andy, think of your kid. There are kids here."

He swerved and marched back, pointing his gun straight at me. "How do you know …"

"Andy, listen. You're not a murderer, I felt it. But when this ends, you will be one. Is that what you signed up for?"

He was shaking. I saw his friends were watching. He spoke without turning his head. "Sarge. Tell me what to do. I don't want to be a murderer."

A short man with a thin moustache and a couple of stripes on his shoulder reacted. He looked a little pale. Before he could answer, the last of the sleepers went up in smoke. As the body slumped, its hair caught fire. There was now an audible high-pitched sound coming from the device, and the scaffolding was rattling.

He jumped into action and snarled, "Get the cages open. Hurry!"

The wolf-rider had taken the key, but they found a metal bar and broke the lock. By the time the people near the container noticed what was going on, Nadia and the others were escaping into the forest. Paul joined me behind the bulldozer, soldiers hunkered down to either side. Over at the container, the wolf-riders were firing toward us. The regular militiamen with them looked on in confusion, no longer sure what they were doing, and took cover. Andy and two others were wrestling with the next cage. They finally sprang the lock, and no sooner had the prisoners escaped than sparks erupted from the mesh walls. The sergeant was speaking rapidly on a radio to someone. "… confirm, they intend to execute the prisoners. Just saw it with my own eyes, sir, it was a close thing."

I called over to him. "Sergeant, I need to get up to the platform. Whatever that thing does, it can't be stopped from down here. I might be able to."

He looked quickly above the cover. "No way, miss, they have full control. There are men up there, no one is getting near it."

"Then we need to get these cages emptied. The ones that are still connected up. The people, they are fuel for the machine. Do you understand?"

"Not in the least, miss."

Andy and the two others scuttled back to cover. "We can't get to the next one, Sarge. And we need to move from here somehow, because if this cage gets juiced, it will get to us through the metal of the dozer."

I tapped the spot–comm. "Bear, are you hearing this?"

"Yes, Annie. Tansy and I can get out through the floor, but I don't know what to do from there. Are the villagers safe?"

"Some have escaped. There are ten, maybe eleven cages where the cables are broken. The others we can't get to, we're too exposed. Sergeant?"

"It's your people inside that container? And you can talk to them?" the sergeant asked.

"Noura here. Simon is at the hospital, he is on the way. Fifteen minutes to where you are."

"Thanks, Noura. Yes, Sergeant, we have two inside that container. There is some help on the way, although I don't know what they can do. What about your colleagues over there?"

"Miss, we're all here voluntarily. All I know is that I didn't sign up for mass killings, and I don't believe anyone else did. The captain is holding fast, and I ain't shooting at anyone.

You are still the enemy, as far as I know. And if you try any of that head stuff on me, I won't be answerable."

"You're an honest man, Sergeant. All I can tell you is that these people don't deserve this. They are some of the best I've ever known."

He leant back and breathed with his eyes closed. I think he might have been praying. After a pause, he spoke. "Wherefore by their fruits ye shall know them ..." Another pause. "I'll talk to the captain. We won't interfere, and if you can clear some cover, I'll get these cages empty. But those people on the platform, they are our comrades as well."

Actually, even from here, I could tell that the people guarding the device were all wolf-riders. I sensed I had pushed him far enough. "Sergeant, we aren't killers. Are we, Bear?"

There was a low rumble. Fortunately, the sergeant couldn't hear it. "She says fine. We'll try to avoid bloodshed."

"*You are very free with promises, Annie. But as long as the human soldiers stay out of it, we stand a chance. Agreed.*"

On the Platform

Tansy was standing on a chair, looking at the screens. "Come on! We don't have time for this. If I'm right, we have about six minutes until the next cage goes up."

We had already tied up the technicians with wires stripped from equipment, so we slipped out through the hole in the floor. The walls of the container slowed us briefly, but there were enough paw-holds that I could climb with Tansy straddling my shoulders.

Once on the roof, we were in reach of the understructure of the scaffolding. The whole thing was shuddering above us, rattling and humming noises filling the space with thunderous echoes. I gripped the scaffolding poles and dragged myself up towards the edge. Tansy leapt from my shoulders onto the platform.

There was a shout and a shot was fired. I heard heavy boots thudding after her and pulled myself up as fast as I could. Growing to my maximum size, I ran after them, past the glowing glass containing Dominic. The one I thought I'd recognised as Leif was struggling with Tansy, who had her teeth clenched around the barrel of his rifle. I left them to it and ran straight at two others, roaring as loud as I could. Before they could react, I ran into them, pushing them over the edge.

Tansy had relieved Leif of his gun and was holding him at bay, hackles raised. He was changing, the uniform collapsing as he reverted to his natural form. I waved urgently toward Annie, and people darted away from the bulldozer towards the cages. And in the distance behind them, there was movement. It was the huge tracked crane from earlier, crawling back. "Noura, is that Simon and the others with the crane?"

"Yes, Mrs Trimble."

Help was coming, but our troubles were not over. At the base of the stairs, I saw Svend. He smiled at me and aimed his rifle. I dropped below the edge just as a bullet ripped the air above my head. I could hear footsteps on the rickety staircase. By now the vibration of the platform was so violent that it was seriously interfering with my balance, and I staggered as I ran towards the stairs, thinking I would dislodge the connectors. Another bullet came flying, and as it hit the glass, a shard chipped away, leaving a small damaged area where it had crazed. Without thinking, I grabbed a loose pole and hit the chipped glass as hard as I could with it. Nothing happened except a bone-rattling jar running through my arms. On the second try, small cracks radiated. As pounding footsteps climbed the staircase, I lifted the pole like a spear and thrust it with all my might at the crack. There was a splintering noise. I ran, followed by the sound of a shattering crash behind me.

Instinctively, I leapt over the edge, and as I fell, everything went into slow motion. Tumbling through space, I saw Tansy and Leif falling, her jaws locked around Leif's neck, their limbs struggling for something to grip. The scaffolding collapsed behind me, planks, twisted poles and silvery cables dancing through a dusty cloud of glass that was lit up by a beautiful golden light coming from the setting sun. An elegant ballet of destruction falling onto the heads of the people below, all running an inch at a time away, doomed to failure as the whole edifice collapsed upon them.

I landed a distance away, the breath forced from my lungs in a slow whoosh. As the debris landed and settled, time returned to normal. I looked up. My hearing wasn't working properly, but I could see people in the cages cheering. Shaken-looking militiamen slowly recovered their wits and started to move towards them, opening the doors. I hobbled over to where I thought Tansy must be. Leif had taken the brunt of the fall, landing badly. He wasn't moving. Tansy was lying across his wolfish body, one rear leg at an angle that looked bad. She was unconscious, but still breathing, and I picked her up carefully.

It was done. There were still confused armed men around, but the danger was over. The crane was entering the clearing, and I waved toward it, recognising Simon and some of the other people in the cab. But Simon looked unhappy. He was pointing at something behind me with urgent gestures.

I turned to look. The towering glass device had gone, but its shape still filled the space it had occupied, an outline of purple light growing in intensity. Dominic still hung there, broken wires dangling, and the raven was in its own segment above, wings outstretched. Above them both was another human body. I could just make out the features of William Carabon. And as my hearing returned, I could hear the humming restart.

"I WILL NOT BE DENIED. MY WILL BE DONE." The voice was Erik's, and it boomed across the clearing. The bird convulsed and expanded massively in size, wings spread in a spasm of pain, blocking the sky. As I watched, a black line shot from its thorax straight down into the debris. Svend was there, trying to get to his feet, and the line penetrated his back. He jerked in agony and the line lifted him into the air, pulling him towards the glow. Two more lines shot out, curving snares sent in different directions. Another of the pack was reeled in, squirming, followed by one of the soldiers sheltering nearby. Shots started from that area, but more and more snares emerged, twisting through whatever cover they had tried to find and dragging them back. As each body approached the raven, they stopped moving, and the purple glow got stronger. I was running now, but all around me I could hear screams from my villagers as they were plucked from the ground. And then there was an intense pain in my back.

Shortly after, everything went dark.

The Wish

Alderman's Well, October 2018   *Annie*

We'd thought for a few moments it was over. When the screaming started, Paul grabbed me by the hand and we ran towards the crane, scrambling up into the cab, helped up by a man in a suit I took to be Simon. We watched helplessly as the monstrous object scooped up scores of people. When we saw Bear lifted, there was a shared groan.

"We have to get out of here, pronto. Get proper help," Paul said. "This cabin won't hold against whatever that thing is."

I was having none of it. "Nope. We are not running. She knew what that thing is—a weapon that needs dead people. It's got those in spades now. I don't know what it is supposed to do, but this is just the start. We have to stop it."

He looked aghast. "We have nothing that can fight that! You there, driving. Turn this thing back at top speed."

Simon rested a hand on the driver's shoulder and shook his head. "This young lady is correct. Even if all we can do is slow it until the authorities find out what is happening. Our friend and guide may be dead, but we are still here." He turned to me. "Do you have any suggestions?"

"Yes. I can talk to them, at least I can talk to Dominic. He's the one at the bottom with all the wires. I'm certain he didn't know this was going to happen. I just need to get closer, like about six feet away. Maybe he can stop it."

The snares were expanding their radius and would soon be within reach of the crane. Simon acted promptly. He detailed three of his team to gather up survivors and take them to safety. They ran off to an uncertain future, and we were about to make our move when someone shouted, "Wait!" It was Lance. "Let me on board, Simon."

Puffing with effort, Lance climbed up into the cab. "I was listening in. I can help. You can start driving now." The crane lurched a little and started moving towards the device. Lance turned to me and held my hand. "Annie, get out there onto the crane. You need to be high enough to reach Dominic. Let us worry about getting you there."

"Lance, I can't do that!"

"You can, Annie, and you will." He closed his eyes. "I wish I'd known about this place before. How strong it is here. Everything seems so clear …" His hand was warm, then hot, and as the heat penetrated, I felt a warm glow of … hope? Support? No. It was love. I don't know how Lance was doing it, but I could feel waves of love pouring into me, first from the people in the cabin, then from everyone around, even while they were still trying to escape.

"Go to him, Annie. We will hold them back somehow."

I swung out of that cabin like some sort of action hero. Adrenaline must have been carrying me. I don't know how I managed to get to the tower of the crane, but as I was swinging precariously around, I clung to the latticework, lightheaded with the feeling. I watched as the black snares hurtling towards me faltered and fell short even as they continued to reach beyond for new victims. With a grinding sound, the crane angled upward, and I rose into the air. We were close now, the bodies so thickly clustered above me that I couldn't see either the raven or Carabon above them. Then we were near enough and I breathed in deeply and hoped to God I wouldn't be caught on one of those snare lines. At least I wouldn't see it coming.

I closed my eyes tightly and entered the interior world of the stone.

🐾 🐾 🐾

There was Dom, as before. He looked strained, muttering incomprehensible words in a staccato rhythm.

"… fuoto gearn unreo …"

"Hey, Dom," I said gently, "I'm back."

He looked up in my direction, exhausted, but the words kept on coming.

"… pyfsi nutch …"

"Dom, stop. You need to stop. Do you know what is happening?"

He nodded weakly, pointed his face upwards, and carried on speaking.

I turned my blind gaze in the same direction. Above us was a nearly incomprehensible sight—a huge open network of human body parts and feathers seamlessly bound in a loose ball. Spinning gently, limbs stretching and flexing, faces open-mouthed. Not in pain, but blankly blissful. I felt my real stomach lurch as Grant's head and upper torso came into view as the thing rotated. Lungs floated behind him, trailing like balloons. He looked at me and I forced the nausea down as he waved.

"Hello, Annie." He sounded as cheerful as the day I'd met him.

"Grant. Dear God, what have they done to you?"

"It's not so bad, Annie. We see everything now. And we have our purpose." He frowned. "Though we wish it were other."

"What is your purpose, Grant?"

From behind me came another voice. "Perhaps I will explain, Annie. You did offer to record my story." The tortured trio of bodies that made up the inner Carabon drifted into view. It was swollen, red, with shards of light spilling out from cracks between the twisted limbs. "I see you have acquired something that does not belong to you. How, I wonder? The Soul Stone was unfindable."

I ignored the question. "Hello again, William. Or is it Erik?"

Three mouths spoke in unison. "Ah, where does one end and another begin? But you are correct, I prefer my original name, and that is the name they will know me by. The name my grateful subjects will chant in my honour. Erik the First. Erik the Last. Erik the Saviour."

Bear was right. He really did like to gloat. "So, my question again, Erik. What is your purpose? And how do I stop you?"

A three-part laugh in distinct tones. The word 'sinister' didn't do it justice. "For reasons I cannot fathom, I like you, Annie. I want to please you. It feels unnatural. Is that Mr Brannigan's work? A useful expansion of his talent that I will be sure to adopt once I have the power that is coming to me." Various hands gestured towards the fleshy network above. "Meet my father, Annie. His name is Francis, and his sacrifice will be the saving of humanity. Between us, we have made a network of minds connected in uncountable ways, capable of solving impossible problems. The bear was once made into something like this by one of her masters. So trusting of her to have told people. It never seemed to occur to her that someone could replicate the process. Would you like to know the beauty of it? I don't even have to know how it will achieve what I want. All it has to do is to act on the wishes of its master."

"I get it. Dominic is the master of this—what, a super-mind? And you are the master of Dominic."

"Poor Dr Hunt. So vulnerable to manipulation. Drugs, hypnosis, a little judicious torture. I can make a man my slave in very traditional ways."

I held my temper. "And I guess the point of all this is what you said. Close the gap. Make it impossible for the ants to get to us."

Erik laughed again. "Such a small ambition. It is much, much more than that. I have instructed my creation to give me supremacy over everything. This world, the new worlds of the insects. Any others that I choose. Under my guidance and leadership, righteous men will prosper. I will eliminate the deviants, along with the weak and useless. Man will once again be supreme over all creation, for now and evermore."

He was mad. But within the ball of flesh and feathers, I could see some of the heads looking towards him, nodding, apparently in agreement. I turned once more to Dominic, pleading with him to stop, but he was unreachable. Then above me, I heard my name, whispered in a repeating echo.

"Annie." As the sphere continued its gentle rotation, I saw the familiar faces of Bear's companions, clustered together, holding tight. A protective grid of hairy limbs surrounded them, attached to the super-mind by a single thick furry thread. Claws ripped at the feathery strands that threatened to engulf them. Their voices merged into that of Bear. "Hurry, Annie. I am fighting it, but I haven't got much strength left. Go to Dominic. Help him. *Be* him."

I understood at once what she wanted. A combination of nausea and excitement swept over me. "You said there's no way back."

"You will be someone new. Your body may even die. I don't know, Annie, but this isn't just about Dominic anymore. You can't let Erik do this."

I looked back at Dominic, torn. He was suffering so much. For a few moments, I thought about my dreams and ambitions—the books I would never write, the things achieved and still to be achieved. They withered and dissipated, illusions that never mattered in the first place.

I reached out my hand and took Dominic's. A thrill ran through me, and he jerked alert, looking straight into me. Behind me I heard an inhuman howl, and, risking a glance back, saw the hideous thing that was Erik trying to get closer, waving its limbs as if it could somehow swim to us.

"OK, Annie, time to wake up Sleeping Beauty." I rested my other hand against his cheek and leaned towards his face.

As our lips met, a thrill surged and raced across me. I sank through the kiss into Dominic, our faces melding together, followed by our torsos, and then everything. Our bodies joined, merged, nerves curling around each other, his arteries threading through mine, bone jostling against bone in exquisite pleasure, until it seemed like every strand of our DNA was united in bliss.

As the glorious sensation of joining faded, we looked around. Hanging above us, the spectacle of Erik and his unwilling partners was screeching in a furious cacophony of voices. We risked a look through Annie's real eyes. The physical body of Carabon was clawing its way down through the press of bodies and cables, his body contorted into unnatural angles, teeth bared. We'd broken his mental hold, but he could still physically attack Annie's body. Then our view was blocked by Bear, hauling herself along her snare line towards us. "Get on with it, Annie!" she shouted, as she turned to face Carabon, claws at the ready.

We closed our eyes again. Above us, the super-mind spun gently, poised, waiting. What to do? Bear had drifted out of view. Our combined viewpoints jostled gently, almost teasingly. Annie's understanding of the people involved filled in the gaps in Dominic's knowledge. Dominic's reading of the evidence provided in his training showed the genuine peril humanity found itself in. Freed from Erik's influence, we were no longer bound by his perverse desires. Here was a chance to change things. But what to do?

And then, in a flash, the answer became obvious. We raised our voices and called out our request, loudly and firmly.

The Testimony of Svend

Greyside, March 2019   *Annie*

I approached the interview with Svend with some trepidation. It meant travelling into Greyside, for a start, and he was reportedly still nursing a grudge. But of all the pack, he had been closest to Erik and was the only person who could give anything like a full account of his activities.

So, escorted by Tansy, I navigated the tunnel again, and made my way through the barren landscape of Greyside to the hollow where the wolves had made their home.

"I'm kind of amazed you can manage the tunnel hobbling along on three legs. Any idea how long it will take the broken one to heal?"

"It will be years in Greyside time. The ants offered to supplement it with robotic elements, but that's all a bit too experimental. I'm managing for now, I'm very adaptable."

"Obviously."

It had been a bright point in the aftermath when we unearthed Tansy alive from the wreckage. As well as Mosen and Grant, we'd lost twelve more of the villagers. Many others had been left with injuries, some of them life-changing. Lower Pichesham was a sombre place at times now, but it was uplifting to see the way the people were pulling together. Work was nearly complete on a new memorial space, an elegant glass and steel construction built inside the shell of St Joseph's, and the newly appointed village committee were busy planning a restoration of Ferry Cottage.

"How are the new people settling in?" Tansy asked.

"There was a bit of backlash to the idea from some of the villagers, but it's settled now. It was rather inspired to suggest offering somewhere for the families of the soldiers to escape any press attention."

"It wasn't my idea originally. It was something the Thing-under-the-Water indicated."

"Well, it has my approval. Andy's wife and daughter are in Dom's old house, and we're finding space for others where we can. Simon is pushing the MOD for approval to reopen the old prison camp. We'll get Andy and the others there when they are sentenced. Keep it in the family."

There had been far more casualties among the militia. Andy had been among the lucky ones who had been caught through a non-vital organ. The honest sergeant had been less fortunate, and I'll admit I shed a tear when we found him. It was his decision that had turned the tide.

We reached the hollow and were greeted by a sullen-looking wolf, who led us inside a large hut. It was pleasant enough inside, warm and clean, even if the air was a little funky with the smell of animals. A wolf who I took to be Svend was strapped into a harness that partly supported his body. Another in semi-human form was passing him food.

"How is the injury, Svend?" I enquired politely. "Any recovery yet?"

He just glared at me. The other wolf spoke. "The ants say it is unlikely. There is still hope long-term with mechanical support, but the spinal damage is profound."

I looked at her. "You are Frida, right?"

"I no longer go by that name." She turned to Svend. "You are to tell them everything. You may not care anymore, but the rest of us want a future."

"I said I would. Stop pestering me."

I settled onto a nearby cushion, got out my notebook, and checked that the communicator was recording the session. "So, Svend. Is it OK to call you that still?"

"Call me what you like. Just get on with it."

Hoo boy, this was going to be fun. "Very well. I need you to explain the course of events that led to the battle at Alderman's Well. Be as clear as you can, because I, for one, am still confused. Bear was convinced that Erik was an ally right up to just days before. What led to Erik's betraying her?"

"There was never a betrayal. After the ants arrived in Greyside, Erik understood where the power lay. He played along, watching for opportunities. He was always on the side of mankind. True mankind, not freaks like you. And certainly not the disgusting insects or their sycophant allies, begging for their leftovers. Animals."

I knew this was a delicate point, but I needed an answer. "You are wolves, not human." He growled. "I mean, you are biologically, at least. I still don't get it."

"Erik was our leader. We all swore the blood oath. Someone like you will never understand what that means. He held us together when all was lost and swore revenge." He stared at me. The anger he felt was real, but diluted with a sense of bone-deep tiredness.

"Revenge? On who?"

"Revenge on the perverted excuse for a human who made us like this, of course. And we had that, after a fashion. But what Erik wanted was our true bodies returned to us. He never forgave and never forgot."

The female gave an impatient sigh. I sensed she did not share Svend's worldview.

I took a breath. "He'd been planning this for a long time?"

"Decades. Not all the details at first. Erik made sure that he and I were in the team that helped infiltrate the US space program in 1949. We were part of the security detail, and that's when we first became aware of Frank Carabon. He had the whiff of otherness that you all share. It was obvious he could see through Bear's disguise, even if he didn't understand what he was sensing. We kept that to ourselves. Erik found it amusing to see what would happen.

"In the end, Frank was never a serious danger to Bear's plan. The ants added their extra booster rocket on top of the human-built one. No other humans had any suspicions, and it worked perfectly. They made it into orbit, and from there never looked back. They finally left the planet in 1974 and we were glad to see the back of them. It made things much easier for us without their constant presence."

"Easier how?"

"Easier to divert the materials we gathered from the field. We stored them in the tunnel at Alderman's Well, in hidden spaces far away from the paths that others knew. The natural background readings kept it all concealed from the sensors."

"But why …?"

He snorted impatiently. "At the beginning, it was just to preserve them for mankind. I should have thought that obvious. The ants had decided we were worthless, not to be trusted with their secret knowledge. Of course we were going to keep some back. That changed after what happened with Frank Carabon."

"Back up here. I'm getting lost. How on earth does Frank Carabon fit in with this? I thought it was William."

The female interjected. "That part is why I am here. Erik had me placed as an information gathering agent inside Scotland Yard. My cover name there was Lucien Trice."

"Wait a moment." I quickly flicked through my notes. "Got it. Frank's statement to the police in 1963? Lucien Trice was mentioned in the notes that Erik gave me."

"Yes. I passed the information onto Erik as usual. I don't know why he took it further. The standard response to anyone who threatened to reveal our activities was a quiet disposal."

Svend chipped in, "Erik sensed something in Frank when we met him the first time at White Sands. He may have disliked him on principle because of his latent abilities, but Frank still impressed him."

The female continued. "Erik had me bring him in for questioning. It was odd. They genuinely bonded over faith. Frank was a devout Bible reader, while Erik still observed the old religion, the only one of us left who still did. Not that it helped Frank in the long run. Erik played on his fear of demonic forces and persuaded him to volunteer for something we'd never tried before. We made our own djinn. Frank knew what it meant, but he had already given up on life. He performed the ceremony himself, and at the crucial moment was killed and embodied into a raven. That raven became our spy in Lower Pichesham, able to pass between worlds and report on what was going on."

"So the raven at the end … Arthur … was Frank. He really was Carabon's father. Sort of."

She nodded. "Frank's only condition was that we take care of his family. We honoured that promise, and when the son came of age, he was encouraged to join the police. William took after his father in many ways, and he was easy to manipulate. I think the modern expression is 'useful idiot'.

We encouraged him in the shaping of Phoenix International, the public face of a secret league of the faithful. It was he who found scientists who shared his beliefs. Guided by the hints that Erik gave, they came up with the technology that you saw being deployed."

Svend took over the story again. "William may have been blinkered, but he wasn't a bad detective. There was a point when we realised he knew more about us than he was letting on, that we had the unnatural bodies we did. It is difficult to maintain human form, and the disguise slips sometimes. He needed to be disposed of. Erik made a massive error of judgement. I pleaded with him …"

"What? What did he do?"

"He said that we needed to keep Frank cooperative. So rather than simply kill William, Erik went ahead with an experiment. We asked William to retrieve the Soul Stone from its hiding place in Ireland. With everything we knew, Erik had convinced himself he could use it to displace William from his body and place his own human spirit within it. He would at last have true human form again."

The female interrupted. "It sounds insane even now. For all the difficulties, we all had good lives. Erik destroyed his wolf body for what was an untested idea."

Svend looked glumly downward. "On that, at least, we agree. Anyway, William didn't suspect a thing until it was too late. And the procedure seemed to work. William was gone, and Erik lived on within William's body. He just took over and Phoenix International continued as if nothing had happened. But the Erik living inside William's body was changed. He became erratic, reckless. He started ranting about religious matters. The people in the organisation saw only their own fanaticism reflected, but we were worried."

I knew this bit. "He was at war with himself. All three of him."

Svend looked uncomfortable with this line of discussion. "I do not pretend to understand. But he was not the same. Still, the work continued. By now, the weapon was under construction. We gathered up people who might be suitable pilots for it. Humans riddled with the stench of ability, taken from the war zones we operated in. Tainted volunteers, Erik called them. The strongest was to be the pilot, and spares were to be used as primers for the weapon. None were particularly promising, but there was time to keep looking." He coughed a little. "I need water."

The female raised a shallow bowl to his mouth. I needed the break. Svend's contempt was grating on me. But there were none of the signs of concealment I had come to recognise. If anything, he seemed to be enjoying the chance to tell his story.

I kept my face neutral. "OK, Svend, I think I understand all that. Move on. Dominic wasn't one of those volunteers, so how did that happen?"

"I terminated a man in Birmingham. It was a routine disposal, just the same thing that we did to anyone looking too closely into Phoenix International. When I was cleaning up his contacts, I saw an address in Lower Pichesham. Your name. I passed it on to Erik to decide, and he chose to deal with it personally."

Farzad. A routine disposal. It was hard for a moment, but I calmed myself. "And Erik turned up in our house. What for? I don't get it. For fun?"

"None of us had been to the village for many years, and he wanted to take a look at the place. His original intention was simply to dispose of you after checking for other loose ends. I suspect he also intended to see if Bear would recognise him. As I say, he had become reckless. But the first person he encountered was Dr Hunt, reeking of power, one of the strongest he had ever known. And then he met you, if anything, even stronger. He changed plans on the spot. He tried to lure you in with the promise of information, even risking giving you something real. It worked, didn't it?"

"Maybe. A little."

"When Dr Hunt turned up at the front desk of the hospital, Erik realised he was the real prize. A powerful user, damaged, open to manipulation. The ultimate tainted volunteer. Here was his pilot. When you arrived at the hospital looking for him, a perfect strong primer for the weapon, I think he took it as a sign from whatever deity he chose to believe in."

"And then Bear rescued me, and you knew the game was up."

"Erik just laughed. Said it was meant to be. The weapon was untested, but ready to go. I had to pull together a force at short notice. It was smaller than I was happy with, but we had the element of surprise. It should have worked."

"I'm glad it didn't." The female spoke vehemently. "You licked his arse for centuries, Svend, and he nearly killed you—all of us—without a second thought. I hope he rots, wherever he is."

Svend ignored her, hanging there in his harness silently for a moment or two. "Are we done? Is that enough humiliation for you?"

I pressed the communicator. The girlish voice of the ants. "*It is enough for our decision.*"

"I have one more question. I know you've been asked before, but where is Erik? What happened to him? The raven was found dead in the wreckage, but there was no trace of Erik."

"Then I tell you once more, I don't know. You are supposed to be the truth detector. Am I lying?"

He wasn't. I turned to the other. "How about you, whatever your name is now?"

"No. I would tell you in an instant if I knew," she replied. "We are free of him now, blood oath be damned."

🐾 🐾 🐾

I took some persuading when the ants came back with their decision.

"So let me get this right. You are offering the wolf pack a whole new planet? Of their own? How is that a fair outcome? It must be thousands of people they have killed over the years. Some oath or other taken a millennium ago doesn't excuse that."

"Annie, you misunderstand the nature of our decision. We did not seek to pass judgement on them. Who are we to condemn a species for following what it believes to be right?"

"You were quite ready to pass judgement on humans!"

"Again, you misrepresent us. We have never judged you as a species on moral issues. We chose the path that we believed ensured our own peace and prosperity while leaving interference with others to a minimum. Similarly here, we are offering the pack a choice. They cannot return to Earth, so they must decide between permanent exile in Greyside, or to take on the role of caretakers for New Earth. It was one of Bear's requests, a refuge for the Earth's biosphere, somewhere that the non-human life of Earth would have a second chance."

"But …"

"The planet needs additional intelligent management for now. Terraforming on that scale is no easy task, even for us.

You should also know that the protoversal link to this planet is much weaker than Earth's. Without the equivalent of Greyside to fall back on, their biology will slowly revert to normal. They may even be able to breed with the non-altered wolves we already have living there. Let them make a future in which they can be themselves, safe in the knowledge that they are no longer a threat to us or to you."

And with that, I had to be content, because when looked at objectively, they were probably right.

Perhaps, reader, you are going a bit crazy by now. How did we stop Erik? What happened to him? Part of the reason I have left these questions to the end is that the answers are unsatisfactory. I will tell you that our combined order to the nexus of minds was, "Tell us what order would give the best outcome we could hope for." In short, we let the most intelligent living thing ever created work it out. And I presume we then told it to act on that, and it did. But the frustrating thing is, we don't know a lot more.

I've put together bits and pieces of information. For a start, the remnants of the device were gone. Every scrap vanished, including the machines inside the containers. The research up at the old prison camp, deleted. The surviving scientists suffered what seemed like amnesia.

The ants are … changed somehow. They seem less certain, as if they don't have all the answers anymore. Erik came so close to undoing everything that they have achieved. If he could do that, then who is to say what someone else could do? Something done once is a lot easier the next time. I like them more than I used to because of this.

As for Dom and I? Despite what Bear believed, afterwards we were back in our own heads. They found us holding each other under some scaffolding planks. Dom wasn't badly hurt.

The wires inserted in him all vanished with the rest of the device, leaving the puncture sites open and bleeding. He looked like raw steak for a while, but most of the scarring has gone now.

We got married a few weeks ago. Not legally, we'll do that later, but we wanted to do something in the new memorial space. Paul gave me away and Sandra and I were polite to each other. Maybe we can be reconciled properly one day, but it was a start. Dom asked Lance to be the celebrant. I still don't know quite how I feel about Lance, but it is hard to stay mad at someone who spreads love and happiness so freely. They are talking about restoring more of the buildings in the old village, given how many new people are arriving. It will be a shame in some ways, but Lance will just have to put up with having neighbours.

Honestly, not sure what the future holds for us. We are going to visit my folks, do the legal thing there for their benefit. Then who knows? A normal life somewhere, incognito? Visit a new planet? It's an option, apparently.

Before we decide, I have to put down everything that happened on record. It won't be me who tells this story to the world. I'm sealing everything up and placing it with lawyers, including some the ants don't know about. Do not open until 2050. That's the date we all agreed on. By the time you read this, all the secrets should be out in the open and this evidence will fill in some of the history.

There's a bit of me that still regrets it won't be me picking up any awards. Whoever gets to break this, good luck and I wish you well.

Annie Maylor-Hunt
Former Journalist

Final Word

Annie offered me the last word in this account. Since I had a hand in writing some of it, I suppose that is reasonable. I'm not really a writer though, so forgive me if my thoughts are a bit out of order.

By the time you read this in 2050 I will be gone, another dried-out husk in the desert of Greyside. This has nothing to do directly with the events at Alderman's Well. If anything, I should be grateful to Erik for the extra time I've been granted. After the battle, Simon arranged for me to be patched up in the veterinary hospital at Chester Zoo. Quite how he squared it away I don't know, but persuasiveness is part of his special ability.

I digress. While I was on the operating table, they found the tumours. Apparently, there was quite an argument while I was still under anaesthetic about whether it would be kinder to end it there. Fortunately for me, Simon was on call.

According to the vets, the growths have been there, growing silently, for years. It's hard to judge, but it is possible I had the beginnings even while I was still a regular bear. Now it's advanced to the point where palliative care is the only option. And since Thing-under-the-Water is a master of that particular skill, I have returned to Greyside to end my days among my books and memories. The

Pichesham Trust is in good enough hands, and I hope it will continue and thrive in whatever form my successors see fit.

The ants have promised me that a full-scale extermination of humans is no longer a possibility from them. Also that they will re-establish a presence on Earth with the aim of helping you avoid the worst of your own behaviour. If that sounds patronising, tough. You should have been better in the first place.

If there are still bears somewhere on Earth in the year 2050, please take proper care of them and their environment. I've done what I can for them now, and at least they have a chance elsewhere. Oh, and be better to your pets. You may need them more than you realise one day.

No more maudlin thoughts. Goodbye and good luck.

The Bear of Pichesham
April 10th 2019

Author's Note

I admit to some moral concerns about having written this book. The flood at the unnamed legal firm was just one of those things. Accidents happen even in the best-regulated offices. The partners felt obliged to make some attempt to dry out the contents of the archive, and when my distant relative was tasked with this, he was grossly unprofessional to have passed copies on to me. But the details, if even slightly true, were sensational. Who am I to withhold such transformative knowledge?

The public has a right to know, but I also must protect my source. Consequently, I have altered and adjusted the content of the book you have just read. The names of people and places have been changed and timings subtly altered. You will not find Lower Pichesham on any map, in England or anywhere else.

I also have a small confession. The intermissions are my fabrications. Somehow, it seemed only fair to give you a bit of a clue to what was coming, but there is no evidence to back them up. The section imagining what might have been going on inside Frank's head at the end—all invented. 'Annie' could have questioned Svend more about the time Erik made the fateful decision to abandon his wolfish body, but if she did, it wasn't in the files. I hope you will forgive the presumption.

For legal reasons, I will further state here that the story is fiction, and any resemblance you may find to any living person is a coincidence.

Jonah Larchwood
May 2023

Acknowledgements

Thanks are due to a lot of people, but particularly the following.

- To my nearest and dearest, whose belief and enthusiasm kept me going in the times when everything I wrote felt like dross.
- To my family and friends for all the encouragement along the way.
- To my daughter Emily, who has taken on the role of designer and made the words visually beautiful in ways that I didn't know were possible.
- To First Book Coaching, and especially to Max Gorlov and Ben Clark. I came to you with an idea and some ambition. I've finished with a story I can be proud of, and a desire to make more.
- To Kim Santini, the artist who made her beautiful painting available for the cover.
- To my beta readers, for their invaluable feedback. The final book is immeasurably better as a result. Karen Bennett; Helen Dunford; Arie Anna Farnam; Matt Grimshaw; Laurence Edward Jackson-Lowndes; Clarence Jennelle; Kim Martin; Jackson G. McGrath; Sasha Pinto-Jayawardena, Marilyn Stevenson; Owen Stevenson; Sam Wallace. For those of you who are also on this writing journey, I wish you many readers in the future.
- To Eleanor Boyall, for the final editing. Correcting my grammar, reminding me that 'discreet' is different from

'discrete' and fixing my dangling modifiers. For polishing and enhancing the text in hundreds of other ways.

- ❧ To Professor Hannah O'Regan and the Box Office Bears project, for appearing on my radar at the right time.
- ❧ To everyone who has offered suggestions, hints and ideas about all the complications of actually publishing a book that have nothing much to do with the writing of it.

And last, but not least…

Thanks to **you**, the reader, for taking the time to get this far. If you enjoyed this story, or were infuriated by it, or had any reaction at all, you can help in several ways.

Please leave a written review on Amazon or Goodreads. This is more important to visibility than you can know. Even if your review says almost the same thing as someone else's, it is a numbers game. Reviews mean readers are interested, and the more there are, the more that the big companies will promote. There is no amount of reviews that is too large. Don't feel like it has to be five stars, because frankly, if you've taken the time to read and review, you are entitled to give it whatever rating it deserves. And it doesn't have to be long or detailed—a few words is enough.

Please follow Jonah Larchwood on social media. I'm on Facebook and Instagram right now, but by the time you read this, I might be on TikTok as well. Who knows? Share my posts if you like them. They aren't all about me, me, me.

You can also sign up for my email newsletter. I promise not to spam you mercilessly, not least because I hate that myself. But those who do sign up will get incentives like early access to first chapters and bonus stories.

Printed in Great Britain
by Amazon

32036411R00189